To Dr. Vincanity!

Hey, try to love a few women ih this town for a struggling Author alright. And if you're not a Parker fan, don't bother reading the very end!! :)

Sign the Book!

Lethal Access

David Thiele

Lethal Access

Western Hemlock
Publishers

Western Hemlock Publishers
Esq. 3 W. Carrillo St. Suite #216
Santa Barbara, CA 93101

First Printing: June 1999

1 2 3 4 5 6 7 8 9 10

Acknowledgment is given to Tracy Blair and partner editors for their editing at:
ABC Editing Services

Acknowledgment is given to excellent
services provided by *Eagle Web Press, Your Town Press,*
and *L.grafix.*

Cover Photo of Seattle by David Thiele
Text design by David Barker and Dan V. Hook at *L.grafix* and David Thiele

ISBN: 0-9671847-0-3

Printed in the United States of America

To my family and friends

Acknowledgments

I first want to thank my mother and father for their incredible generosity of love and encouragement. They have always done all they could, and I'm thankful to have them as parents. I'd also like to thank my mother and father for offering me a place to stay in case this book would not have turned out. Even though I don't quite need a place to stay, I wouldn't mind another box of homemade cookies.

I want to thank my brother and sister-in-law for always inspiring me to work hard and set high standards. I don't believe I've ever met a man more ambitious than my brother, and I'm proud to admit it. Although, I hope this doesn't mean I was adopted.

A person shouldn't go through life with out good friends. I'm very thankful to have friends which I am able to truly rely on for anything, and I hope we build upon our friendships even more as the years go on. However, for those friends of mine reading this right now, I don't want any of you to think this means you'll be getting this book for free.

I'd also like to thank all the people who were involved in helping me publish this novel. There is an incredible amount of work involved with the entire process of publishing a novel which most people tend to overlook. In order to succeed, and in order to overcome each hurdle along the path to success, one must never stop fighting. I'd like to thank those people who helped me keep alive that spirit of fighting. I'd especially like to thank Dave Barker and Dan V. Hook for their long hours in helping to creatively design the cover.

Lethal Access

Chapter 1

Bedpans and rubbing alcohol: the stench infiltrated my nose the moment I walked through the front doors. No matter how bad the smell, it didn't keep me from coming here. As long as she was here, nothing would keep me away. As always, after a few minutes I got used to the smell. All I could think about was whether or not she'd recognize me. I was pleased with the pleasant aroma of the bouquet I bought. I always brought her flowers; what could be better than flowers? Perhaps this time I'd outdone the flowers. The box under my arm represented three years of my life, but at least I was done. I wasn't sure I'd do it again; was anyone entirely sure about what they chose to do with their life?

I walked down the long, halogen-lit hallway, toward her room. Suddenly, I noticed someone's feet extending through the door of a patient's dark room, toes pointing upward. It took me a moment before I realized that an elderly lady was lying flat on the tile floor. I dropped the flowers and box, yelled to the front desk for help, then hustled into her room. I checked her pulse by gently pressing my index and middle finger against the left side of her neck. To be sure she was breathing, I put my hand under her nose and loosely over her mouth. I could feel her pulse, but no breath. I lowered my head and put my ear next to her nose. Still nothing. I decided to give her mouth to mouth, but when I pinched her nose and opened her mouth, she suddenly gasped for air and opened her eyes in a panic. Three nurses ran into the room ready to go to work, but realized all was well. I switched on the light and grabbed a pillow off the bed for the elderly woman. I slowly lifted her head and placed the pillow underneath it. The nurses examined her to make sure she hadn't been injured. The elderly lady smiled and said thank you in a soft, grandmother-like voice. I smiled and held her hand to give her a little comfort.

Another elderly lady, appearing to be more a visitor than a patient, rushed into the room with a look of terror on her face. When she realized everything was under control, she sighed in relief. She sat next to me on the floor, and gave the other lady a soft hug. After the nurses determined that the lady hadn't been injured, they helped her into bed. Angry and upset, I walked out of the room and waited in the hallway. All I could think about was how I'd feel if it were my mother lying on the floor. This place filled me with fury; not the best time for Fred, the overweight, supervising nurse, to approach me.

"What happened," Fred asked, brushing past me and directing his question to the nurses? Still in the hallway, I could hear them talking, telling each other what a good job they did. Then one of the nurses said something about the guy in the hall.

I'd known Fred for more than three years; ever since my first visit to this care facility. At first I liked the guy; he seemed sincere, caring and generous. But soon I learned that he couldn't care less about the patients here. Most of the time he sat in his little cubbyhole office and watched game shows. The last time I was here I saw him take a stapler off a secretary's desk and slip it into his bag. I'd bet that much of the money supposedly used for patient's medicine ended up in his pocket.

Fred peeked around the corner and nodded for me to come into the room. I walked in, stood in front of Fred, and restrained myself from tearing into him. He leaned toward me and whispered that Mrs. O'Conner--the woman I presumed I had helped--asked to see me. I ignored the others, although I could feel them all watching me, and dragged a chair next to Mrs. O'Conner's bed.

"Oh don't bother sitting dear, please stand up so I can see all of you."

I wasn't certain what she intended to do, but I guessed that most people in nursing homes didn't get a great deal of attention, so they enjoyed any companionship could get.

"How's this?" I asked, standing directly in front of her.

She reached for her glasses on the nightstand. When she lifted her arm, I could see her face grimace. The other elderly lady grabbed the glasses and helped her put them on.

"Thank you Olivia," Mrs. O'Conner said.

Perhaps they were sisters. I wished my mother had someone to visit occasionally. That would help calm me.

"Stand up, stand up now," Mrs. O'Connor said, "nice and straight, c'mon now, like a grown man should!"

Her voice was surprisingly chipper. I didn't know what to do or say, so I just smiled.

"Ah yes, you're much more handsome than in the pictures."

Confused, I asked, "In what pictures?"

"A few years ago when your mother was feeling better, she showed me pictures of you. She would talk about how well you were doing in school. She's quite proud of you. Very proud."

"You know my mother?"

She looked offended by my question. "Well I should, after-all, she sleeps only a few rooms down from me."

I was surprised that Mrs. O'Connor recognized me from the pictures my mother had shared with her.

"You know that's the one thing I regret," she said. "I never had any children. But if I did, I'd wish they were as handsome as you. Now then, I don't want to take away any more time from your mother. Thank you for helping me, and be good to your mother. You're all she talks about."

"I'm sure my mother is grateful to have a friend like you, Mrs. O'Connor." I leaned over and gave her a kiss on the cheek.

In a more tranquil mood, I tried to leave the room, but Fred grabbed my shoulder and started to thank me. I interrupted him before he could say another word.

"Listen, Fred," I said, trying to keep my voice low, "do you have any idea how long Mrs. O'Conner was lying on that cold floor?"

Fred swallowed hard. "Um . . . no."

"Neither do I, but I don't work here, do I?"

"No sir, you don't."

"For all you know she could've cracked her head open when she fell, maybe even bled to death, had I not seen her!"

"I understand where you're coming from," Fred said, "but I promise you we do routine checks and I can reassure you our staff is . . ."

Something caught my eye. I turned around and didn't hear the rest of what Fred had said. The nurses were gone, but Olivia was standing next to Mrs. O'Connor.

Looking at Olivia, I asked, "Are you Mrs. O'Conner's friend or sister?"

"Just a friend. I come here all the time to visit her. Why do you ask?"

I walked over to the bed and picked up Olivia's black purse lying next to Mrs. O'Conner's pillow. I grabbed the empty needle she'd tried to stuff in her purse. "What did you just inject into her arm? Are you a nurse, or a doctor?"

"You don't understand," Olivia said. "I'm…"

"She's one of our health care volunteers," Fred blurted.

"That's interesting," I said. "Do you have any proof?" My questions didn't give them any time to think. It's how I was trained.

"Well, uh, no, but that's because she's a volunteer," Fred said.

I knew that Fred was lying, and I could feel my anger rising. But before I could say another word, I heard Mrs. O'Conner's voice.

"John!"

Her stern tone took me by surprise. How did she know my name?

"John," she said again, a little softer this time, "please let it be, she's helping me with my arthritis pain." She reached toward me with trembling fingers, so I gently squeezed her hand.

"I'm sorry." A dozen questions whirled through my mind. Why would someone without a medical license administer injections? Isn't that what the nurses are supposed to do? Realizing that the elderly women were upset, I let it go. Maybe Olivia *was* just trying to help.

Without saying a word, I picked up the bouquet of flowers and the box, and left the room. Fred's voice echoed behind me, whining an apology. I was sure he'd rehearsed this apology with a hundred people. I ignored him and kept walking.

There I was again, outside my mother's room. I could see her through the small window in the door. She didn't realize it, but I could feel her depression. Maybe the next time I see her I'd be able to wipe my conscience clean and give her what she deserved. My hand grasped the doorknob, but I couldn't go in yet. It hurt to see her like this, to imagine what it must be like. What hurt most was my inability to improve her situation. I could feel my chin quiver, tears welled in my eyes. I couldn't let her see me like this. I took a long, deep breath, turned the doorknob, and walked in. She was staring at the TV, but it wasn't turned on. I sat next to her and waited for her to notice me. She turned to me, then gave me a big smile.

"Hello there, is it time for my pills already?" She thought I was a nurse.

"No pills tonight, only a visitor."

"A visitor? Who's coming to visit me?"

I tried to maintain my composure. "It's John, Mom. Remember me?" I picked up the picture on her nightstand. "See," I said, pointing to myself in the picture, "here I am, right next to you and Dad."

"John, my sweetheart! What are you doing here? Shouldn't you be studying?" She brushed her hand against my cheek. I handed her the flowers and the box with a red bow around it.

"That's what I came to tell you Mom. I'm finally done. Now I can follow in dad's footsteps." I waited a long time to enjoy this moment, but there was something wrong. I could see it in her face. "What's wrong Mom?"

"I'm sorry John, I can't remember what you've been studying. "She was ashamed. I still couldn't accept that my mother had Alzheimer's disease.

"I understand, Mom." I didn't really understand how anyone could comprehend her anguish. I pointed to the package with the red bow. "Open it, Mom." She tore the wrapping paper slowly. Before it was even opened, I could see the delight in her face just because she'd received a present.

Her eyes looked like saucers. "My, oh my." She shook her head from side to side. "It's your degree from Illinois State University Law School. John, you're a lawyer. My Johnathon is a lawyer!"

"I haven't passed the bar exam yet, Mom, but I'm finished with law school." A pang of tension struck me as I thought about how hard I'd studied during the last few weeks.

"I'm so proud of you, John. You truly are a blessing." She leaned forward and gave me a hug. I didn't think of myself as a blessing; perhaps a blessing in disguise. Few people would label lawyers a blessing, but if my Mom believed I was, then I was.

We spent the evening talking about my childhood years; something from the past that my mother clearly remembered. It was painful when she forgot simple things, or when she couldn't recognize a face, but it felt like a knife in my gut when she kept talking about dad as if he were still alive. I didn't remind her that he was dead. Why subject her to a painful memory she'd forget by tomorrow? Once in a while I had to conceal my tears. I missed my dad so much. Eventually, the medication took hold and she fell asleep. I left the framed law degree on her nightstand, put the flowers in a vase filled with water, and left.

I always felt sad when my visit was over, but tonight was particularly painful. I was leaving the city for quite a while, and the thought of my mother remaining here, taken care of by cold strangers, made my departure even worse. I wasn't sure which tortured me more, her disease or loneliness. Few things are worse than being alone. For her to be isolated in a room, day after day, with nothing to look forward to except nurses visiting with daily medicine, that made my stomach turn.

From outside the door I whispered, "Someday I'll change this whole mess, Mom. I promise." No one could hear this promise, but when your heart knew it would be kept, who needed to hear it? I took one last look at my mother through the small window, and then headed home to sleep. One last night in the Windy City of Chicago.

Chapter 2

It was an unspoken understanding between my stepfather and myself that I could not stay at home. In his eyes, he was kind enough just to have let me stay to study for the bar exam I took a little while ago in the State of Washington. I had to fly over to the West Coast for three days while I took it, and then came back here to pack my things and leave to Washington for good. I often imagined how diffcrent things might have been if my real father were still alive. He was the reason I entered law school. I could still remember him talking about how great it'd be for both of us to work together in court and win cases. With great excitement he once told me that we would make history by preserving true justice. I was uncertain if such a thing existed; nobody believed in lawyers anymore. That was not to say I didn't believe in my father. He was one of the last decent lawyers. I didn't have the heart to tell him I didn't give a damn about law. That's when I knew I was going to be doing a lot of acting.

Unfortunately, I never got the chance to tell my father how I felt. There were many feelings I never shared with him. I was amazed how quickly a life could be taken. He was on his way home from work. His firm had celebrated an insurance claim victory for one of their clients that evening. The next morning the police found his car wrapped around a telephone pole. My mother married Steve Barker, the money-hungry-scoundrel I have for a stepfather. He claims to have known my father for years, said they were great friends in law school. Perhaps that was how he manipulated my mother into marrying him. I'd bet my poor mother never anticipated being confined to a nursing home at forty-eight years old. She finally realized how much Dad meant to her when Steve began treating her like a bank teller, helping himself to her money. Steve managed to devise a plan that entitled him to all my mother's money, including my father's Firm. My father was so proud of that firm. I was sure Steve found a way to swindle me out of my birthright as well. I'd rather not stick around here anyway. Watching Steve scheme was enough to run anybody out of town.

My stepfather seemed happy to drive me to the airport, as if every second I'd be gone would be a pleasure. I stood in the middle of the airport, not knowing a soul. It was better that way. I wasn't really in the mood to talk. I walked to the ticket counter and checked in everything I owned: one piece of luggage. While waiting for the boarding call, I decided to have a seat. I wondered what it was like in Seattle. I didn't get to see my relatives, or the city of Seattle, when I went there to take the bar exam because I was too occupied with taking the tests. But I had been there once for Thanksgiving, a long time ago. All I remember was being smothered with kisses and hugs from all my relatives. I never even got the turkey leg, which my Mom made sure I got when I was a little kid. I was going to meet my Uncle James, my father's brother and closest friend at the Seattle airport. That was probably why I got along with him so well; it was like still having my father around. Like my father, Uncle James has his own law firm. He offered me a position when I was still in law school. It was the only offer I ever got, so I wholeheartedly accepted.

Sitting across from me was an elderly lady knitting some kind of a sweater. Considering the *unique* colors, I didn't think her grandchildren would be wearing them. Suddenly I recognized this lady. She was the woman from the nursing home. I considered striking up a conversation, but decided not to. She noticed me. I smiled and tried to look away.

"You're the young man from the nursing home," she said. "I'm thankful you were there to help. I really don't trust the staff there."

"Well, that makes two of us. And considering the type of accessories you carry in your purse, I'm not so sure how much you can be trusted either." I expected some explanation of the needle. Instead, she just laughed, as if the needle-incident never happened.

"Ever been to Seattle?" she asked.

"For Thanksgiving," I said politely. "But that was quite a long time ago." I didn't feel like mentioning the short trip I had taken recently for the bar exam.

"Where do they live?" she asked.

"Where does who live?"

"Whoever you're visiting."

"My relatives live in a suburb just outside Seattle, in the country." I wondered why I was answering her nosy questions. "How about you, any family members in Seattle?"

"My entire family lives there, including me. That's why I was curious where you lived."

"How nice," I said sweetly.

The loudspeakers crackled above me. "Now boarding rows twenty through thirty."

"Well, that's me," I said, quite relieved. "Sorry we didn't get a chance to talk longer. Have a good trip." With a smile I turned and walked away.

"Maybe we'll see each other on the plane," she said.

I found my seat on the airplane, took off my shoes, and quickly tried to make up for lost sleep. When I awoke, the old woman was tugging at my shirt with a big grin on her face, and a horrendous pile of knitting on her lap.

"Time for dinner young man. Eat. You need your energy." Half the passengers could hear her shrill voice. "I think it's chicken."

"So how did you end up next to me?" I asked.

"I asked a young blond woman sitting next to you if she'd switch seats with me." She made it sound like a good deed. Like she did me some huge favor by getting rid of whomever this potentially beautiful lady may have been. With my luck the blond might have been my future wife. Maybe the flight attendant would make them switch back. I could only hope.

Throughout the flight, the grandmother talked nonstop. But I had to admit, I enjoyed it, well, some of it. I was surprised to find that she knows so much about Seattle, but then again, she does live there. As we talked, the scene with the needle kept interrupting my thoughts. It irritated me, but I decided not to let it bother me too much.

When we arrived in Seattle, I helped Olivia with her tangled web of knitting, and walked her to where her son, Danny was waiting for her. The elderly woman wasn't so bad after all. Chatting with her helped me to forget about other things, like my indebtedness for eighty-four thousand dollars, and some change. I had nothing to show for it except a worthless piece of paper and three wasted years of my life.

I heard a voice from behind me. "Hey Johnny, is that you!"

I turned and saw my Uncle James Bowman. He'd gained a little weight since I last saw a photo, but it looked good on him. He had the appearance of being well accomplished and friendly. He almost looked like Santa Claus in a business suit. Without the beard. After greeting each other with a bear hug, we retrieved my suitcase and drove to his house.

Uncle James' house is in a beautiful countryside location with an abundance of flowers planted along the terrace. Flower boxes hang in front of all the windows. The home is a three-story estate. On the north side of the estate there is a medium-sized pool surrounded by a well-maintained garden. On the south side there is a small pond with a little dock and a small rowboat. As I admired this beautiful home, I couldn't help but wonder how many law suits it had taken to pay it off.

Uncle James took me inside to meet the rest of the family, whom I hadn't seen since I was a kid. Aunt Heide greeted me the way she did long ago, with a firm hug and warm smile. My two cousins had changed a lot. I barely recognized them. James Junior, the cousin I once played with and climbed trees within the back yard, was behaving like an absolute jerk. I didn't fit into his little club of rich, bratty, polo freaks, and he forgot how to say anything except, "Ah yes, Johnny, so, how's the weather back in Chicago?" Charleen had changed as well, but probably for the better. She used to be a "Tomboy," but now she was a pretty and ladylike woman. To my surprise, however, she had a two-year-old daughter who was quite adorable. Charleen told me that she was much too young at the time, and didn't know what she was getting into in the relationship, but she didn't regret having a child. Had she not made a mistake, she wouldn't have her beautiful daughter. The father was no where to be found. The last she'd heard, he was working as a bouncer at a strip bar. From what I could tell she seemed to be doing fine as a single parent.

After a delicious dinner, Aunt Heide showed me to my room. She told me to stay as long as I needed to, which is good because being in debt eighty-four thousand dollars, and some change, could keep me off my feet longer than expected. The bedroom is spacious with a private bathroom. Best of all it has a balcony with a great view. Uncle James came up to wish me a good night, and to warn me to prepare myself for some hard work in the next few months. After hearing endless speeches in law school about how firms expected their employees to put in eighteen-hour days, six days a week, I was prepared for the worst.

Chapter 3

My Uncle's firm is on a main street where there's a lot of foot traffic. I suspected that this had been a main objective when he started the firm. It isn't an overwhelming building. However, it's not a poor establishment either. Of the twenty-seven members of the firm, only a few are established senior partners. Mr. Bowman, which is what my Uncle asked me to call him while working, introduced me to three members who occupied offices next to mine. Each of them gave me a friendly hello and a firm handshake. After only a minute, they seemed to squirm and jitter, as if I had stolen far to many seconds of their endless day. The rest of the members are hidden somewhere in the maze of offices and hallways, but I'm sure I'll eventually run into them.

Mr. Bowman welcomed me to my new office; he told me that after some time I might be able to get a larger office. By the looks of things, I had already done my time. The office has two large floor-to-ceiling windows overlooking the main avenue with all the foot traffic. There is a large oak desk, a small fridge, and a huge fern plant hanging in the corner. I pray that someone else will take care of the plant. I couldn't keep a plastic cactus alive if my life depended upon it.

"So what do you think?" Mr. Bowman asked. There was a look of curiosity in his eyes.

"Well, I really don't know what to say, uncle, I mean, Mr. Bowman. It's more than I expected." The office put me in awe. I didn't know how he expected me to answer, let alone remember to call him by his professional name. I had to admit, my problems were beginning to gain a little balance.

"You don't have to say anything, John," my uncle said. "We're glad to have you here. Just don't let us down. All right?"

"You can count on me, Mr. Bowman." I tried to say this with confidence, although I was uncertain how it would be possible for him to count on someone who didn't even know whether or not he'd passed the bar exam.

"I knew I could, Johnny. Oh, I almost forgot. I told James Junior to stop by around lunchtime to take you to the Cricket. It's a sports bar, a good local place to get some relief from law and enjoy some good food."

"Sounds great, Mr. Bowman." I tried to sound thrilled.

"Good, I thought you'd enjoy catching up on things with him. And I'll also have the secretary give you some files to look at, just so you can get the feel of things."

I nodded my head and gave him another handshake to let him know I really appreciated everything he'd done for me. He returned a polite smile and then left me alone in my new office.

A little after noon, James Junior strolled into my office. As if his office down the hall wasn't twice the size of mine, with a hundred more gadgets to play with, he tried to admire mine. At least he was making an effort to be nice. But I still didn't like his attitude.

We left for lunch. The Cricket was a laid-back place, like Harold's, a local pub near where I went to law school.

"You don't mind if I just call you, J?" I asked. It was what I called him when we were kids, and I figured it might renew an old friendship. Or maybe it was just wishful thinking.

"Call me what you like," James said. His snobbish tone made me feel that I shouldn't have asked. Yet if I would've simply blurted it out, it would've been a whole different story.

"It sure has been great seeing everyone again." I said, trying to talk about something with depth, yet careful not to place too much attention on J. I wouldn't want to inflate his ego.

"Yes, we do enjoy seeing you as well, John. It's been quite some time."

I wondered if he really gave a damn.

"So tell me, John, where did you go to law school?" He asked this with a smirk on his face, as if he didn't know. This was the last subject in the world I wanted to discuss. Good old James Junior has told everybody that he graduated from Harvard law, a university I only dreamed of. Not that I wasn't able to go there because of my grades, I didn't have the money nor the connections like Junior. I could blame it on my father's death, but I got through law school nonetheless, so I guess I can't blame it on anybody.

"I decided to go to Chicago State." I made it sound as if this was my choice.

"Did I ever tell you I went to Harvard, John?"

"No, J, nobody ever brought it up back home." I shrugged a little, trying to give the impression that Harvard was no big deal, as if I were a man who had a broad spectrum of options. "Your Dad's firm seems to be doing well," I said, hoping to end further talk about law school. Suddenly, I noticed J's face turn serious, almost blank white. "What's wrong J?" I wondered if I had started the wrong conversation.

J leaned toward the center of the table, and began to speak in a low voice. "My father's firm is in trouble."

"How are they in trouble?"

"Money. The banks have been trying to close it down for the past year now."

"But why? I thought your father's firm was doing well, especially now."

J leaned in a little closer. "About two years ago, Greg Finley, a lawyer working for my father's firm, was involved in a scandal. He was working for an insurance company worth more than you or I will ever see. Greg handled the insurance company's borderline cases. These were disputable cases; ones the insurance company couldn't just settle. There's little doubt that Greg was good at handling cases like this. He created just enough apprehension that the opposing attorneys would doubt how well their case would hold up in court. This would force them to settle for whatever they could get."

"No scandal in that." I said, trying to keep the story moving.

"Whenever Greg won a case, he claimed 15% of the prosecuting party's original settlement, as well as any extra fee. So, instead of the insurance company having to pay the whole sum of a lawsuit, they only had to pay 15% of it. It saved them a lot of money, and Greg delivered his promises almost every time."

"I still don't see the problem, J." I hoped that I wasn't humiliating myself by overlooking something obvious.

"Well, Greg got greedy. When he was working on the insurance company's lawsuits, he gained access, with permission, to all of the company's client files. In addition, they gave him the data required to access all company and banking account numbers. These account numbers were used by the insurance company to organize client files, as well as for billing. Greg didn't need the files for the account numbers, but for information to help build his case against any sort-of prosecuting law firm. However, things changed quickly when he realized what he actually had the potential to do. Since he had all of the account numbers and routing numbers of the insurance company and the clients, all he had to do was transfer unnoticeable percentages of the billing into a private account that couldn't be traced."

In total disbelief, I asked, "But how could he possibly get away with something so obvious?"

"Greg wasn't subtle, he did it right under their noses. The first bill would be completely legitimate, under the authority of the Bowman Firm. He billed the expected 15% of whatever the prosecutors sued for by mailing the bill to the insurance company's accounting office, just like our firm, or any other firm, would normally do. Then he would wait forty-eight hours; the amount of time for the legitimate bill to be processed and confirmed by the company before it went to the bank account. At the same time the first 15% was being withdrawn and transferred from the insurance company's bank account to the Bowman's account, Greg would bill the second time by bypassing the insurance company's in-house accounting system and going directly to the bank. He did this without having to use any official names or codes, only with account numbers given to him by the insurance company. Since the same amount was withdrawn twice on the same day, with all the proper account numbers, the insurance company believed it was the same 15% they had processed forty-eight hours earlier."

"Didn't the bank realize that they were making double transfers?" I asked, still trying to figure out how someone could defraud a multimillion-dollar insurance company.

"The bank was aware of both transactions, but since they were being transferred through cleared account numbers, and because all transactions were posted monthly, the bank didn't suspect anything unusual."

"So, what happened?" I asked.

"This hotshot accountant started working for the insurance company. He examined the Bowman files and noticed that money was being transferred to both the Bowman account and Greg's private account. When he informed the president, all hell broke loose. The in-house lawyers took it all the way; corporate lawyers live for scandals like this. Greg left the country before my father was even aware of this fiasco. Because the Bowman firm employed Greg, my father was legally responsible. During the time span of two years, Greg had embezzled 1.8 million dollars."

"But James is covered by insurance, right?" I could feel a knot in my stomach, as if I was on trial.

"He's covered by Trueity, the company that Greg swindled. But because Greg committed fraud, the responsibility is my father's. No insurance policy covers fraud associated with an insurance collection. It would be like someone buying health insurance, then purposely injuring themself." Veins appeared under J's skin. I sensed that J had thought about schemes like this many times, but never quite had the balls to pull it off.

"Doesn't James have the money? I mean, 15% may have been a substantial amount, but not more than what any secure firm is able to make. And your father's firm appears to be financially stable. Besides, he hired me, didn't he?" I said this to lighten things up.

"Shortly before this happened, my father had expanded the Bowman firm, adding over three times the number of lawyers. All the additional staffing, health insurance costs, office space, and Christmas bonuses, placed my father on a narrow bridge of financial security. Although long-term the investment looked extremely promising, initially his expenses tripled. My father's expansion showed his clients that he had faith in the firm and the people he hired. Business was really starting to boom."

"Until Greg?"

"When Greg's little scheme was publicized, everything went down hill. We lost a lot of clients, because many concluded that the firm was no longer trustworthy." J couldn't look at me. "John, we're on the brink of . . . bankruptçy."

"But why did James hire me if he's doing so poorly?"

"Well, you're his nephew, but don't feel too special. He recently hired two other attorneys because he gets a tax break. The loss will help him survive for another few months."

I suddenly realized that my job was in jeopardy. "Is there any way out of this mess?"

"There is if you can find a way to win back our old clients, and get us some new ones."

J's last words, as well as the prospect of searching for a new job, consumed my thoughts for the rest of the day. At six-thirty, Uncle James and J walked into my office, both with smiles. We left early, probably because it was my first day. Or perhaps because their client list was so small there wasn't much to do. I continued rehashing what J had said earlier in the day. However, when I walked into the Bowman home my mind shifted to one thought: food. The wonderful aroma of ham, potatoes, gravy and a dozen other wonderful smells filled the air. I hadn't been this pampered in years, and I certainly hadn't had the chance to be part of a loving family like this since my father died.

At ten-thirty, after having a few glasses of wine and still craving seconds of Aunt Heide's triple layer German black forest cake, I went up to my room. Since it was a clear night, and I loved fresh air, I decided to sit outside on the balcony. I tried to clear my head, but my thoughts flashed back to the Bowman firm. I couldn't help but wonder what was going to happen to me, my job, and my debts. I wondered why I ever became a lawyer. I hated law and lawyers. And now, I was one.

At times like this I missed talking to Susie. She always found good, even in the worst situations. I remembered once working an eighteen-hour shift, then studying for another thirteen hours to prepare for a three-hour test. I had failed the test, and didn't have enough money for an aspirin. Susie had told me it was better that I lost my job because it gave me more time to study. And that failing the exam was good because I would take my studying more seriously. I didn't know how my life going to hell was a good thing, but somehow Susie helped me to find some good in my failures.

I missed her. I missed her being in my arms. I could almost feel her soft cheeks against mine, her deep eyes looking into mine. Sometimes I got caught up in some kind of a hell-like dream, unable to awaken and stop the ache from piercing my heart. Dreams of Susie grew longer and more agonizing as time went by. I hated to do anything that reminded me of her. She's gone, and by now there's probably someone else enjoying her love.

Chapter 4

"John, John, wake up!" I awoke to the voice of a frantic lady. I glanced at my alarm clock, still trying to determine if I was dreaming, and noticed it was three-forty-five a.m. I dragged myself out of bed, threw on an old pair of sweat pants and a T-shirt, and stumbled downstairs to the kitchen. Aunt Heide and Charleen looked like nervous wrecks. James and James Junior were nowhere in sight.

"What's going on?" I asked.

"It's James," Aunt Heide said. Her voice was unsteady and her eyes were in tears.

"Has something happened to Uncle James?" I asked.

"We need to go to the hospital," Charleen said.

"Will someone please tell me what happened?" I could feel my voice tighten.

"We'll explain on the way to the hospital," Aunt Heide said.

I knew better than to argue. She tossed me the keys to her Mercedes and we headed for the hospital.

Still trying to find out what had happened, I asked, "How serious is it?"

"Junior found James lying on his office floor unconscious," Charleen explained. "He immediately called for an ambulance, but we're not sure how long he'd been lying there."

"Was he injured or bleeding?" I asked, feeling somewhat frenzied.

"We're not sure," Charleen said.

"Why was Uncle James in his office so late?" I asked.

"After you went upstairs last night," Aunt Heide said, "he received a call from Dwayne Albertson and Richard Murphy, two senior partners of the Bowman firm. They told James it was urgent they speak with him immediately. After a couple of hours we got worried and called the firm, but there was no answer, so we called Dwayne. He told us he had been home for hours and that James and he had left at the same time. Junior drove to the office and found James unconsious on the floor. That's when he called us."

We arrived at the hospital emergency room, and I parked the Mercedes as close to the entrance as possible. The receptionist informed us that James was in one of the trauma rooms and we'd have to wait in the lobby until the doctor came us.

The waiting seemed endless. I never hated hospitals so much, but lately they'd caused me nothing but grief. The only employee in sight was a wrinkled old nurse who looked so lost she could have been a patient herself.

Finally, after about thirty minutes, we were escorted down a long hallway to where Junior was waiting. He was slumped in a chair, hands covering his face. I felt sympathy for all of them. Aunt Heide and Charleen embraced Junior, but only for a moment. The nurse led us into room one-seventeen where James lay unconscious. She introduced us to Dr. Grunnkeil, the family physician, and Dr. Jennings, a neurologist. Dr. Grunnkeil is a middle-aged man with a heavy German accent. Dr. Jennings is a tall slender lady, looking to be about thirty-five.

After a brief explanation of Uncle James' condition, the doctors permitted us to be alone with him for a few minutes. Aunt Heide was next to the bed long before the doctors finished speaking. I walked over to the bed myself, and suddenly it hit me. Uncle James, *my* Uncle James was lying in that bed.

Uncle James didn't look like he was alive. It seemed strange staring at a man barely breathing with a weak pulse, without personality or energy, a man who usually was so lively and happy. Aunt Heide and Charleen held his hands; tears streamed down their cheeks. I could feel Aunt Heide's pain and could see how much she loved him. Junior was standing next to me. I felt awkward, even angry, but all I could do was stare. It was a feeling of complete helplessness.

After a few minutes, Dr. Grunnkeil opened the door and peeked inside. Without saying anything, he smiled and we knew it was time to talk. Junior whispered something to Aunt Heide. She nodded, gave James a kiss on the cheek, grabbed Junior's hand, and went to the door. I tried to offer as much comfort as I could to Aunt Heide, Charleen, and Junior, but keeping myself together was hard enough. I put my arm around Charleen and gave her a firm hug, then we joined the others in the hallway.

We stood opposite Dr. Grunnkeil and Dr. Jennings, waiting impatiently to hear what they had to say. As she studied her graphs and charts, Dr. Jennings was deeply absorbed with her notes; her glasses were resting at the tip of her nose. Dr. Grunnkeil let out a sigh, and began to explain how fortunate the situation was. I couldn't understand how my uncle being unconscious was fortunate, or maybe I just didn't want to understand. He told us that James had sustained a fractured skull due to a severe blow to the back of his head. Dr. Jennings explained that the EEG did not show any brain damage, however, she cautioned that some brain injuries were not immediately detectable. Dr. Grunnkeil warned that it could take some time for James to awaken, and that there was a slight chance he'd remain in a coma. With the proper care, love from his family, and prayers, the doctor believed that James would, however, recover soon.

Still trying to process all that had happened this miserable evening, I asked Dr. Grunnkeil if Uncle James' head injury might have resulted from his fall.

"It's tough to say for sure. He could have slipped and fallen, but on the other hand it could've been a deliberate blow to the head."

Obviously shocked by the doctor's words, Aunt Heide asked, "Are you saying that this was an attempted murder?"

"It's a definite possibility. Actually, it might not be a bad idea to call the police and ask that an officer be posted outside Mr. Bowman's door. I can support you in any way necessary if the police hassle you."

"Don't worry, Mom," Junior said, patting her on the back. "I've already notified the police and they'll be at the office at eight a.m. to take a report. They also said that they'll send someone down here to keep an eye on Dad's room."

After shaking hands with both doctors, Junior and I went to get some coffee for all of us. During law school, coffee had become an essential dietary supplement, particularly during times of stress.

Walking through the hospital halls, I couldn't help but think about Susie. I remembered her warm smile whenever we met during her fifteen-minute breaks. I listened to her detailed stories when she so excitedly told me about all that had happened in the operating room that day. She'd tell me about all the medical miracles she'd witnessed. I guess her intensity and drive was what first attracted me to her. Ironically, those were the same characteristics that forced her to leave me.

In a way, it seemed almost comforting to know that she was on an island somewhere in the Pacific curing and healing helpless children. At least she didn't leave me for another guy. I didn't know how many times I waited for her to call me from the airport to tell me she decided to come back home. It never happened, but life goes on.

With the taste of bad coffee still in our mouths, Junior and I gave Aunt Heide and Charleen a hug and kiss, and then headed for Uncle James' office. I guessed that Junior's new BMW cost more than my eighty thousand-dollar debt. Considering the financial state of the Bowman firm, I couldn't help but wonder how he could possibly afford such a vehicle. Or perhaps it's just another tax write off.

The drive to the office was quiet. When Junior and I parked in front of the Bowman firm, the police hadn't yet arrived. The office was throbbing with activity; all of the partners and their support staff were busy at work. I could sense an air of uneasiness; everyone seemed to be on edge. With what had happened to Uncle James, and the Bowman firm on the verge of bankruptcy, how could I blame them?

Junior and I took the elevator up to James' office.

Shaking his head, Junior pointed to the bloodstained rug in the middle of the room. "This is where I found him."

I gawked at the soiled Oriental rug, unable to fathom why anyone would do such a thing to Uncle James.

There was a soft knock at the door. A secretary peeked inside. "There are two police officers at the front desk asking for you, Mr. Bowman. Should I show them in?"

"Yes," Junior said. By the grim look on his face, I guessed that speaking to the cops was the last thing Junior wanted to do.

The secretary led the officers into the room. One looked to be about forty-five, out of shape, and had a mean look on his face, the kind of snarl I'd seen a dozen times when receiving a traffic violation. The other officer was a mid-thirty-ish young woman, very attractive; not the type of person I could have envisioned holding a gun to someone's head.

"I'm Lieutenant Bob Fischer," He said, and then pointed to the young woman. "This is Officer Danny Brumm." Fischer found his way to the liquor cabinet, filled a glass with ice, then poured gin and tonic into the glass as if he owned the place.

"Rough night, huh?" he said, slowly stirring his drink. Without giving us a chance to answer, he turned to Danny and ordered her to take notes and photographs.

Fischer pulls a fat cigar out of his pocket. "Mind if I smoke?"

"This is a nonsmoking building." My tone was icy.

Fischer slowly slid the cigar under his nose and inhaled deeply, licking his lips. His eyes surveyed the office and he gave Junior and I the once-over.

"Before you found him, Mr. Bowman, who was the last person to be with your father?" By the tone of his voice, Fischer, I suspected, was trying to intimidate us.

Just then Dwayne pushed the door open, stomped into the office, and said, "Richard and I were the last ones to see him." Richard followed close behind like a well-trained dog. I recognized them from some enlarged, framed photos with their names labeled underneath them which I saw hanging in one of the hallways.

"Dwayne Albertson!" Bob shouted. His bulldog face softened to a smile.

I guessed it was the first time he'd smiled since last handcuffing a murder suspect.

Giving Fischer a quick hug and a firm handshake, Dwayne said, "Good to see you again, Bob." Dwayne fixed his stare on Fischer's gut. "I see you're still working out hard in the gym."

"Just keeping up with you Dwayne," Fischer said. "Must be nice having the little woman prepare those healthy, low calorie meals for you."

"So how's the family?" Fischer asked.

"You know Marcie. Always finds time to max-out the credit cards. And how's your family?"

"Still paying off my daughter's braces. And Holly still has a problem with my innocent helpings of whiskey." So far these guys sounded like a bunch of drunkards.

Danny folded her arms across her chest, obviously annoyed at this untimely reunion. "What were you and Richard doing here with Mr. Bowman last night?"

Peering at Danny as if insulted by the rookie's question, Dwayne said, "We had a conference."

"What sort of conference?" Danny asked.

"Who the hell do you think you are?" Dwayne yelled.

"We don't have to be in a courtroom for me to ask these questions, Mr. Albertson. Now, please explain exactly what you were doing here in the middle of the night."

Looking at Fischer for support, Dwayne said, "Tell me she's joking."

"Listen, Danny," Fischer said, "Dwayne and I go back a long way. And for you to ask him such a..."

"Excuse me, Lieutenant," I interrupted, "Officer Brumm is merely doing her job. I suggest you allow your obviously competent partner to continue." I glared at Fischer, warning him to back off. "I believe the young lady asked you a question, Dwayne."

Cracking his knuckles, Dwayne said, "Richard and I met Mr. Bowman to discuss an important client. I'd love to share the gist of the conversation with you, officer, but even a rookie cop must know about client-attorney confidentiality."

I couldn't believe Dwayne's rudeness.

"When the meeting was over," Dwayne added, "I think it was twelve-forty-five. I went directly home." He fixed his stare on Officer Brumm. "If you have any further questions, I'll be in my office. And Bob, if you have to come here again, don't bring the rookie. Until James is out of the hospital and physically able to run the firm, I'll be acting president of this firm."

Dwayne and Richard said goodbye, then left the office.

I was still uncertain how I felt about Dwayne, but I didn't think I'd be getting along with him any time soon.

Chapter 5

Surviving the rest of my day with a coffee cup in my hand, I tried to make a dent in the mountain of paperwork dumped on my desk from everyone, except perhaps the janitor. I guessed that the new guy got all the grunt work. Besides, as long as I was earning a paycheck, it really didn't bother me. Actually, the day went by rather fast. I hadn't eaten anything all day, and the coffee was starting to take its toll on my stomach. Junior, who I was actually pleased to see, peeked his head through my office door at seven p.m. More than likely we shared the same needs: food and sleep.

Before we headed home, we stopped by the hospital to see Uncle James and to comfort Aunt Heide the best we could. Charleen had to pick up her daughter at the babysitter's house and prepare dinner, so she'd left the hospital in Aunt Heide's car just before Junior and I arrived. After spending some time with Uncle James we drove Aunt Heide home.

I felt sorry for my aunt. It was as if every breath she took was a struggle, like a child trying to catch her breath after having cried for so long there were no tears left.

Entering the front door, the aroma of chicken helped ease my empty stomach. I wasn't sure if Charleen had prepared dinner herself or picked up take out. It really didn't matter. I was so accustomed to late night vending machine snacks at the law school cafeteria that almost anything tasted like a home cooked meal.

Not much was said during dinner. Aunt Heide ate very little. I understood what she was going through. After my father had died, my mother and I went through a period of silent dinners and plates barely touched. At times my mother hadn't eaten for days. And when she had, she hadn't been able to keep it down for long. I could only hope that Uncle James awakened from his coma and spared this family any more pain.

Charleen served cherry-covered cheesecake with a scoop of ice cream on the side, and even Aunt Heide took a small sliver. As for me, I didn't hesitate for one moment in helping myself to a third piece. I felt a little sleepy after eating, and slowely sunk deeper into my chair.

As I stuffed the last piece of cheesecake into my mouth--having only thoughts of crawling into bed and going to sleep-- the phone rang. I tried to dismiss the fact that it might be for me, until Charleen handed me the phone with a grin on her face.

"It's a model who says she knows you." Said Charleen, obviously joking.

"Hello."

"Well hello their you sweet thing you." It was a lady with a loud, raspy voice. I pulled the phone away from my ear.

"Come again?"

"Don't you remember me? We had a lovely conversation on the airplane."

"How could I possibly forget you, Olivia?" What I remembered most were the piles of bright red yarn tossed about in every possible direction.

"You're a kind young man, but flattery will get you nowhere."

Did she think I was actually planning to get somewhere with my flattery?

"The reason I'm calling, John, is to invite you to dinner with my family. I've told everybody so much about you that I could hardly call it family dinner without you."

I could picture the whole event now: A dozen grandchildren racing through the house, sneezing, wheezing, crying, screaming at the top of their lungs; all wearing a pair of Grandma's hand knitted socks. And in the middle of all the havoc I had to convince Olivia's son-in-law that his bright red sweater really didn't look that bad, even though it was three sizes too small.

"I'd love to, Olivia, but things have gotten a bit hectic and I don't know when I'd be able to make it. Perhaps you'd give me a rain check?" I couldn't help but feel relieved that I talked my way out of it. Or so I thought.

"John, can't you spare a couple of hours and make an old woman happy?"

"I'm sorry, Olivia. I promise to make it up to you." I was starting to feel guilty. But not enough to accept her invitation.

"Okay, John. But I'm going to hold you to your promise."

"I'm counting on it Olivia."

She was a sweet lady, but I didn't owe her anything. Just as I set the phone down, wondering how she'd gotten my number, the phone rang again. Thinking it was Olivia, trying to wear me down with another attempt, I picked up the phone.

"May I speak with John Bowman please?"

I didn't recognize her voice. "This is he."

"Mr. Bowman, this is Linda Black from the Lake Shore Collection Agency of Chicago. I'm calling to remind you that you have thirty days to repay your loan to Mr. Blackwell."

"Excuse me? What are you talking about?" I had no idea what this was all about. I hadn't heard from Mr. Blackwell since I quit working for him, right after graduation. He owned three restaurants and didn't want to pay a CPA to do his books, so I did his accounting. I'd heard rumors that he ran a few under-the-table businesses, but I hadn't done any paper work for them, so I never paid much attention. Blacky had paid me well and always took care of me when I needed help. I never stuck my nose where it didn't belong. I had no intention of getting a close look at his buddies or their baseball bats.

"You signed an agreement with Mr. Blackwell to pay him the debt you owe in full one month after securing a job. Failure to pay will result in legal action."

"Mr. Blackwell would never file a lawsuit against me. I verbally agreed to send him monthly payments until the debt was paid in full, but I never signed a formal agreement. Let me speak with Mr. Blackwell so we can get this cleared up."

"I'm sorry, Mr. Bowman, but that's not possible."

"Blacky never refused to talk to me. Why should it be different now?"

"Mr. Bowman, Mr. Blackwell can't talk to you because he's in jail."

I knew it would have happened sooner or later. "He's in jail? Why?"

"All I know is that Mr. Blackwell is collecting all his debts so he can pay for legal representation. I'm calling to remind you that you owe him sixty-five-hundred dollars."

"I understand." I tried to think of what I could pawn to help pay the debt. Blacky was one of the few people I'd intended to stay in touch with. And now he'd sent a bill collector after me. I wondered what he'd finally done to get himself in jail. Probably another underage strip joint. It was hard to believe that I had to scrape up sixty-five hundred dollars to get a man like him out of jail.

Everyone but Junior and I had cleared out of the kitchen. I poured both of us a glass of orange juice. We sipped our juice in silence. I was embarrassed that Junior overheard my conversation, but I wasn't ashamed. I did make it through law school. And that's all that mattered.

With the help of student loans, my first few years in law school were worry free. Little did I know that my last year wouldn't be approved for a loan. Did it really make any difference whether I owed eighty-four thousand or a hundred? Blacky had helped me out with a fair job and monthly loans to help pay bills. The descent thing would be to pay him back. How that was possible was another question. Someday, perhaps, I'd handle a case that would generate a substantial fee. For the moment, I was running out of time.

"If you don't mind me asking," Junior said, "how much do you owe?"

"Sixty-five-hundred."

"Is this guy a loan shark?"

I shook my head.

"We could probably dig up some dirt on this guy. It might free you from your debt."

"But not from my conscience."

"I understand," Junior said. "I'd give you the money myself, but I've already given everything to help my father. Even my car belongs to the bank."

"I appreciate the gesture, Junior."

"I'll have a word with the senior partners of the firm. I'm sure they'll help you out." He jabbed my shoulder in a playful manner.

"Sounds good, Junior."

Maybe a good night's sleep and a few generous senior partners could change my whole perspective on things.

Chapter 6

Having tossed and turned throughout the night, awakening every half-hour, I managed to stay in bed until five-thirty. By the time I took a long shower, watched the morning news, and drank two cups of coffee, the rest of the family was up and about.

After breakfast, Junior and I hopped in his "bank owned" Beamer and drove to the office. Our minds are preoccupied with many things; too many for us to engage in conversation this early in the morning. Of course I couldn't blame him if he were thinking about his dad; that's where my mind would be, and if fact, that's where my mind is partly. I'm also brainstorming for different ideas on how to pay off Blacky. Ironically, I have no idea what my salary is. Uncle James and I never had a chance to talk about it. Considering the financial situation of the firm, I was happy with food and a place to stay.

We finally made it to the office. Junior patted my shoulder and told me not to worry about my situation, as if it were no big deal to owe sixty-five hundred dollars to a man whose bodyguards looked like Schwarzenager and Rocky. I entered my beautiful and much undeserved office, and waited impatiently while Junior talked to the senior partners.

Even though I never signed, or at least didn't remember signing, any sort-of legal contract binding me to paying back Blacky at a particular time, I *did* have a lot of IOU's. I leafed through copies of the IOU's I'd signed for Blacky. After careful evaluation, I was unhappy that the little slips of paper were pretty cut and dry. I had hoped that my debt was less than the woman from the collection agency told me, but unfortunately, it was not. Each one had a brief explanation of what the money was borrowed for. Most were for rent and bills. I remembered signing all the statements, and they added up to sixty-five hundred.

While waiting in my office, I frantically tried to think of anyone who might owe me, or at least let me borrow some money. From old friends and acquaintances--many I wished I hadn't met--I looked up phone numbers, hoping they hadn't changed. Unfortunately, those people who still lived in their crummy old places, didn't have any money. And those, who most likely had well paying jobs, were long gone.

After what seemed like a day at the doctor's office, my secretary knocked at the door and told me the senior partners were waiting for me. Trying to control my nerves, I walked down the hallway, turned right, hopped up a short flight of stairs just in time to see Junior open the door to the conference room and disappear behind it. My heart began to pound. There was nothing for me to do but wait for Junior. After what seemed like an eternity, Junior opened the door and walked out of the room. He stared at the floor for a minute, and then lifted his head to eye level. He was as white as a ghost.

"Are you all right Junior?"

"They're merciless. Absolutely merciless."

I gawked at Junior as his words whirled though my mind. What did he mean by merciless? Junior, still shaking his head, slowly trudged back to his office. I stood there, unprepared to face these well-trained sharks who are supposedly on my side. Smelling my blood through the door, Murphy waved me in, as if I was some helpless steer about to be slaughtered. When I entered the room, three senior partners were sitting at the conference table. They introduced themselves. Mr. Brentwood was a tall, stern-faced man, and Mr. Stillens, shorter than Mr. Brentwood, was bald, but still healthy looking, and had a poker face that could probably even fool Dwayne Albertson.

"Have a seat, John," Dwayne said. His face was cold, just like his soul. Obviously, he was still angry because I couldn't control my mouth when the rookie officer was questioning him about Uncle James' so called accident.

"If Junior said something that created tension between you," I said, "don't take it out on him. He shouldn't be blamed for my mess." I sounded like some high-school kid trying to get one of his buddies out of trouble.

"Junior's got his own problems," Dwayne said. "You should be more concerned with your own dilemma."

"About the loan?"

"The loan isn't the problem John," Dwayne said. "We're jointly loaning you seven-thousand dollars. A little extra to get yourself some attire suitable for this law firm." He peered over his glasses at the shabby suit I'd borrowed for a wedding reception back in law school. My study partner had never asked me to return it, and I *accidentally* forgot about it.

"I don't know what to say. It's more than generous of you. But I don't understand what the problem is."

"We received the results of your bar exam," Dwayne said. "You failed."

The room was silent. My three-year nightmare became a reality, I failed. I had the Washington Bar exam Associates send my results to my Uncle's firm in care of my Uncle's name so that: first of all I could claim a Washington address since I wanted to take the bar exam in Washington, and second of all I'd be able to see the results somewhat faster if I had them delivered to the firm. However, I didn't plan on having the Senior Partners of this firm opening my mail. I guess they figured they had a right to it since it was in my Uncle's name, and Dwyane *is* now the acting President instead of my Uncle, but it still pissed me off. I'm not exactly in any position to argue with them at this point either. What greater humility than standing before three highly educated, well-respected lawyers, and knowing I failed the bar exam. "Could the score have been miscalculated?"

"We've contacted the examination board and asked them to recalculate. It's a long process, and they're usually not wrong about these sort-of things, so I suggest you not take anything for granted, and begin studying for the next exam."

"I understand."

"We understand that it's hard to face failure, so we've agreed to keep quiet about it and we're going to help you study for the exam. However, there is one golden rule among the "true" members: an eye for an eye, and a tooth for a tooth. There have been past members who considered themselves "true" members, but did not see eye to eye with us when they were asked to return a favor. We do not tolerate those who swim against the current. We are all open with each other, John, so if you have something to share please don't feel intimidated by us."

"It seems quite clear," I said, feeling more skeptical than ever.

"We're not asking you to do anything inhumane," Dwayne said, "but when the time comes, we expect you to return the favor. Perhaps one day one of us will need to borrow money from you to pay off a loan shark." They all chuckled.

"Sounds fair to me," I said.

Dwayne Albertson shook my hand and poured me a drink. Although my instincts were telling me not to get involved, I was relieved that I could now pay back Blacky.

While trying to manage the never-ending paper work on my desk, the frustrating thought of the bar exam occasionally passed through my head. To have failed that damn exam made me nauseous. Maybe a law career wasn't meant to be. Whatever attributes my father and uncle possessed certainly were not passed on to me. Maybe I should have stuck with the saxophone. Even as a poor, starving musician, at least I would have enjoyed my work.

Chapter 7

I left the office at seven and decided to stop by the local bar and grill. From what Dwayne said, Junior had enough on his mind without having to worry about me, so I left a note with the secretary and told him that I'd find my way home.

When I arrived at the restaurant, I lost myself in a corner table and ordered a plate of barbecued ribs. The food was pretty good and the place was packed with people of all ages. With the exception of me, most appeared to be having a good time. At the back of the restaurant was a small stage. No one was playing at the moment, but I guessed it was a little early. It was the kind of place that catered to unheard of bands. I could hear some familiar Bob Marley tunes in the background. It wasn't the best sound system I'd ever heard, but the music, along with a potent Margarita helped improve my mood.

I didn't usually go to bars alone, but then again I'd never begged for a loan from lawyers, seen my uncle on his death bed, or failed the bar exam. Worst of all, there wasn't one eligible woman to help me dance my sorrows away. Even the waitress looked at me as if I was an alcoholic.

After two margaritas, three Mexican beers, a bloody Mary, and a rack of ribs, I ordered dessert. About a quarter of the way through my scoop of fried ice cream, a comedian with a guitar took the stage. From his hyped-up behavior, he looked as though he'd drunk five cappuccinos. Either that or I had one hell of a buzz. I tried to ignore him, but his loud voice was a bit overbearing. Finally, I gave in and listened to his third-rate jokes while I enjoyed the rest of my ice cream.

Suddenly I heard a loud voice coming from the bar section. Much to my surprise I saw Junior yelling at the bartender. By the way Junior was swaying back and forth, I surmised that he was wasted, yet still trying to convince the bartender that he was sober enough to order another drink. I decided that Junior and the artender needed my help. I didn't feel too steady myself, and I didn't think the comedian was happy when the audience directed their attention toward my bad sense of balance rather than his thirty-year-old jokes.

"Hey Junior," I said. "Have a seat at my table and I'll order you something to eat." A bouncer was approaching, ready to do a number on Junior's loud mouth.

"Johnny! What are you doing here?" His words slurred and he was barely able to stand. With less balance than myself, I slowly helped him stumbled toward my table. I waved to the waitress and ordered Junior a burger, and both of us a pot of coffee.

"What's going on, Junior?"

"Just having a good time, Johnny!"

"Is something wrong?" I asked.

"No, Johnny. What are you doing here?"

"You know what I'm doing here. Quit fooling around and tell me what's going on."

His face got serious. "They have no compassion."

"What do you mean?"

"If you're not careful, Johnny, they'll do the same to you."

"Junior, you're not making any sense. What are you talking about?"

"The firm assigned me to represent an international computer company, called Xiborlink."

"What's so bad about that?"

"They're being sued by a company that claims Xiborlink stole one of their computer chips. Our firm has been fighting this computer company for quite a while."

"It sounds like the kind of case you'd like," I said.

"It is!"

"Then what's the problem?"

"I'm working with the production division and they're located in New Delhi, India. In order for me to clearly understand the case, I need to be there." Junior put down his coffee, reached for my Mexican beer, and gulped the last mouthful. I could understand why he had no interest in sobering up.

"When do you leave?"

"Tomorrow morning at nine."

"Can you refuse?"

"Sure. If I want to lose my job!"

"But your father owns the firm. Doesn't that give you some power?"

"Before I joined the firm, my father signed a contract with the senior partners entitling them to controlling power if anything ever happened to him."

"What about Heide? As your father's spouse, doesn't she have any authority?"

"Legally, mom owns 50% of the Bowman firm. She still needs dad's authorization to override their contract. Either that, or she'd have to secure another 1%. So unless my father dies, and full ownership is passed on to my mother, I'm screwed."

"How can they ask you to leave the country when your father and family need you here?"

Junior didn't answer. He shook his head and stared down at his untouched burger. Although Junior had poured out his heart to me, I still wasn't going to tell him that I failed the bar exam.

The silence continued, so I waved to the waitress and asked for the check. After leaving a generous tip to make up for our obnoxious behavior, we headed outside to catch a cab ride home. Junior was dozing all the way home. I couldn't believe that the Bowman firm could be so cold-hearted. Junior wasn't such a bad guy. At least now I could understand his poor attitude. I might start getting one myself working for people like them.

After hitting the snooze button a few times, I finally made it out of bed at six forty-five, only to discover that I had awakened with a terrible headache. Junior was already in the process of bringing his suitcases out to the car when I strolled into the kitchen wearing my regular sweats and a T-shirt. Everyone was awake, and of course Heide was teary-eyed as she watched her boy leave.

Charleen didn't want to wake her teething two-year-old, so Junior and Charleen said goodbye at the house. Aunt Heide drove us all to the airport where we bid our final farewells to Junior. I gave Junior a bear hug just to let him know that everything would be okay. I knew he was hung-over, so I tried not to slap his back too hard.

Fortunately, Junior is letting me drive his Beamer until he returns, or until the bank repossesses it, whichever came first. Aunt Heide gave me a lift to the office, which is where the BMW is. Although she didn't talk about it, I could tell she was going to go straight to the hospital tt be with Uncle James.

I headed for the library and picked out the books I needed to study for the next bar exam. I grabbed a big mug of coffee, and then hid in my office wearing my sweats and T-shirt. I really didn't care what anyone thought about my sweats. I wasn't a lawyer yet anyway, so why should I dress like one?

After a few hours, my secretary knocked on the door, then walked in carrying a huge cardboard box with books piled almost higher than her chin. It was almost funny, but I decided not to laugh.

"The senior partners sent these for you." Her voice sounded strained from the weight of the books. "Where would you like me to put them?"

I remembered my manners and hopped out of my chair. "Let me help you with those."

"New suit?" She said, with a wide-eyed smirk on her face.

"Are you jealous?"

"Hardly!" At least the secretary has a sense of humor.

"Know of a good pizza place?" I asked.

"What kind do you like?"

"Hawaiian."

"I'll call it in for you."

"Don't go through all that trouble. I can run over and pick it up."

"Nonsense! If I order it for you, it'll be a business expense." She winked and smiled as she walked out the door.

While waiting for the free pizza to arrive, I looked through the box of books. Each one had notes and bookmarks. It reminded me of college, when all I studied were the underlined parts, hoping to pass. I wished it were that easy.

Chapter 8

For the rest of the day I studied with complete enthusiasm; like I had when I first entered law school. I took a quick break around four-thirty, drove to the post office and mailed a sixty-five hundred-dollar check to Blacky. I went back to the office, polished off the rest of the pizza, and studied until eleven p.m. It had been a long day, but if I kept studying at this pace, I'd pass the bar exam with a record-high score. I still haven't gotten my first paycheck, nor did I have any idea what I was being paid. I could only hope that studying during work hours wasn't a problem. Until someone told me it was, I wasn't going to worry about it.

I headed toward the back of the building and walked out the door. With the exception of Junior's BMW, and perhaps a couple of other cars, the parking lot was all but empty. The few cars remaining belonged to partners whose lives revolved around the firm. I wondered how such people could live with themselves. Their kids grow-up without them, their wives sleep with aerobic instructors, and what the hell do they have to show for all the hard work when their lives are over? No thanks! That lifestyle is not for me. As soon as my eighty-four thousand-dollar debt is paid off, my law career is over. I intend to get a real nine to five job, live a normal life, and maybe even eat some American hot dogs with my kids at a baseball game.

Suddenly I there's a voice in the shadows. "Is that you, John Bowman?"

"Who the hell's asking?" I took a few steps backwards and clenched a fist.

Without saying another word, a man walked out from the shadows and handed me a folder.

"What's this?" I asked.

"It's from Blacky." He disappeared into the shadows.

"I already paid Blacky. What else does he want?" I got no reply.

Is this what my life has come to, dodging shadows in the night?

I tried not to think about Blacky's friend and enjoyed the smooth drive home. Besides, I know for certain that Blacky, although he may try to intimidate me, would never have any reason to have someone harm me.

I got home at eleven-forty. Everybody was in bed except Charleen. She sat alone at the kitchen table, holding a mug of either coffee or hot chocolate, I couldn't quite tell.

"Up kind of late aren't you?" I asked, wondering why her eyes looked glossy.

"Getting out of work kind of late, aren't you?" Charleen smiled.

"Yeah, quite the work load. Why aren't you in bed?"

"Michelle has been keeping me up."

Michelle was no where in sight, and she was the most well behaved little girl I'd ever seen. "You're worried about your Dad?"

Charleen nodded, and a tear ran down her cheek.

It was a clear evening, warm with a nice breeze. "Want to go for a walk?" I asked.

Charleen didn't answer. She stood up, put her arm around me, and we headed outside. We ambled down to the lake and sat on a bench facing the water. For a few minutes, we both were quiet. Then Charleen opened up and poured out her heart to me. She missed her Dad so much that her anxiety twisted even my stomach into a knot. With her brother away, it was even worse. We spent the early-morning hours exchanging stories and trying to cheer each other up. It did both of us some good. I even told her about failing the bar exam. It's strange, for some reason I completely trust Charleen in that she would never see me as less of a person simply for failing the exam. That's a rare thing to find in a person. Usually, people enjoy seeing others fall, especially when it's someone they know as a friend or relative. Charleen is a good woman, and I think she'll make a wonderful wife for some lucky guy out there.

I wished that Uncle James were up and about. It would make life a lot easier for all of us, especially for the family and the Bowman firm.

Chapter 9

Nothing but thunder and lightening, all morning a steady downpour. Maybe because I knew that I was not missing any fun-in-the-sun, the rain helped me to concentrate on my studies and put me in a bookworm mood. Studying was precisely what I'd be doing right now if the senior partners hadn't summoned me to a casual luncheon.

Feeling as stressed as a laboratory rat being studied by a mad scientist, I endured lunch while the senior partners scrutinized my every move. Not exactly what my life thrived on.

"Why aren't you eating, John?" Dwayne said. "Your uncle would be upset if I weren't taking good care of you."

I forced myself to be polite. "Thanks, but I ate something earlier."

"At least have a drink with us."

"Sure, why not?"

"That's more like it. What can I get for you?"

"Ice water would be great."

Dwayne's face tightened when he realized I was playing with him. He waved to his secretary to fetch me some water as if she were his personal maid. I was amazed that guys like these still existed. I was almost more amazed that women still went along with that sort-of crap.

"We've got a surprise for you, John," Dwayne said. "Ordinarily, we wouldn't do this for a new member, but considering your relationship with your uncle and your dire financial situation, we feel it would be a good step for your career."

"I feel honored, but I'm not sure what this all means." I couldn't help but feel that Dwayne was now toying with *me*.

Dwayne handed me a three-inch-thick folder. "We're going to let you handle the Sharpner/Peterson case. It should be cut and dry. Mr. Peterson, a wealthy sixty-eight year old businessman, is divorcing his thirty-five-year old wife. He's pretty sure all she ever wanted was just his money. He wants revenge; wants her out of his house with barely enough money to pay for a taxi."

"But I haven't passed the bar yet."

"We understand your dilemma, but you still need to earn your keep. Compared to everyone else's workload, this case is easy. All you have to do is gather enough information to put up a good fight against Sharpner's divorce attorney. Another partner will represent you in court. And you'll still get a fair percentage."

Trying to show initiative, even though I had none for this sort-of thing, I told the partners that I wanted to begin working on the Sharpner/Peterson case. I left the luncheon and headed for the Cricket. It was a rather wet walk due to the heavy rain, but once inside, it was warm, and quite busy with people. I sat close to the bar and ordered a BLT sandwich since I didn't really eat at the luncheon with the senior partners. As I tried to organize my insights, my mind was tangled with thoughts of studying and the case.

I couldn't believe that Dwayne asked me to handle a divorce case. Every lawyer knew that divorce cases were never cut and dry. It wasn't a job for a lawyer; it was more suited for a shrink.

You'd think a busy establishment like the Cricket would get some better comedians. What was the deal with this guy? Every time he told a joke he took a break and sipped his water.

Suddenly the comedian didn't seem to bother me. I focused on a woman at the bar. Her dark brown hair, green eyes and overall looks blew my mind. Her boyfriend seemed to be too busy talking to his buddies to acknowledge her. She stood in the background, unappreciated. If she were standing by my side, I'd make damn certain that everybody knew she was the most gorgeous woman here. And I'd make certain she knew it too.

Chapter 10

As I walked down the hallway, the hospital appeared to be deserted. Heide had asked me to pick her up after I was finished with work. Uncle James had been moved to the second floor, room two-o-two. I was told the hospital moved the more stable patients to the second floor. Hopefully, this had eased Aunt Heide's mind. As always, I found Aunt Heide sitting beside Uncle James, clutching his hand. I decided to sit next to Heide and spend a little time with both of them. I had hoped my uncle would've been out of his coma by now, but I'm not going to stop hoping. This family has evoked feelings in me that were almost indescribable. They seem like a second family to me. Ironically, since I arrived, things had been quite unstable. The firm is on the verge of bankruptcy. Junior is in India. And Uncle James is confined to a hospital bed in a coma.

We visited with Uncle James for about twenty minutes, then headed for home.

"We need to talk, John," Aunt Heide said.

"What is it?"

"I talked to one of the senior partners today, Dwayne Albertson. We may be forced to close the Bowman firm if things don't start looking up. Dwayne and the other members offered a fair amount of money in exchange for all files of our clients and their cases. They would then open their own firm with those clients. It's not a great retirement plan, at least not one I would have predicted. We wouldn't be able to live extravagantly, but it would be enough to get by on with out too many headaches. And perhaps, considering all the hassle we've endured in the past couple of years with that firm, it would be the best choice we have."

"When are you going to do this?" I asked.

"I'm going to wait and see what happens with your Uncle James. Right now it would take a miracle to reverse everything that has happened."

I was surprised that she was able to see things so clearly. If I were in the same situation, all I'd be able to do was pray.

Dwayne's offer seemed a little obvious to me. This was exactly what the partners were waiting for. They kept all the connections and paper work, and if they could persuade the clients to stay with them, they'd become much wealthier than if they ever stayed with the firm. It amazed me how much greed could take over one's soul.

It's Saturday morning and even though working at the office is encouraged, I decided not to go to work today. Instead I drove the BMW to downtown Seattle to shop for clothes with the extra money I got from the senior partners. With only five hundred dollars, I have to look for inexpensive attire considering the prices of suits these days.

As soon as I got out of the car, I saw Olivia Potter. She had called me yesterday evening but luckily I was in the shower. I tried to duck out of sight, but there was no place to hide.

"There's my Cutie Pie!" She yelled from across the parking lot.

I decided to be nice. "Hello, Olivia. How are you doing?"

"I'd be a lot better if you returned my calls, you silly boy." Olivia gave me a big kiss on the cheek as though I were her grandson.

"Sorry Olivia, I've been so busy lately, I haven't had time for anything but work."

"Is that what you call working so hard right now, strolling around all the stores?"

She may be old and wrinkled, but she sure wasn't afraid to throw stones.

"You got me on that one. How can I make it up to you?"

"For starters you can invite me on your shopping spree. You are going shopping aren't you?"

"Yes, actually I am." Keeping her company might not be a bad exchange for her good taste.

After explaining to her what I was looking for and how much I intended to spend, Olivia grabbed my arm and dragged me through all the little shops. I wasn't sure if going into these shops was for my benefit, or if Olivia just wanted to show me off as her new grandson.

We looked through ten clothing stores before we found one with the style clothes I was looking for. Unfortunately everything was priced double of what I had to spend. I tried on a dark green, double-breasted suit with a matching tie. Then I slipped into a dark blue suit. I paid for the dark green suit and put the other one on lay away. Maybe when I got my first paycheck I'd be able to pay off the blue suit and buy a couple more.

"Well," Olivia said, as we headed back to the car, "all we need to do now is make dinner plans."

"Actually," I said, "I'm going to be quite busy for the next few weeks, so I don't really have enough time." I was certain that guilt was written all over my face.

"Nonsense John. Next Saturday at seven." Olivia patted me on the back and left me standing next to the BMW.

"But wait," I yelled, "I don't even know where you live!"

"I'll take care of it." A glimmer of power sparkled in her eyes.

Chapter 11

Throughout the day on Sunday, Aunt Heide and I tried to contact Junior. Unfortunately, we didn't get through. I was sure everything was fine, but I had hoped we'd be able to reach Junior to ease Aunt Heide's mind.

For a Monday I was feeling quite energetic. Surprisingly, the office was not busy. The senior partners had another business luncheon today. I hadn't heard what it was about, but I was sure it had something to do with money or power and who will get the most of it.

I decided to review the Sharpner/Peterson case. In law school, we did practice trials on dozens of divorce cases just like this one. I never would have predicted that I would ever really file one. I always believed I'd secure a job that involved real court cases, and not a bunch of grunt work. Strange how things ended differently from what I had imagined. I telephoned Mr. Peterson and set up an appointment for Wednesday. If he was expecting to keep his fortune away from his wife, I wasn't going to have good news for him. Mr. Peterson hadn't bothered to get a prenuptial agreement. If I had been in his shoes, and married a thirty-five-year-old woman, I would have made certain that I had a prenuptial.

For the rest of the day I studied for the bar. I was beginning to get a feel for what law was all about, and felt confident I'd pass the exam. Then again, I had the same feeling before I took the bar exam for the first time. I headed home at seven p.m., making it through the entire day without seeing any of the senior partners. If only things could go like this every day.

As usual, things were quiet when I got home. I made myself a sandwich, then took a shower. The hot water felt good after a long day of studying; it helped to relieve the stress. I said good night to the family, then went to bed at nine-thirty.

There's a loud knock at my door. "John, wake-up."

Charleen walked in my room, as frantic as I'd ever seen her.

"What's going on?" I asked, waiting for my pupils to adjust to the light.

"The hospital just called!"

"Is Uncle James okay?"

Halfway out the door, Charleen shouted, "C'mon, Mom is still on the phone!"

I awakened in a heartbeat and dashed down the stairs. I didn't know what time it was, but it didn't really matter. Sliding into the kitchen, I stood next to Charleen. We were both completely out of breath. Aunt Heide was nodding her head, listening, while the doctor did most of the talking. It was impossible to know what was going on. Finally Aunt Heide hung up the phone.

"That was Dr. Grunnkeil." Aunt Heide's face lit up with a big grin. "James has regained consciousness."

I could almost feel my heart jump. By the looks on Aunt Heide's and Charleen's faces, I suspected they felt the same. We hugged each other for a long while. It was as if we'd just won a long-fought war.

Still wearing pajamas, Aunt Heide grabbed her trench coat and draped it around her shoulders. "Dr. Grunnkeil said we can visit James right away."

I didn't bother with a jacket. I was wearing an old pair of shorts and a T-shirt, so I slipped on my thongs, and really didn't care what anyone thought of my outfit.

When we arrived at the hospital, Dr. Grunnkeil and Dr. Jennings were waiting for us. Both doctors looked happy.

"So far everything looks good," Dr. Jennings said. "Mr. Bowman appears to be fine, but we still need to be cautious. He's not fully stable yet."

We followed the doctors into the room. Uncle James' eyes were closed, but by the look of the bed, I could tell that he'd been moving. I glanced at the EKG monitor next to his bed. His heart was beating with an even rhythm. Aunt Heide and Charleen sat on the edge of the bed. Aunt Heide softly touched James' cheek and his eyes slightly opened. He appeared to be somewhat sedated, but managed to smile. Charleen didn't hesitate to give him a gentle hug. James moved his fingers toward them and Aunt Heide and Charleen each held a hand.

I decided to quietly leave the room for a bit to let the moment become a memory. Both doctors were down the hallway with smiles on their faces. Obviously, they were delighted to have delivered such good news to the family. I wandered toward the snack bar, just down the hall from my uncle's room. I really needed a cup of coffee, but didn't want to miss an opportunity to say hello to Uncle James. I had no idea what time it was; there were no clocks in sight. Time didn't matter anyway. I was just relieved that Uncle James was conscious.

Just as I sat and poured three packages of sugar in my coffee, I saw Aunt Heide and Charleen walking out of the room displaying big smiles. I was a bit surprised that they hadn't visited with my uncle longer.

As Aunt Heide and Charleen walked toward me, I stood up and gulped a mouthful of my coffee. "James asked to see you, John," Aunt Heide said with a smile, still as happy as ever that her husband is finally conscious. "It sounds serious."

Without saying a word, I nodded my head and walked to my uncle's room. I pushed the door open and tiptoed over to the bed. His eyes were closed so I gave him a gentle pat on the hand. He turned his head and opened his eyes. He looked barely awake.

"John," he whispered. His voice was strained. I leaned forward to more clearly hear him. Uncle James gripped my arm somewhat tightly, probably using every bit of strength he has. "John, get out of there!"

"What do you mean?" I asked, feeling my stomach twist into a knot.

"The firm! Get away from that damn place!" He began breathing heavy.

"Uncle James, please, take it easy. You're still weak, and whatever the problem is with the firm I'm sure we can work it out in a couple of days."

"John, you don't understand. I used to trust them, now look what has happened to me." He said, still breathing hard.

"Did someone from the firm do this to you?"

Uncle James was now wide-eyed and speaking very sternly. "Please, John! Get the hell out, and make sure you take Junior with you!"

I could see him struggling to breathe. Suddenly he was gasping for air and his palms were pressed against his chest. The EKG monitor stopped the intermittent beeping and hummed a steady tone. I ran out the door, into the hallway, and yelled for help.

Running down the hallway toward the doctors, I screamed again, "Help! Quick!"

"What happened?" Dr. Jennings asked.

"He's having a heart attack!"

Dr. Jennings didn't hesitate. She brushed past me and ran into the room. Dr. Grunnkeil followed behind pushing a defibrillator. I stood in the doorway and watched in disbelief.

"Clear!" Dr. Jennings yelled. Dr. Grunnkeil rubbed the shock paddles together, then pressed them against my uncle's chest. Nothing. Two nurses entered the room; one took my arm and led me into the hall. Just as I left the room, Dr. Jennings yelled clear again.

With tears running down their cheeks, Aunt Heide and Charleen came running toward me. "What's going on in there, John?" Aunt Heide asked.

"James is having a heart-attack."

"Why is this happening?" Aunt Heide screamed. "WHY?"

I didn't know what to say. I stood there, holding my aunt and cousin.

The doctors walked out of the room; their faces grim.

"I'm so sorry. We did everything we could," Dr. Grunnkeil said.

"You bastards! Why couldn't you save him?" Aunt Heide pounded her fists on Dr. Grunnkeil's chest. Then she turned to me. "Damn it John, what did you say to him? You knew he was weak, why couldn't you have just left him alone?"

I didn't know what to say. I tried to say something, anything, but except for my slow flowing tears I was frozen. I felt horrible, I shouldn't have gone into that room. "I'm sorry Heide, I'm so sorry." I finally was able to utter with out even being able to look at her eyes. Right now, I was the enemy.

For a moment, we all stood there, silent, overwhelmed with disbelief and sorrow. Then Aunt Heide grabbed Charleen's hand and charged down the hall.

The doctors apologized to me. I shook their hands, then shuffled down the hallway to where Aunt Heide and Charleen were holding each other.

"What did you say to make him die?" Aunt Heide yelled at me.

"Please, Aunt Heide, how can--

"Why did you let him get so excited? You knew how unstable he was!"

"I'm sorry. Please believe me. I never meant for this to happen."

I could feel my heart sinking. Aunt Heide turned away and jogged toward the car. Charleen and I followed close behind. Before we got into the car, Charleen gave me a quick hug. And that's when it hit me hard, nothing but tears poured down my cheeks. I'm sure if it was because of the way Aunt Heide felt about me, or if it was because of James, or perhaps a combination of both. All I know is it felt good to know that Charleen didn't blame me.

The drive home was silent. We got back to the house just past four a.m. None of us went to bed. We all retreated to our own private space. It might have been better for the three of us to talk, but for now maybe it was better for each of us to mourn privately.

I walked out the back door and sat on the swing hanging from the oak tree. I could see moonlight reflecting off the pond. I didn't know how long I sat there, but when the sun peeked over the horizon, Aunt Heide appeared out of nowhere. I stood up, but didn't know what to expect. She put her arms around me and gave me a hug. It felt comforting. We sat on a bench and didn't speak for a long time.

"I'm so sorry I said all those things, John," Aunt Heide's voice was raspy. "I hope you understand that I was in shock and didn't know what I was saying."

I couldn't find appropriate words, so instead, I gave her another hug and could feel tears streaming down my face.

Chapter 12

I awoke to a slight breeze, realizing that I dozed off while sitting on the swing. It was Tuesday morning; probably the worst Tuesday of my life. There was a blanket around me, and I guessed that Aunt Heide must have wrapped it around my shoulders. When I walked into the kitchen, Charleen and Aunt Heide were sitting at the table. I sat beside them with the blanket still draped around me. Charleen was feeding Michelle and Aunt Heide was talking on the telephone. I closed my eyes for a minute and tried to discern what had happened with-in the last twenty-four hours. It felt unreal, like some kind of sick nightmare. Uncle James was like a second father to me. I would never forget what he'd done for me.

"I've been trying to get through to India," Aunt Heide said. "It's pointless. No matter how many times I call, I can't reach Junior." Her eyes welled with tears. "I spoke with the senior partners--Dwayne Albertson in particular--and they're going to handle the funeral arrangements and try to get a hold of Junior"

My aunt was one tough lady. After all she'd been through, she still had the strength to coordinate whom to call and what to say. At least the firm was doing something for Uncle James for a change. Why those idiots sent Junior to India was beyond me. He should be here with his family, now more than ever.

After spending a little more time with Aunt Heide and Charleen, I took a quick shower, threw on some clothes and headed for the office. I was a bit curious how the senior partners would act around me. I walked in the main entrance at eleven a.m., and the place seemed to be in an uproar. Standing at the main entrance and observing the chaos, I saw Dwayne Albertson. Everyone's attention was suddenly drawn toward me.

"I'm truly sorry about your uncle, John." Dwayne said. "He was a good man and we're all going to miss him."

I tried to read his eyes while he gave his little speech. Lawyers are such good actors, and more specifically, good liars.

I felt awkward with everyone gawking at me. "I'm sorry too."

"If there's anything we can do, John, let us know."

"I appreciate the gesture, Dwayne."

I felt as though a spotlight were shining on me. To avoid further conversation with Dwayne, I hopped on the elevator and went to my office. I tried to clear my head, so when I called Mr. Peterson to cancel the appointment, I'd sound like a professional. My office no longer was appealing to me. The oak desk, the tall windows, and the fern that amazingly managed to stay alive seemed foreign. I wasn't sure if this was because Uncle James had died, or if something else was happening. Either way, my office felt cold.

I prepared myself mentally, then telephoned Mr. Peterson. At first, he was upset, but after I explained the circumstances, he was more than understanding. He sounded like a decent man, very sympathetic. He had an enthusiastic voice, sounding much more energetic than a typical sixty-eight year old. I wasn't sure how well he knew Uncle James, but I invited him to the funeral. Because I had no details of where and when the funeral would be held, I transferred him to my secretary.

After speaking with Mr. Peterson, I grabbed my first cup of coffee and focused my thoughts on Uncle James. It was hard not to get emotional. I didn't see anything wrong with shedding a few tears now and then. I guess it proved that I wasn't a hard-ass lawyer like everyone else around here.

After pondering another twenty minutes, I decided to speak with Dwayne Albertson and take him up on his little offer. I knocked twice on his oak door. Before he responded, I walked in. It wasn't that I didn't have manners, I just didn't feel like using them around people like Dwayne.

Dwayne was sitting at his desk, sipping what looked like gin and tonic. Quite an odd way of showing his condolences.

I sat in one of the cushioned chairs facing him. "There is something you can do for me, Dwayne."

Dwayne grinned like a clown. "I'm glad you feel you can come to me, John."

"I'd like to pay off all my debts, including any return favors that might come up in the future." My tone was firm and steady.

"That's one hell of a favor. How about this? Hold off on repaying us, and as far as the favor is concerned, well, let's not worry about that now. It's a vicious world, John, and we have to stick together."

My voice got forceful. "I want a clean slate. No debts and no favors!"

Dwayne lit a fat cigar. "Most people would consider it a privilege to owe us a favor, but if this is what you want, consider it done."

Dwayne puffed on his cigar. "I must tell you though, I have lost some respect for you, John."

"Why do you say that?"

"I thought you wanted to be part of our team." He sneered. "But there's still plenty of time to convince you of that, isn't there?"

I shook my head and smiled. "By the way, how do I get in touch with Junior?"

"I wish I knew. We haven't heard from him for quite some time now."

"Thanks." Feeling relieved that the seven-thousand dollar debt was lifted off my shoulders, I walked out the door quite satisfied.

Chapter 13

I entered the family room and found Aunt Heide and Charleen sitting next to each other with Michelle cuddled up between them. They both turned their heads and smiled. I walked behind the sofa and massaged their necks, one hand on each neck.

"We can't hold on to the Bowman firm much longer." Aunt Heide said. Charleen's head snapped toward her mother, obviously shocked by this announcement.

The thought of the senior partners taking over the firm incensed me. "Do you think the senior partners can preserve the firm's reputation and client list?"

"Even if they can't, I'm in no position to bargain," Aunt Heide said. "Their offer is generous. Besides, now that James has passed away, how could I possibly keep the firm alive? Things may be a little tight now and then if I take the offer, but at least we can keep the house and not have to worry about losing everything. It's their problem now, let's let them deal with the headaches." Aunt Heide stood up, squeezed my arm, said good night and lumbered up the staircase.

I sat next to Charleen. Considering how quiet she was, I assumed she was pondering my Aunt's words. To lose this firm--a company her father had spent a lifetime building--must have been difficult for her to accept.

"Will you continue working for the firm?" Charleen asked.

The question caught me off guard. "I haven't really thought about it. I don't really want to, but until I find another means of income, what choice do I have?"

"You're welcome to stay here as long as you like. My mother may not say it, but she really enjoys having you here. And that goes for me too. It's especially hard right now without Dad or Junior around, and you've been very supportive." Charleen picked up her daughter and said good night.

It felt good to be appreciated. I wished it were under different circumstances.

Chapter 14

There was thunder and lightening in the distance, but no rain. Nobody paid much attention to nature's sound and light show. I had no idea Uncle James knew so many people. I'd say there were over three hundred somber faces gathered around the grave.

The senior partners were standing opposite us. Not one of them could look at Heide, Charleen, or even me. As far as I was concerned, they were a pack of cold-hearted scoundrels. They were, however, decent enough to have paid for the funeral. I wondered what they had in mind for the firm. Whatever it was, I was sure it would make me nauseous.

I tried not to cry, but I couldn't suppress my emotions. Every time I looked at the coffin, or Aunt Heide, or listened to the pastor's words, tears would flow. Charleen stood beside me, squeezing my hand, resting her head against my shoulder from time to time. Other than my father's funeral, this was the most difficult experience of my life. Uncle James was one of the kindest men I'd ever met.

Both Uncle James and my father had served in the Navy during the Vietnam War; therefore, they were entitled to a military service. Three shots rang in the air as five sailors pointed their rifles to the sky and squeezed the triggers in harmony. They folded the American flag and handed it to Heide. She could barely hold the flag. It was an impressive, yet poignant display of respect.

A final prayer was said next to the gravesite. Afterwards, several people paid their condolences to Aunt Heide and Charleen. The crowd slowly dispersed, and Aunt Heide, Charleen, and I walked back to the black limo. Just as Heide and Charleen stepped into the limo, I heard someone call my name.

"Excuse me, John."

I turned and looked at an unfamiliar face.

"I'm Mr. Peterson. I'm terribly sorry about your loss. James was a good man."

"Thank you."

"If you or your family needs anything, please don't hesitate to contact me."

I forced a smile. "I'll keep that in mind."

"Oh, by the way, let me know what firm you'll be working with and I'll consider letting you handle my case."

His words hit me like a hammer. "What was that?"

"Aren't you leaving the firm?"

"What gave you that impression?"

"I called you yesterday just to let you know that I would be attending the funeral, but when I tried to leave you a message, they transferred my call to a new lawyer. I assumed you were no longer with the Bowman firm."

Before I could answer Peterson's question, or even begin to understand what was going on, I heard a loud crack of thunder and heavy rain poured from the sky.

Peterson handed me his business card, pulled his trench coat over his head, and disappeared in the heavy rain. I stood there dumbfounded, rain drenching me. Finally, I got inside the limo.

My stomach felt like it had risen to my throat; my thoughts were overwhelming. When I looked at Aunt Heide or Charleen, I felt a wave of tears. But when I thought about the senior partners and what they were trying to do, rage overpowered me. I knew now, more than ever, that they were nothing more than sharks.

Chapter 15

Friday morning I walked through the front doors of the firm, my rage hadn't diminished. I headed straight for Dwayne Peterson's office, but his secretary intercepted me.

"None of the partners are here right now." She handed me an envelope. "They asked me to give this to you."

Not in the best of moods, I tore open the envelope. I read, not entirely in shock, a termination letter. It explained that due to the recent change in ownership, and an effort to reduce expenses and restructure the firm, my services were no longer needed. I tore the letter in half and dropped it on the floor. There was nothing I could do, so I went to my old office to gather my personal belongings.

"John," the secretary said. Her voice was a bit softer. "The senior partners asked me to clean out your office. The box is in the library closet. I'm sorry, John. Oh, I almost forgot. A Mr. Blackwell called for you. Said he was an old friend." She handed me a slip of paper with his phone number written on it. Not exactly the first person I wanted to hear from right now.

I walked into the library and found a cardboard box with my belongings stuffed inside. The file for the Sharpner/Peterson case was gone, and of course, all the study books the senior partners had let me borrow were also gone. Feeling full of spite, I surveyed the shelves and picked out every book I could find to help prepare me for the bar exam, and threw them in my box. There were a few other books of interest, so I tossed them in the box as well. As I walked out the door, laboring to carry the heavy box, the secretary stood in front of me with a big smile. I assumed that she approved of my little act of larceny. I nodded and returned the smile, knowing that under the circumstances, she'd probably do the same thing.

I drove home feeling angry, yet somewhat satisfied. When I walked into the main entrance of Aunt Heide's house, I found four suitcases in the foyer.

I heard my aunt yelling from upstairs. "John, would you come up and help us out for a sec.?"

I dashed upstairs and into my aunt's bedroom. Charleen was sitting on a suitcase while my aunt was attempting to secure the locks; quite a comical scene.

"What the hell's going on?" I asked.

"I booked a flight to Colorado," Aunt Heide said. "Most of my family lives there. It's been difficult without James. I guess I need a little time to recuperate."

I helped Charleen fasten the suitcase. "It'll be lonely without you, Aunt Heide."

"Charleen will be here to keep you company, and you better take good care of her while I'm gone."

"No need to worry about that."

I dragged the last suitcase downstairs, and the three of us sat in the family room. Aunt Heide opened a bottle of red wine.

We sipped wine and talked. I wasn't sure whether or not the wine lifted my spirits, but it sure tasted good. Reluctantly, I told them that I was no longer with the Bowman firm. I didn't tell them I'd been terminated, but I was certain they both knew. Aunt Heide took me by the hand and led me to Uncle James' office. She told me that I could use it whenever I needed to.

"Dwayne Albertson went through the office collecting papers, files, and books that he felt were part of the firm's records," my aunt said.

The heartlessness of the senior partners never ceased to amaze me. I thanked Aunt Heide for everything she'd done, kissed her good night, and went to my room. I was emotionally and physically exhausted.

Chapter 16

Charleen and I gave Heide a ride to the airport, then we waited with her until her plane left for Colorado at ten a.m. Taking a trip to visit with her family was a wise decision. Charleen, too, would have benefited from a trip, but she had her father's blood; a natural instinct to face difficulties head on.

When I got home, I hit the hammock in the backyard until two p.m.

"Hey there, sleepy head," Charleen shouted with a grin, making very sure I was awake. "Someone's on the phone for you. Sounds important." She dropped the cordless on my lap.

"Hello."

"Johnny Boy. How ya been?"

I'd never forget that voice. "Hey Blacky."

"Haven't heard from you for a while." His tone had a sarcastic ring.

"Been kind of busy. What can I do for you?"

"Did you check out those files I delivered to you?" Blacky asked.

"What do you expect of me Blacky? I paid all the money I owed you. Now you want me to do extra work?"

"If you help me with this one, John, you'll never hear from me again."

"What about your lawyer? Isn't this his job?"

"My lawyer's okay, but I need you on this one, John. Did you look at the file?"

"I haven't even opened the envelope"

There was a long silence. "I see."

I was walking a thin line. Blacky wasn't the kind of guy to mess with. "I'll take a look at the file and call you in a couple of days."

"I really appreciate this, John."

"Yeah, well, just so long as you realize this is your last favor. And realize that I won't be putting that much effort into this either." I hit the disconnect button and went into the house.

I grabbed my box of belongings and retreated to Uncle James' office. It felt eerie sitting at my uncle's desk. I wondered how many hours he'd spent in this room examining cases and planning strategies. Underneath the law books I had so conveniently "borrowed," I located the envelope Blacky's crony had given me. As I sorted through receipts, IOU's and other papers that made little sense to me, I found a letter with my name on it. I recognized Blacky's handwriting. He explained in great detail that for over two years he'd been serving liquor at one of his restaurants without a license. Considering all of his contacts, this made no sense to me. It had already cost him over two hundred thousand dollars, and if he decided to reopen the restaurant, it would cost even more. I had no idea what he expected me to do.

Time slipped by quickly, and before I realized it I was late for dinner with Olivia. Perhaps I'd get lucky and she'd also forgotten about it. I hadn't heard from her, so without feeling guilty I fell on the sofa in the living room and turned on the television, ready to lounge around for the rest of the evening. When the doorbell rang, I was certain it was Olivia. Charleen beat me to the door.

Charleen walked into the living room with a sinister grin on her face. "I don't suppose you would know why a chauffeur is looking for a Mr. John Bowman?"

I jumped off the couch and peeked my head out the door. "Can I help you?"

"I believe you had a dinner appointment at seven p.m. with Olivia Potter and her family."

I suddenly realized that I hadn't taken a shower today. "Can you give me a few minutes to get ready?"

"A few," the chauffeur said, looking me up and down with a disapproving look.

I ran upstairs, hopped in the shower and tossed the soap and shampoo around until I was fairly clean, and then dried off. I got dressed as quickly as I could, threw on some casual clothes, dragged a comb through my hair, and dashed down the stairs. The chauffeur gave me another once-over, but I couldn't read his eyes. Hopefully, I looked presentable. I gave Charleen a friendly peck on the cheek and told her not to wait up for me.

As I sat in the spacious back seat of the limo, enjoying the quiet ride and the luxury, I sipped fine champagne and nibbled on exquisite chocolate. I had no idea where we were going, and frankly, didn't care. We arrived at the harbor in downtown Seattle, where the fairies dock, and the chauffeur drove onto the open deck. I decided to get out and stroll around for a bit while being on the fairy. The view was spectacular. As we left the docks and headed across the water, I watched a beautiful sunset. I noticed the chauffeur standing a few feet away from me, so I asked where we were going. I thought it curious that he didn't answer me, but maybe he hadn't heard me. He looked in his seventies and appeared to be a cultured gentleman.

I got back into the limo just as the operator negotiated the fairy against the dock. As the limo pulled away from the fairy boat, I read a sign that read, 'Welcome to Mercer Island'. I remembered Aunt Heide and Charleen talking about this island. They had said if it wasn't such a long trip from Seattle they would have moved there many years ago when the Bowman Firm was thriving.

With little effort, the limo driver drove along the curvy road as if he could have made this trip in his sleep. Before long we turned into a long driveway. I turned my head and gawked at a home that made Aunt Heide's house look like the maid's quarters. We pulled up to the main entrance, and quite to my surprise, Olivia rushed outside and opened my door. I got out of the limo and the spunky woman gave me a firm hug.

Putting her arm around my waist and guiding me toward the front door, Olivia said, "You look as handsome as ever, John."

Wearing a ravishing black evening gown, Olivia's ensemble made my tan Dockers and button-down shirt look like a pauper's outfit. "You look quite stunning yourself, Olivia."

When we walked into the main entrance, I couldn't believe what I saw. Hanging above the foyer was a magnificent chandelier--must have weighed two thousand pounds--reflecting a rainbow of colors from the last bit of sunlight pouring in the tall windows facing the bay. I had no idea what Olivia did for a living, but it was obvious she had a lot of money.

"I'm so happy you made it, John. I can't wait for you to meet my family." She took my arm and escorted me to the other side of the house. I didn't know what the mouth-watering aroma was, but whatever it was that she was cooking smelled wonderful. Olivia and I strolled into a massive dinning room. There were about twenty people gathered around the dining room table, but two seats were vacant. I guessed they were for Olivia and I. Everyone stopped talking and directed their attention to me. I felt uneasy, as if a spotlight were shining on me, but Olivia took the time to introduce me to each guest seated at the table. Olivia showed me to my seat, then excused herself, and walked out of the room.

The room again was silent. A middle-age man--one of Olivia's son-in-laws--cleared his throat and turned toward me. He didn't smile; his look was almost mean.

"Are you still in school, John?" he asked.

I thought his name was Tim, but decided not to risk it. "Actually I'm finished with college."

"What do you do for a living?"

"Well, I deal with people who have problems." For some reason, I decided not to tell him that I was a lawyer. Technically, I'm not until I pass that damn bar.

"What sort of problems?"

Walking into the room, and likely saving me from an interrogation, Olivia said, "It's not necessary to give our guest an interview."

"I'd like you to meet my grand kids," Olivia announced. "Brian, Ted, Terry, and Kim." The children were neatly dressed and well behaved. Each walked over to me and politely shook my hand. They excused themselves and went into the kitchen where I assume they were eating their dinner.

"Those sweeties belong to John and my daughter-in-law, Brenda," Olivia said.

Brenda, I surmised, was the attractive lady with the proud smile on her face.

"Where are your two sweet-ones?" Olivia asked Tim.

"My son is most likely getting in trouble with his friends, and Lisa is working on a project."

Olivia excused herself, went back into the kitchen, then returned with two large trays filled with salads and shrimp appetizers. Half the guests jumped up and tried to help Olivia.

"Sit down!" Olivia shouted. "I was a hard working waitress long before any of you were born. I didn't need your help then and I hardly think I need it now."

Everybody sank into their chairs as if they'd just been scolded by thier third grade teacher. In this family, Olivia obviously had the final word on everything.

Olivia served us the salad and appetizers flawlessly. I was impressed with the pride Olivia displayed. She didn't seem at all like the sweet old lady on the airplane with a ball of red yarn hanging out of her carry-on. Instead, Olivia was tenacious and self-reliant, a feisty woman, aware of everything going on around her. In spite of this tough exterior, it was evident to me that she loved her family, and that they reciprocated that love.

For the most part, there was little conversation while we all enjoyed the first course. As I quietly listened to the chitchat, I noticed that Olivia's blue eyes were always looking my way. As though she was admiring one of her grandsons. I couldn't quite understand why, and it made me feel almost ackward at times, but I decided not to think too much of it.

"Perhaps I could use a bit of help," Olivia said, her stare fixed on me.

I quickly helped Olivia clear the table, and pushed the serving cart with all the dirty dishes into the kitchen.

"Why don't you hire someone to help with the household chores?" As soon as I asked this question I knew I was being presumptuous.

"I have some hired help. But I prefer to do all the cooking myself. There's nothing quite like watching my family enjoying a home-cooked meal prepared by grandma."

Olivia opened the oven, pulled out a large turkey, and set it on the counter. I tried to help, but she gave me the 'don't your dare' look. She took out a carving knife and began slicing the golden-brown turkey.

"Anybody special in your life, John?"

"Why do you ask?"

"Just being a little nosy."

I hated questions like that. I knew it was time to change the subject. "How did your limo driver find me?"

"Oh, you're such a kidder, John. You lawyers are all alike, always suspicious of things."

"How did you know I was a lawyer?" I asked, becoming exactly what she just accused me of, being suspicious.

"Really John, you should be able to figure things like this out. You *did* go to law school. Remember Mrs. O'Conner? She's known your mother for quite some time now. And you know how old women can be, we like to talk. We like to talk a *lot*."

She's right, I should've figured that out. Olivia wheeled the serving cart into the dinning room and placed the turkey in the center of the table. With all the food and people at the table, it looked and smelled like Thanksgiving. I suppose Olivia likes it that way, she likes being surrounded by her family. One by one we all helped ourselves. Olivia announced that she wanted to say grace before dinner, which seemed a little strange to me. Why hadn't she said a prayer before the salad and appetizers were served? I could only guess that it was some kind of family tradition, and every family does things a little differently than others. Either that or maybe she'd just forgotten.

We ate dinner and exchanged small talk. By the gratifying look on Olivia's face, I was certain she was pleased that we all ate dinner with great enthusiasm. Everyone--including the grandchildren--thanked her for such a wonderful meal.

As I was just about to gobble my last piece of turkey, Olivia shouted, "There's my girl!"

I lifted my head and couldn't believe my eyes. The gorgeous woman I had seen at the Cricket only a few days ago was standing ten feet away from me. And this time she was without her unappreciative boyfriend.

She gave Tim a kiss on his cheek. "Hi, Daddy."

I wondered how a grouchy old man like that could have a daughter like her.

"Come over here and give your grandmother a hug," Olivia said.

I watched in awe as this ravishing beauty floated across the room and hugged Olivia.

"John, I'd like you to meet my sweet grand daughter, Lisa. John is a very bright young man."

"Don't let her fool you," Lisa said, "I'm not that sweet."

"Olivia hasn't been wrong about anything so far." I couldn't take my eyes off her. "On the other hand, she's been known to exaggerate, so maybe I should wait and see."

"In that case," Lisa said, "I guess I'll have to judge for myself and see just how bright you really are."

She was flirting with me, and I loved it!

Olivia winked at me. "She's still not married, John."

Now I was beginning to understand.

"Grandma!" Lisa shouted. Her face flushed red.

"And that's the way I like it," Tim added. "She doesn't have time for romance." He raised an eyebrow and burned a hole through me.

"Oh Tim, what do you know?" Olivia blurted. "All you do is work. I can't remember the last time I saw you smile. Let Lisa live her own life."

"Thank you, grandma," Lisa said. "I can take care of myself, Daddy."

"Have a seat, dear, there's plenty of turkey left."

Lisa sat across the table from me. I tried not to gawk at her, but she was the most gorgeous creature I'd ever seen.

"Your father said that you're working on some kind of special project?" I asked.

"It's been quite a headache lately, but I'm making a little headway."

"Any new breakthroughs, Lisa?" Her father asked.

"I'd rather not talk about work right now. It's been a long day and I'm a little stressed out."

"John, I almost forgot," Olivia said. "I have something for you." She handed me a coat hanger with gift-wrap hanging down to the floor.

"You didn't have to get me anything Olivia."

"Don't be silly," Olivia said. "Open it."

I already had a pretty good idea as to what it was. It's a bit obvious when it's on a hanger. I tore away the wrapping paper and found the dark blue suit I had put on lay-away.

"I'm speechless, Olivia. What did I do to deserve such special treatment?" I gave her a hug and kissed her cheek.

"Try it on for us, John," Olivia said.

Feeling beyond embarrassment, I said, "Now really isn't a good time."

"Now John, I went through all the trouble of getting you that suit, the least you can do is try it on for us."

I didn't have much of a choice. She was a brilliant litigator.

Olivia ushered me out of the dining room, down the hall and left me in a huge bedroom. I felt like I was ten years old. When I put on the suit, it fit perfectly. A little red in the face, I sauntered back into the dining room and stood in front of Olivia, as well as everybody else.

"Quite the handsome young man. How does it feel?"

"Feels great. Thanks again Olivia, you're very thoughtful."

"Are you beginning to feel like a first class lawyer?" Olivia asked.

"I sure feel like one."

"You're a lawyer, John?" Lisa asked. "Who do you work for?"

Not wanting to give an in-depth explanation, I said, "The Bowman firm."

"This is a joke, right?" Lisa snapped. Everyone in the room was staring at me.

"Remember James Bowman, the famous attorney who just died?" Olivia said softly. "Well, John is Mr. Bowman's nephew."

Lisa's eyes filled with tears. "Why did you invite him to dinner? And you gave him a suit? Have you abandoned the whole family, Grandma?"

"He's not part of that Lisa," Olivia whispered. "I promise you."

Lisa stormed out of the room. Half the people at the table followed her down the hall, each of them giving me a disgusting look as they passed by.

"What the hell did I do?" I asked.

"It's not you, John. You're not part of it," Olivia said.

"Part of what?"

"Just forget about it, John."

"I don't want to forget about it. Please, Olivia, tell me what this is all about."

"Lisa is working on a project for Schlau computers, our family-owned company. It's a small organization and most people have never even heard of it. A few years ago we developed a revolutionary computer chip. While we were in the process of perfecting it, one of our employees pirated the idea and sold it to a competitor. They duplicated the chip and are now claiming rights to it."

"How can they claim it? Do they have a patent on it?"

"No. But neither do we. We had a pending patent, but when the other company filed their own patent, the whole situation turned into a nightmare."

"Can't you take them to court?"

"We did. And lost. The court decided that we had not produced sufficient evidence to support our claim. We are in the process of filing an appeal, but until the case is tried again, the court ruled that both companies have full rights to produce and sell the chip."

"Are you producing and selling the chip?"

"We've been manufacturing the chip, but no one will buy from us."

"What do you mean?"

"We can't compete with the advertising power of our competitor. They're twenty times bigger than we are. We've tried everything, but all efforts have failed."

"Is your company still solvent?"

"We're still generating income from other products. But once this new computer chip reaches its full potential it could increase our revenue dramatically."

"Wouldn't your competition also be able to develop the chip?"

"I'm certain that they already are. However, Lisa has developed an innovative theory that could surpass even our competitor's development."

"Does the theory work?"

"We don't know. The financing necessary to test Lisa's theory is unavailable. We are a financially secure company, but we do not have the enormous resources required to research and further develop Lisa's thesis. If we abandon all reason and invest all of our money into Lisa's idea and it fails, we're out of business. It was the Bowman Firm that defended our competitor. And they didn't merely beat us in court; they humiliated us and tarnished our reputation through vicious tactics."

"I assure you, neither my uncle nor I knew anything about this case. My uncle would never allow his partners to conduct themselves in such a way. I have no idea how the Bowman Firm handled this case without my uncle's knowledge, but your family is way out of line. My God, it was only two days ago that the man passed away."

"I'm sorry, John. It was not my intention to upset you."

"Olivia, I thank you for the lovely dinner and the beautiful suit, but I think it's time for me to leave."

I gave her a quick hug, and walked down the long hallway to get my clothes. Several family members were standing in the hall giving me dirty looks. I ignored them and left as quickly as I could. When I stepped outside, the chauffeur spotted me and immediately pulled the limo up to the front door. As we drove away, I didn't look back.

Chapter 17

Charleen woke me up early and convinced me to go to church. I hadn't been to Sunday service in quite a while. The parishioners were mostly white, and the African-American preacher was well received by the crowd. Occasionally I would drift off, but Charleen managed to bring me back by jabbing her elbow in my side. Charleen's daughter looked adorable. She wore a white dress with pink lace and had little pink bows in her hair. Michelle looked like she belonged in a storybook.

When we got back home from church, Junior had left a message on the answering machine. He said that somebody in production had helped him out, but because of a bad connection the rest of the message was unclear. At least we knew Junior was okay. I had no idea how he'd be able to grasp all that had happened since his departure. I hoped he'd be back soon.

I examined Blacky's file well into the late evening hours. Then I switched gears and studied for the bar exam for a few hours. If I ever wanted to pass that bar and get out of debt, I had to balance my time carefully between work and study.

Monday morning started out slowly, but I kept busy by studying and reviewing Blacky's file. At two I called Mr. Peterson and left a message with his secretary. He returned the call around four. He told me that the Seattle Associates Law firm, formerly the Bowman firm, invited him to lunch to discuss his case. Mr. Peterson had accepted the invitation, and at the law firm's request, he chose where they'd met. He decided on the priciest restaurant in Seattle. After ordering the most expensive dish and listening to their propaganda, he bid them farewell and said that he'd chosen another attorney.

Not yet knowing whether he had chosen me as his attorney, I asked for an appointment. He agreed to meet me for lunch, Thursday at noon. I told him that he could pay for his own lunch. He chuckled and said okay.

◇ ◇ ◇

Early the next morning I was awakened by a phone call from Dwayne Albertson.

"What the hell do you think you're doing?" Dwayne yelled in my ear.

"What have I done now, Dwayne? Shoplift some books perhaps?"

"Don't get smart with me, John. You know exactly what I'm talking about. I could end your career for soliciting one of our clients. You haven't even passed the bar exam yet."

"I may not be a lawyer yet, but I still understand the law. I didn't do anything wrong, Dwayne. Peterson left your firm on his own."

"Listen, kid, one of these days you're going to mess up. When you do, I'll be there to make sure it goes down on paper."

"What are you going to do, Dwayne, try and take my law firm away?" I asked, hoping he would understand my sarcasm. Dwayne hung up on me. He sure has a temper like none other I've seen.

I got sick of the same routine, so I grabbed my books and Blacky's file and headed to the park. Charleen and Michelle accompanied me. I enjoyed feeling the warm sun on my back. I hadn't seen much sun in law school, I figured it was about time to make up for lost hours in the sun. Charleen and her daughter found a group of parents and children to mingle with. I didn't mind; I had plenty to keep me busy.

I read over Blacky's file again and wrote my advice on a piece of paper. It was crummy advise, but what did he really expect with the situation he was in. The restaurant he had been operating without a liquor license had been losing money for two years. I suggested that he not be concerned with reopening it. Instead, he should sell it and use the proceeds to pay off his court fees and fines. I already knew that he wouldn't like this advice, but it was the only solution that made sense. If he wasn't happy with my free advice, then it would have to be his problem.

After writing the letter to Blacky, I layed down on the grass and daydreamed for a while. I couldn't stop thinking about Lisa's beautiful green eyes. She was the kind of woman who made it impossible for me to concentrate on anything. Yet occasionally, thoughts of Susie drifted into my mind. I often wondered how she was doing. Susie no longer had a stronghold on my heart. I didn't know if this was because I hadn't seen her in a while, or because perhaps I'd looked into Lisa's green eyes.

Chapter 18

By Wednesday I gave in to my heart and sent Olivia a bouquet. When I wrote the card, I kept it simple and made certain she would not perceive that the flowers were in any way an apology. I told her that I appreciated the wonderful dinner and maybe next time we could also enjoy a better conversation. I hoped she realized that the incident in no way impaired our friendship.

After leaving the flower shop I headed for a local bookstore to pick up a bar exam preparation book. The book offered questions similar to those on an actual exam. It helped a student to determine how well they would do on a real exam. As much as I'd studied, I still needed to practice on realistic questions, which would help me better prepare for the exam.

I came across a going-out-of-business sidewalk sale as I was driving along. I couldn't resist searching for bargains, it's how I furnished myself for quite a few years with barely any money at all. I spotted the store located across the street from what was once the Bowman firm. I tried not to let it bother me and parked the Beamer in front of the store. I have found many useful, inexpensive items at similar sales. At the moment my money was running low, but it didn't hurt to look.

After searching through the overcrowded store, I found a big white teddy bear with a long red scarf for only twelve dollars. I decided to buy it for Michelle. Quite to my dismay, the checkout line was all the way out the door. After more than twenty minutes, standing behind the worst smelling woman I'd ever encountered, I paid for the teddy bear. When I walked outside, the Beamer was gone!

I looked up and down the street, hoping I'd see a cop. "Damn it! DAMN IT!"

"Hey man, your name John?" I turned and saw a longhaired teenager wearing a black leather jacket.

"Who's asking?"

"I know who took your car."

"Why didn't you do something?"

"Listen, man, he said he was from some car collection agency. He laid a fifty on me and told me to give this letter to the first pissed-off guy I saw."

"And then what?"

"He broke in the car and drove off like he owned it."

"Damn it!" I yelled again.

"Sorry man. Sure was a nice car."

There was nothing for me to do but flag down a taxi and go home. Opening the door to the taxi, I saw Dwayne Albertson standing in the front window of his office, staring at me. He was holding a glass in his hand--probably southern whiskey. Dwayne took a long swallow of the drink and disappeared into his office. I couldn't help but think that Dwayne somehow initiated the repossession of Junior's Beamer. He and his sleazy buddies were a disgrace to the legal profession.

I glared at him until he walked away. Confused and angry, I stood there for a few minutes trying to gather my thoughts. Then, I tore open the letter. The BMW had been repossessed because the Bowman

Firm had defaulted on the auto loan. I wasn't surprised. I had a gut feeling something like this was going to happen sooner or later. Bunch of Jackasses, I hope their new firm goes under.

Chapter 19

Charleen's daughter was sleeping when I got home, so I slipped the teddy bear next to her head. When she woke up the next morning, she paraded around the house and wouldn't let the bear out of her sight. I was glad I at least made one person happy. Charleen was upset when I told her what had happened with Junior's car. It wasn't so much the car that bothered her; it reminded her of how hard her father had worked to keep the firm afloat. She'd been quiet for the past few days, but she had every right to be. I knew first hand how hard it was when your father passed away.

I telephoned Mr. Peterson first thing Thursday morning and told him what had happened. He chuckled until I mentioned that Dwayne was watching the whole thing from his office window. I was uncertain why Mr. Peterson disliked Dwayne and his associates, but it was fine with me. I still wanted to meet Mr. Peterson for lunch, but I told him I'd have to take a taxi. Quite to my surprise, Mr. Peterson insisted that he'd pick me up. I didn't argue.

Mr. Peterson picked me up in his 911 convertible. We decided not to eat at the Cricket because neither of us wanted to risk a confrontation with Dwayne nor any of his associates. Besides, the Cricket was in downtown Seattle, and Mr. Peterson didn't wish to drive that far. Mr. Peterson drove his Porsche more like a sixteen-year-old than an elderly man. I enjoyed the drive as much as he did.

He drove me to a restaurant just on the outskirts of Seattle. He had taken so many back roads I had no idea where we were. The restaurant looked similar to the Cricket, and it also had a stage for entertainers. I was surprised that Mr. Peterson had chosen this particular place. Most of the patrons looked like eccentric students, or aspiring artists waiting to be discovered.

We were seated in the middle of the crowded dining room, and the moment we sat down, Mr. Peterson said, "So, shall I brief you on my marriage from hell?"

"I'm all ears." I removed a note pad and pen from my shirt pocket.

"Linda, or as you know her, Miss Sharpner, had a clear agenda when she married me. I was so toasted on champagne and vodka, I can't even remember the ceremony. Three months ago I invited a few close friends, some business associates and their spouses to Las Vegas for a little bash. Linda and I had been casually dating for a while, and I decided to invite her."

"What happened?"

"Linda's plan was to get me drunk, then slip the old ring on my finger."

"Can you remember any of it?"

"Except for the ceremony, I can damn near remember the whole thing. We were sitting in the hotel lounge and Linda was ordering one drink after another. Each drink seemed a little stronger. I didn't notice that I was out-drinking her three-to-one. She kept joking about running down the street and getting married at the first chapel we saw. I, of course, laughed at the idea. However, after everyone else retired for the evening, Linda convinced me that we should get married. I was too drunk to think logically, and before I knew it, I was in a chapel in downtown Las Vegas. Twelve hours later I woke up with one hell of a hang over, and a wedding ring on my finger. Her intentions were obvious from the start. She's after my money, and it appears that she's going to get it unless you can help me out of this mess. I know the odds are against me, John, and I don't expect miracles, but I'd love to see her get what she deserves: nothing!"

"How long were you and Linda married?"

"It'll be three months next week. If there had been even a little love between us, maybe things would've worked out. Don't get me wrong, my ego is not crushed. I'm sixty-eight years old. What do I really have to lose at this point in my life? I've accomplished everything a man can accomplish in a lifetime, and now it's my turn to have some fun."

I couldn't quite share his point of view. I didn't understand how a man could be happy with so much wealth and so little love. He was going to die a wealthy, lonely man.

"Do you have your marriage certificate and the name of the chapel?"

He handed me the certificate, and the name and address of the chapel.

We both ordered the chef's special: barbecued ribs.

I contemplated telling Mr. Peterson that I hadn't yet passed the bar exam, but decided not to. If the case progressed to the point that we had to go to court, I'd have to enlist the services of a real attorney. How

I'd explain this to Mr. Peterson, I didn't yet know. The only thing I knew for certain was that I was feeling a bit devious.

Chapter 20

I promised Charleen I'd have dinner with her and Michelle, but she wasn't home yet, so I grabbed a couple of apples out of the fridge just to hold me over. Although I wasn't overly concerned with spending a great deal of time on the Peterson case, I found myself somewhat intrigued and curious as to how I'd handle it. With Dwayne watching my back, I had to exercise extreme discretion.

Before I bit into the second apple, Charleen walked in the door. Immediately feeling guilty for making me wait, she apologized. I told her it was no big deal. After all, she isn't responsible for my stomach. Charleen had run into an old crush from high school. Unfortunately, after talking to him for only fifteen minutes, she decided that his good looks didn't make up for his perverted personality. He didn't know it yet, but she'd given him her x-boyfriend's phone number instead of her own. I'd have to say that was a very good call.

Because today was Charleen's last day of summer school at the University of Seattle Washington, we decided to celebrate. Since neither of us had much money, we agreed to buy an inexpensive bottle of champagne and celebrate at home. Without violating client confidentiality, I shared a few thoughts with Charleen on the Peterson case. Charleen didn't think there was much hope of keeping Miss Sharpner out of Mr. Peterson's piggy bank, but said it was worth a try. The fall semester didn't begin for another three weeks, so Charleen offered to help with research on the Peterson case. She said it would help prepare her for law school.

The champagne looked good pouring out of the bottle, but it sure didn't taste good. I toasted to Charleen's next three weeks and set the glass aside. We raided the refrigerator, but there wasn't much to eat. Charleen found a pizza in the freezer and threw it in the oven. I promised to go grocery shopping later today. My budget for the next three months was about five dollars a day; not much. Especially not that much if I have to keep taking a taxi into town. If my money ran out, I'd be forced to ask Aunt Heide for a small loan, but considering her financial situation, it would have to be a last resort.

Two minutes after Charleen threw the pizza in the oven the doorbell rang. I told Charleen to stay sitted and relax, and opened the front door.

"Olivia. What a surprise." Although I had gotten her flowers, my tone was still less-than-friendly. I didn't want to get invited to another diner.

"I know you're upset, John, but please let me make peace with you."

We walked into the kitchen and I introduced Olivia to Charleen. Concluding perhaps that Charleen was competition for her grand daughter, Olivia didn't seem too happy. When I told her we were cousins, her face lit up.

"I'll make this brief, John," Olivia said. "I deeply apologize for the fiasco at dinner. To more clearly help you understand what's going on, I'd like you to come to my office at Schlau Industries. If you're still upset after you see our situation, then I promise I'll never disturb you again."

"I'm not sure I have the time, Olivia." I wasn't going to let her paint me in a corner.

"By the way, thank you for the flowers, John. They were beautiful." Olivia stood up and walked toward the front door. "Well then, I'll see you within the next few days?"

"I can't make any promises."

I was glad Olivia wanted to make peace, but I wasn't excited about going to visit her company.

Charleen had a puzzled look. I debated whether to tell her the whole story, but didn't have the patience.

Chapter 21

I wasn't sure Mr. Peterson would have appreciated Charleen helping me research his case, but then again, he'd probably be more upset if he discovered that his attorney hadn't yet passed the bar exam. Throughout the weekend Charleen engrossed herself with the Peterson case, searching for a way for him to reduce his loss. I, on the other hand, continued studying for the bar. I insulated myself from all distractions. If I failed the exam again, my future as an attorney is over.

Monday and Tuesday were more of the same: Charleen working on the Peterson case, and I submerging myself deeper into law. On Wednesday morning Mr. Peterson telephoned, anxious to hear what I had found. I could no longer deceive him, and the last thing I wished to do was tell him what was going on through a telephone conversation, so I convinced him to meet me for lunch tomorrow.

As soon as I got off the phone, I sat with Charleen and reviewed what she had found. I couldn't take the case to court myself, but if I were able to produce enough evidence for Mr. Peterson, and convince him that I'd refer him to a competent lawyer who could win the case, then perhaps he'd show his gratitude with a small check. I was quickly running out of money, and desperation forced me to practice creative law.

Neither Charleen nor I could find anything to improve Mr. Peterson's position. Everything looked legal and legitimate. Mrs. Sharpner, a crafty one indeed, had persuaded Mr. Peterson to pay off all the debts she'd incurred prior to their marriage. I was amazed that Mr.

Peterson, obviously a shrewd businessman, could be duped by such a transparent scheme.

Unable to find any hard evidence to help Mr. Peterson, it was time for me to shift into fifth gear and make a few telephone inquiries. In law school I'd learned that not everything was black and white, and asking the right questions uncovered more than what was written on paper.

Calling Miss. Sharpner was futile, so I didn't waste my time. The only other person that could help the case was the justice of the peace who had performed the ceremony. Fortunately, the chapel telephone number was printed on the marriage certificate. Charleen handed me the cordless telephone and picked up the extension in the kitchen.

"Las Vegas Chapel for Sweethearts, this is Rhonda. How can I help you?" She had the squeakiest voice I'd ever heard. I glanced at Charleen, who was listening on the other phone, and crossed my eyes. Charleen shook her finger at me, warning me to be a little more serious.

"My name is John Bowman. May I speak to George Shundrich please?"

"One moment please."

I was surprised that she didn't ask who I was.

"This is George"

"George Shundrich?" I asked just to be sure

"Yeah, who's this?"

"John Bowman. Mind if I ask you a few questions?"

George cleared his throat. "Depends on the questions."

"Five months ago, you performed a marriage ceremony for a highly intoxicated couple. Sharpner and Peterson were their names."

"About twenty couples a night stagger into this chapel."

I thought for a moment, and then asked, "Do you have a fax machine, Mr. Shundrich?"

"Nothing's for free. Besides, I haven't got all night."

"If you answer my questions, I'll FedEx a check for a hundred." I had no idea where I was going to get a hundred bucks or even if he could help me.

"Trust ain't too common here in Vegas. How do I know you'll send the check?"

"I'll fax you a copy of my driver's license and a major credit card." My Visa was maxed out, but I hoped my gesture would put him at ease.

There was a long silence. "Don't bother with the license or Visa. My fax number is: 702-555-1665."

While keeping him on the line, Charleen faxed him the marriage certificate and a photograph of Peterson and his estranged wife. I listened to organ music in the background, probably for the next couple about to tie the knot.

"I rarely remember names," George said, "but this pair I could never forget. She was staggering all right, but he couldn't even stand up. I doubt if he remembers anything. She had to keep slapping him on the back just to keep him from passing out. I expected to see them back here the very next day. I guess things didn't quite work out."

I looked at Charleen, and she had the same bewildered look as I. "I'm not quite following you."

"I was just closing for the night when Ms. Sharpner wedged her foot in the door and insisted that I marry them immediately. I explained that we were closed and promised to give her a discount if they came back the next day. She wouldn't listen. I then explained that Nevada required two witnesses in order for a marriage to be legal, and that my assistants had left for the evening. This didn't faze her either. She offered to triple my fee if I'd perform the ceremony and issue a license. I finally gave in, but I told her there was no way I'd make anything offical. She agreed. So I performed the ceremony, gave her an illegitimate certificate, and took my money. She never did show up the next day to make it official. Fine by me, I didn't have to waste extra time on them."

"So Mr. Peterson and Ms. Sharpner are not legally married?"

"Not unless they went to another chapel."

"But I don't understand, this marriage certificate looks completely lefitimate to me. I don't see anything wrong with it."

"Well it's *meant* to look real. You know, for people that decide to play a joke on somebody when they go back home. But if you'll look on the back, third paragraph down, in the fine print, you'll notice a statement reading that it's an unofficial certificate.

I quickly skim through the third paragraph on the back. There it is, the statement George was referring to. "Thank you, thank you, George. My check will be in the mail first thing in the morning!" I couldn't wait to hang up the telephone so I could hug Charleen.

"I couldn't have done it without you," I said. "I owe one, a huge one."

Charleen and I neatly organized the file and then I wrote a detailed account of my findings, along with specific recommendations for Mr. Peterson. I guessed that he'd be a bit perturbed when I announce that I'm not a "real" lawyer. But when I tell him he's still an eligible bachelor, and always was, he'll quickly forgive me.

At eight p.m., while Charleen and I were knee-deep in paperwork, the doorbell rang. Before answering the door, I peeked out the front window. Quite to my surprise, I saw three uniformed cops and a man in a gray suit. I opened the door.

"What can I help you with?" I asked.

The man in the suit flashed his badge. "We're looking for John Bowman."

"Well, you just found him."

"You're under arrest, Mr. Bowman." He proceeded to read me my rights.

"May I ask why?"

"For defrauding the Seattle Associates Law firm."

"Is this some kind of perverse joke?" Apparently not. The suit turned me around and slapped handcuffs on me.

Charleen heard the commotion. "What's going on?"

"Dwayne and his buddies are playing dirty pool."

Chapter 22

I had never seen a cop drive so poorly. After rolling through stop signs, breaking the speed limit more than once, and nearly smashing into a taxicab, we pulled into the police station. Quite ironically, I noticed Dwayne Albertson's car parked adjacently to the police station. It was much too conspicuous to have been a coincidence. I guess Dwayne wanted to personally welcome me to jail. The police, obviously, were in cahoots with Dwayne. Why, I didn't know.

The police led me to a tiny room with two chairs, one table, and no windows. It felt like I was trapped in a nightmare, but couldn't wake up. The three uniformed cops closed the door behind me. Without saying a word, one cop pointed to the chair. I sat and waited. After gazing at the white walls for what seemed like an hour, the door opened. Two guards entered and took their positions at either side of the door. Following them were two men wearing suits. Right behind them was Dwayne Albertson.

"Are you John Bowman?" The older guy in the suit asked.

"You don't remember who you just had arrested by your men?" It was risky being a prick, but I was in no mood to be cooperative.

"I'm Lieutenant Milihan, and this is my partner Grobbie." He pointed to the younger guy in the suit. "I presume you've met Mr. Albertson."

I didn't say a word.

"Your father and I were good friends," the older suit said. "I remember him speaking of you often. I'm sorry we have to meet under these conditions. Normally, with the overwhelming evidence against you, the judge would set bail in the morning and you'd either post it, or stay in the lock up. But like I said, I knew your father and his family, so I'd like to hear your side of the story."

I fixed my stare on Dwayne. "What sort of lie got me arrested?"

"Black and white doesn't lie, John," Milihan said. He held up a piece of paper. "This signed document says that you borrowed seven thousand dollars from Dwayne's firm. It also says that if you left the firm, either by termination or voluntary resignation that the note was due immediately."

"Dwayne excused that debt."

"Can you prove that?"

"I've got a document at home that verifies this debt was cleared."

"Sorry, John." Milihan said.

"What do you mean?"

"You also owe a two-hundred dollars for each day you drove the BMW."

"What! Who the hell thought up this cockamamie story?"

Milihan showed me another document I didn't remember signing, to prove I was responsible for cost on the BMW.

"So now what?" I asked

"I'm sorry, Mr. Bowman," Milihan said. "We're going to have to keep you here until you can get yourself either a really good lawyer, or the money to pay this all off. At this point, you'll probably need both. And if you don't have any money saved up that can pay this debt off, then

I also suggest you ask someone to look for that paper work you were talking about."

My eyes shot daggers at Dwayne. He just stood there with that annoying little smirk. I wanted to thrust my fist into his face. Dwayne, Milihan, and the rest of the crew gathered their things and headed for the door. The two guards walked me out of the room. I left without saying a word.

They led me down a long hall. When we reached my cell, they uncuffed me and pushed me into my new home. I never believed anything like this would happen to me. Inside the cell there was another poor slob sleeping on one of the cots. He didn't look threatening, but then again, you never know. Right now, all I wanted was sleep. As I lay there, pondering what had happened to me today, it dawned on me that perhaps Dwayne had irrevocably slammed the door on my legal career. Ironically, my career hasn't even begun.

Chapter 23

"Let's go, Bowman. Wake up." I heard a voice, but I was still half-asleep. Disoriented, I awakened and found my body tangled in sheets that smelled like moth balls. Suddenly I remembered that my bed was in a jail cell.

"What time is it?" I asked, curious why the cops would disturb a person behind bars.

"It's twelve-thirty and you made bail." The guard said.

"How? Who?"

"You'll have to wait and see for yourself." The guard unlocked the cell and swung the door open.

With tangled hair and breath that would kill a skunk, I ventured out of the cell. I followed the guard to the front desk, signed my bail papers, and picked up my personal items.

I almost ran down the hallway for the main entrance I was so happy to get out of there. I still had no idea what just happened, or who got me out of there, but I had no intention of revisiting that place.

I walked out the door and couldn't believe how wonderful it was to breathe fresh air. Even though I had only been in jail for a few hours, it felt pretty damn good to be free. Just as I was about to wave down a cab, I saw a limo pull up. Behind the wheel was the same chauffeur Olivia had sent to pick me up for dinner. I had a feeling she'd do something like this. I walked over to the limo and stood in front of the passenger's door. The chauffeur got out and made his way around the car to open my door. Just before he reached for the handle, I opened the door myself. I wasn't sure why, but I didn't feel like putting up with the chauffeur right now.

I could tell the chauffeur was somewhat perturbed by my actions, but I could care less. I immediately recognized the route we were following; we were heading for Olivia's house. I caught a glimpse of myself in a mirror behind the mini-bar. I looked and felt like yesterday's laundry. If only I'd had a toothbrush, at least I could get rid of my bad breath. Who was I trying to impress, Grandma Olivia and her precious grand daughter? Perhaps Olivia might still think I was adorable, but there wasn't much of a chance that Lisa would ever talk to me again. Didn't want to either.

After almost falling asleep on the fairy ride, we finally arrived at Olivia's estate. Before I even really got a chance to react, Olivia ran down the steps and opened the door for me.

"How about some coffee darling?"

It was one-thirty a.m., but I wasn't going to sleep any time soon. "If you don't mind, I could use it." She leaned into me and gave me a hug.

We headed toward the kitchen and Olivia pulled out a chair for me. She opened the cupboard, set two mugs on the counter and grabbed the already-made coffee.

"How do you take your coffee, John?"

"Black, please." I usually didn't drink it this way, I usually didn't drink it at all, but tonight I needed a little extra jolt. The house seemed empty, especially compared to the last time I was here. Slouched back in my wooden chair, I glanced out the window and noticed the chauffeur walking up a flight of steps to his living quarters. Other than an occasional late night drive, he didn't have a bad life. If maintaining the vehicles was the worst of what he had to do, his job was pretty damn good. At this moment, I would do anything to be in his shoes.   Olivia slipped the coffee in front of me and sat opposite me.

"Thank you," I said. "For the coffee *and* for getting me out of jail."

"Oh John, you're such a sweetheart."

"I have absolutely no idea how I'm ever going to repay you."

"Believe me, John, you'll have quite the opportunity."

"You name it and I promise I'll do my best." I said this knowing I might regret it. I trusted her though, at least for the most part I did. How could I not trust a woman who'd done so much for me?

"I have a project for you." Olivia said.

"What sort of project?"

She slid a folder across the table and opened it. "You're perfect for this case."

It was the case her company had lost to my uncle's firm. They wanted to move forward with an appeal.

"Olivia, even if I could understand the technical details of this case, I still wouldn't be able to handle it because I still haven't passed the bar exam. Besides, how could you expect me to stand toe-to-toe with the senior partners of the Seattle Associates?"

Her face was serious. "John, you can't let those men just walk all over you."

"Olivia, I thank you for everything you've done, but there is nothing I can do right now except pray I can find a job as a paralegal." A paralegal is about the only thing I'm qualified to do with out having passed that bar exam. "Besides," I continued, "I have no intentions of letting anyone walk all over me, but I have to take certain steps before I'm capable of taking a stand right now. The first of those steps is passing the bar exam."

Olivia sat silently for a few minutes with a somber face. She reached around behind her and grabbed a nine-by-twelve envelope from the counter. "I've done a little research of my own, and I think you'll be quite happy with what I found." She handed me the envelope.

I tore open the end of the envelope and removed a letter from the Washington State Bar Association.

"Where did you get this?"

"Read it out loud."

Dear Mr. Bowman: we are pleased to inform you that your bar exam score was ranked the fourth highest in the history of the State of Washington. Each year thousands of law students take this exam. Those who pass have the privilege of practicing law. The Governor of Washington recognizes those who surpass the median score. You are cordially invited to attend a dinner on September fifth, which will be sponsored by the Washington State Bar Association. Please notify us if you are unable to attend . . .

"Is this letter real?"

"Of course it is, John."

"Considering that I've already received a letter informing me that I failed, it's a little difficult for me to understand."

"Who told you failed?"

"The senior partners."

"The senior partners lied to you. They wanted to keep you in a position where they could manipulate you."

"How the hell did the senior partners pull this off?"

"Are you familiar with the Finley case? The one that did your uncle in?"

I didn't know where she was getting her information, but her sources sure were reliable. "Greg Finley embezzled a couple million dollars from an insurance company, right?"

"One-point-eight million to be exact," Olivia said.

"What does Greg Finley have to do with my bar exam?"

"Nothing. However, the method he used to embezzle the money has everything to do with you." Olivia raised an eyebrow. "And it also has everything to do with me."

Confused and frustrated, I asked, "Where is this going, Olivia?"

"Remember the evening you joined my family for dinner?"

"How could I forget?"

"When we originally designed the computer chip, it was meant to be used as a security system for the general public. But Lisa found a way to quickly break down digital codes. We can break down a ten-digit code within ninety seconds and a fifteen-digit code within four minutes. The security system is quite simple. The technology allows two opposing computer chips to work in harmony. One breaks down digital codes, and the other creates them. In order to enter a computer system with such a security setup, try to envision two doorways. The front doorway is the one used by the computer user. The back doorway is the one that potential hackers use to steal information. Both doorways are armed with digital security codes, which is where the defense chip comes into play. As I'm sure you know, John, a digital security code is very common with many different products. However, the Schlau security system has two-digit codes arming the "front doorway," and five-digit codes arming the "back doorway." Each code contains ten figures, totaling a twenty-digit code system at the "front doorway" of a person's computer, and a fifty-digit code system at the "back doorway." To ensure failsafe security, the chip automatically changes the codes every ten minutes. This does not give a hacker sufficient time to break the codes. We placed a twenty-digit code system on the front doorway to allow the operator to use the computer. In order for the person stationed at the computer to get into their files we designed a system that would protect the personal files yet still allow for entry; not an easy task. The first thing we did was set the timing of the digital code setter at the front door one minute behind the back door. Since we at Schlau made it possible to break down a ten-digit code within ninety seconds, we assumed that hackers could do the same. Although it was unlikely that anyone could enter a computer's front doorway from an outside line, and even more unlikely for that person to break the codes within two minutes, we had to consider that it could be done. So we developed a backup plan. If a hacker broke the digital codes and accessed the computer's personal files, then both the back and front doorways, and even the direct line to the person stationed at the computer would be in a dead lock mode. The owner of the computer would be able to access their files for a short period of time, but the dead lock would prevent the hacker from accessing the information. To clear the block, the security system has to be re-booted. This should only be done after the owner has secured new computer lines. Reasonably speaking, there is virtually no better security system available."

Somewhat overwhelmed with the quantity of technical information Olivia just shared with me, I still had no idea how any of this is related to me.

"Listen, Olivia, your security system sounds like a real winner, but *please* tell me how all this relates to my passing the bar exam."

"The company that pirated our idea is creating the potential to turn the tables."

"By using a security system?"

"It has evolved into something more complex. In the same way our computer chip breaks down codes to make it possible to access files, it can also break down the codes of an entirely different security system."

"So you're saying that whoever stole the idea now has the capability of breaking into the files of banks, courts, government, and whatever the hell else they want?"

"Well, it's a bit more complicated than that, but for the most part, yes." Olivia's lips tightened and she shook her head. "It's also how the results of your bar exam were manipulated."

"Why would your company market a chip that could be removed from a computer by just anyone and used to steal and alter private data?"

"Not just anyone, John. Using the chip by itself in the manner in which we designed it would not work. But using the idea behind the chip and then creating an entirely new process and system enables the user to do many things. It's not a process or system that could be created quickly by just anybody. It takes time, money, and more than anything else, knowledge."

I paused for a moment and tried to comprehend Olivia's story. "There's no way that's possible, Olivia. I can understand how someone could use this computer chip to access data from an unsophisticated security system, but it's inconceivable that anybody could access security systems used by banks and government agencies. I'm sorry Olivia, but you're stretching your conspiracy theory just a bit too far for me."

"Trust me, John. With the proper connections our chip could be a very dangerous tool."

"I don't know that much about security systems, but I do know that anybody with anything valuable is probably going to be conscientious enough to understand how to protect it."

"The highest risk for banks is not at gun point, it's through illegal bank account transactions done by computer."

"I agree, Olivia, but whenever a bank's computer system gets tapped, it's never by an average Joe. Most often it's an inside job, spearheaded by the individual or company who set up the security system for that particular bank. And let's just suppose you're right about the Schlau chip being used to enter bank computers, it still doesn't mean that someone could do the same with government files. The odds of something like this happening are slim."

"I guess we're going around in circles, John." Olivia looked at the wall clock. "Why don't you get some sleep, dear? We've been talking for a long time, and you must be getting tired. You can stay in the guestroom. We'll talk more in the morning."

"Sounds delightful."

Before I crawled into bed, I telephoned Charleen to let her know I was okay. She had a million questions, but I cut her short. I was tired. Olivia showed me to the guestroom.

I put my arms around her, squeezed her tight, and kissed her cheek. "Thanks for everything, Olivia."

Chapter 24

"Shit," was all I could manage to get out of my mouth as I saw the time on the digital alarm clock, eleven-twenty-two a.m., and realized that I had thirty-eight minutes to make it to my lunch with Peterson. It would take me at least a half-hour just on the fairy, then another twenty minutes to Blue Whales, the English pub where Peterson wanted to meet me. Sitting upright in bed thinking about what to do for a minute, I decided to call Charleen and have her try to contact Peterson to let him know I was running late.

I found a phone sitting on the dresser next to the door and quickly dialed Charleen. She wasn't there, or wasn't answering; either way it was no good for me because I didn't have Peterson's phone number and I knew that he purposely didn't have his number listed.

I quickly put on my jeans and shirt, splashed some water on my face, and rinsed my mouth with mouthwash I found in a bottle in the medicine cabinet before heading downstairs to find Olivia.

"What's wrong dear?"

"Olivia, I'm terrible sorry but I'm late for an appointment and I need to get a ride back right away."

"I'm sorry John, I didn't realize you had to go anywhere today or I would've kept Edwin here. He's my chauffeur. Unfortunately I already promised him the day off."

I was frantic. "Is there anybody else home that could give me a ride?"

"Sorry John, I thought you would be with me until Tim came by this evening, and I thought you could ride back with him."

"Tonight?"

"I'm sorry sweetheart. I wish I could do more to help."

"What about a taxi cab," I asked, trying desperately to find a solution.

"They would have to come across the fairy first and that's another good half-hour, but if you'd like I could call one."

"No," my voice was disappointed, "but thank you anyway. By then it would be too late to even make the effort."

"Usually Edwin takes his bicycle on his days off, but today he took the limo for some repairs he wanted to have done in town. Otherwise you could have taken the limo." Olivia stared thoughtfully out the kitchen window. "Of course now, there is old Richard," she said.

"Who's Richard?"

"Richard was my husband. He passed away a few years ago but I still have his pride and joy. I'm not sure if it still runs. The last time Edwin checked it was over six months ago."

"Do you think it would be okay if I borrowed it for the day?" I was pushing my limit with Olivia's generosity.

She gazed out the window for another long minute, then turned to me. I felt like I was at an interview for a new job.

"If any one of my sons knew that I let you use that car they would absolutely kill me," she said, "so make darn sure you don't put a scratch on it. They'd never let me hear the end of it."

She reached into a drawer and pulled out a set of keys, tossing them to me.

"Olivia, are you sure this is Okay?" I asked, understanding the sentimental value. This was not something to take lightly.

"Just be careful dear," she said with a smile and a pat on the shoulder.

I gave her a smile. I glanced at the kitchen clock and hurried for the door.

"Third garage door to your right," I heard Olivia shout after me.

I had about thirty minutes to make it to the pub. I was sure I wouldn't make it on time, but if I rushed it I might not be terribly late. I'd slept well, but not nearly long enough. The idea of leaving the house without a shower bothered me even more. But I thought Peterson would understand -- if I could make it there on time, that is. I pulled open the garage door and found a dusty white sheet draped over what appeared to be the car. The garage was cluttered with all kinds of lawn and garden equipment, as well as boxes of who knows what. I grabbed the sheet and yanked it off... a Malibu! A convertible Malibu! If I had to guess, I'd say it was a sixty-five or sixty-six. The burgundy paint job looked like new, and the off-white leather interior didn't seem to have a single flaw. After drooling for a minute, I hopped in.

To my surprise, it started up right away. I backed it out of the garage carefully, then tore down the driveway to catch the fairy. I turned on the radio; it looked like the original, with only a dial and no tape deck. I finally found a decent tune. I turned up, but not louder than the old speakers could handle.

After crossing over on the fairy and breaking through traffic, I finally made it to the Blue Whales. I could feel the air-conditioning when I walked in, which felt great after being in the hot sun for the last forty-five minutes. I glanced down at my watch to check the time. I wasn't too late; quarter after twelve. I looked around for Peterson but couldn't find him anywhere. I decided to wait for a little while. It just seems to be the way it goes; every time you have to rush and sweat, the other party doesn't even show. Although I'm sure Peterson wouldn't leave me hanging.

I'd never been to the Blue Whales before. When Peterson gave me directions over the phone he'd mentioned they had good blues music, hence the name 'Blue Whales.' I made my way to the restroom to freshen up a bit. I wet my hair underneath the sink, and dried off with the hand dryer. I didn't have a comb, so I rustled my fingers through my hair. Who cared if it wasn't perfect? Peterson certainly wouldn't, at least not after I told him the good news. I took one more look at myself in the mirror, seeing my tired-looking eyes, and headed back into the restaurant. I glanced around for Peterson, but before I could spot him I heard him call my name.

"John, how you doing?"

I finally spotted him walking towards me from behind the corner of the bar.

"How's it going Mr. Peterson," I said, shaking his hand.

"Sorry I didn't meet you right away when you came in, but I had to make a quick phone call while I was waiting," Peterson said, elbowing me in the side and pointing to his watch with a big grin on his face.

"I'm sorry I'm so late. If you knew what I'd been through lately you would think I'd be in a mental hospital at this point," I said, shaking my head in disbelief at the last twenty-four hours.

"Is everything going to be okay," Peterson asked, giving me a concerned look.

"Well, I'm not in jail so things can't be that bad."

Peterson laughed, not realizing the truth behind my remark. He led me to where he was sitting. There were so many papers spread out across the table that it looked more like his desk than a table. He quickly shuffled them all into a pile and slipped them into his briefcase.

"Good news or bad news?" Peterson got directly to the point.

"Well, to tell you the truth I don't even think you're going to get to court on this one."

"That bad, huh?"

"No, that good," I said with a smile that I was sure stretched further than my ears.

"Are you joking," Peterson asked, his voice serious.

"Mr. Peterson, you were never married to begin with. Well, at least not to Miss Sharpner you weren't."

"John, I know what I saw. The certificate clearly stated that I did indeed get married to Miss Sharpner."

"Mr. Peterson, I apologize for not being prepared. As soon as I can get my final report to you with all the records to prove my point, I will. Until then you're just going to have to take my word for it.

I called the priest from Las Vegas, and he told me himself that your wedding was unofficial. I didn't believe it myself until he had me look at the back of your wedding certificate, which stated it clearly in black and white. Mr. Peterson, you're not married. Better yet, if you really wanted to be cold and heartless, you could nail Miss Sharpner's ass to the wall for a whole list of illegal attempts involving you and your reputation."

I looked around to see if I could get a beer, feeling pretty damn good about myself.

"John are you sure about this? I mean, you're not just trying to pull this out of thin air are you?"

"Mr. Peterson, as soon as I get back home, I'll either fax over the information or bring it to you myself."

"I've got to be honest, I never thought for a minute that you, or anybody for that matter, would ever be able to get me out of this one. You saved me, John. Of course you know I'll still want to see those papers, just to be sure. Not that I'm doubting you, it's just..."

"No need to explain, Mr. Peterson. I fully understand." I felt the same way about what Olivia had told me last night.

"Bartender," Peterson shouted, "two double shots of whiskey and whatever this young man here would like to eat!"

This was a side of him I had not yet seen. I'd have hated to see him handle his Porsche now, with all the extra energy he seemed to have picked up.

After we ordered our food, Peterson lit a long, thin cigar and puffed on it occasionally. He offered one to me, but I told him I'd take a rain check. We talked about all of the possible options he had, which included suing her for what she had done to him in the past few months.

Even though I was sure Peterson could have gotten away with it, he didn't seem to be too turned on by the idea. I couldn't say I disagreed with him. I don't like to play the system, and I'm sure that Peterson felt the same way. Either that or he didn't feel it was worth being bothered with. Whatever the case, it didn't matter to me. Charleen and I had done our parts, and a fine job of it.

We finished lunch at about one-thirty, concluding with a handshake. I told him I'd get all the information over to him as soon as I got a chance. Peterson told me he'd call me within the next few days to let me know how things went with Sharpner and her lawyer. I was sure they'd go just fine. Even though he didn't mention anything about payment, I felt sure he had it in mind. I'm just not sure if I'd be able to accept anything right now considering that Dwyane Albertson is watching me like a Hawk, just waiting for me to screw up.

I said good-bye to Peterson in the parking lot. I stood back for a moment looking at Olivia's Malibu, then dug into my back pocket for the letter that Olivia had given me; the one from the Washington State Bar review office. Leaning against the side of the Malibu, I read through the letter again. I could hardly believe something like this could be true. I suspected that was the reason why I'd given Olivia such a hard time about it. I looked at the address of the office, 1012 Washington St., only a couple of blocks from where I was now. I decided to take a little walk down there to see if what Olivia had told me had any truth to it. Besides, I could still feel a slight buzz from the drinks Peterson ordered, so I thought it wouldn't be a bad idea to put off driving for a while longer.

The Blue Whales is located just across the street from the Seattle docks, making the walk over to the Washington State Bar Review Office a nice one. The road doesn't follow the water, it cuts in and away from it gradually. Their building must have a good view, even if not directly on the water. Every building in the area is at least five stories high, which gives a clear view for miles in at least one direction or another.

I finally arrived at 1012 Washington St., and walked into the main hallway. I was on the ground level, and began to scan through the office name listings. They all seemed to be related to law in one way or another, and I was sure they all had connections to money as well.

Finally I found what I was looking for. The Washington State Bar Review Office is on the seventh floor. The building only had eight floors, so they probably have some of the best views of the building. This probably meant that they were also making some of the best money. Unfortunately, almost every cent came from poor law students that had no choice. They had to 'donate' money to the Washington State Bar Association if they ever wanted to take the Bar exam. I just felt sorry for others like me, who failed the bar the first time around and had to take it again. Unless Olivia was by some small chance right about what she told me, I would be doing just that.

The elevator doors opened up to the seventh floor, and I walked in feeling out of place in my jeans and T-shirt. Everyone around me was in a suit and tie. The floors were marble, and tall windows with evergreen trim were cut into the mahogany walls. I walked to the reception desk. A middle-aged woman wearing a head set looked up.

"Can I help you sir," she asked with a smile.

I was surprised; she didn't give my casual attire a second glance.

"Well," I started, pulling my folded letter out of my pocket again, "I was wondering if you might have a copy of this letter, or something else that would show whether or not I passed the bar exam?"

I returned her smile politely, and handed her the letter. She looked it over for a moment, then lifted her eyes to mine with her glasses hanging at the tip of her nose.

"Did I do something wrong?" I asked, beginning to feel paranoid. Perhaps I committed a crime against her that I was unaware of.

"So, you're John Bowman. Your name sure has gotten around this office," she said, making me feel even more uneasy. I didn't know whether to expect something good or bad. I used to get into so much trouble as a kid that the Principal would finally have to see me. Sure enough I always heard the same thing, "so you're John Bowman." I hated those words. I watched her roll over to the desk behind her on a cushioned chair and grab a file that was sitting on the counter. As she wheeled back over to me I saw my name on the front cover of the file. I began to feel intimidated.

"We've been trying to get a hold of you ever since we got your results, Mr. Bowman. But it didn't matter what phone number or address we could come up with; none of them led to you. You're not allowed to keep this, but I'll let you take a quick look at it." She handed me the original letter. Unbelievable. This stated exactly the opposite from what the senior partners had for me. It didn't say anything about where I ranked, or how high or low; it simply said, "Congratulations, you have passed the Washington State Bar exam." There was also a second letter. The exact same letter which Olivia had a copy of.

"I am so happy I can finally stuff your file away," she said, sounding frustrated, "it gets tiring sending out the same letter to different addresses every week and never getting a response."

"May I see the addresses that you were trying," I asked, handing her back the letter from her file. She handed me almost two full pages of addresses.

"Every single address on here is bogus." I said, baffled at where any of these addresses could possibly have come from.

"I could've told you that, sweetheart." She said with a grim smile.

"Why didn't you just try to contact me through the firm?" I asked, curious as to why they hadn't just used a little common sense.

"We did, but they told us you just disappeared without leaving a phone number or address. I'm sure we could've gotten a hold of you through a private investigator, but let's get real -- we were the ones that were trying to do a favor for you and invite you to a formal dinner. Aside from sending out a letter to a new address every now and then, we gave up on you. Can you hold on for just a few more minutes? I'm sure Richard Pullen wants to see you."

"I guess I could, as long as it's only good news," I said, trying to lighten the mood.

She walked off around the corner, leaving me with my thoughts while it all sank in. I couldn't believe Olivia had been right. I couldn't believe I passed. I couldn't even believe I'd been invited to a formal dinner.

"Ah, so he finally decided to show his face." A man walked around the corner.

My first thought was that I was looking at Albert Einstein. Either that, or Orville Redenbacher. He was about 5'2" and thin, with thick framed glasses, long, bushy gray hair, and a red bow tie. He already seemed like quite the character, and I hadn't even met him yet.

"I'm Richard Pullen, Chairman of the Washington Bar Examiners," he said, reaching out his hand to me.

"Pleasure meeting you, Mr. Pullen." I shook his hand.

"Call me Richard. The pleasure is all mine. We've heard all kinds of things about you lately, John." He motioned for me to walk down the hallway with him, away from the listening ears.

"You mean last night?"

"John, you know as well as I do that before we're allowed to let any person become sworn in as a lawyer we have to do a personal background check. This includes everything, from traffic warnings and accidents to much more serious things. We already did a check on you and we didn't have a problem with you at all, but now we've heard you've become wrapped up in a bit more than just traffic violations. This puts us in a very awkward situation. When we heard you were down at the police station we were relieved to have finally found you, but by the time we arrived you had already left. That's why I'm so glad you showed up here. At least now we can get a look at the troublemaker."

Fortunately, he said it with a smile. He led me to his office and motioned to a small conference table. His office had a whole gallery of football and baseball memorabilia, including the Seattle Seahawks. It looked like the Packers shared a lot of the fame on the walls, and everything else that Richard could fill or cover.

"You look a little tired, care for some coffee," he asked, making me feel like I already needed a relaxing vacation even though I hadn't found a job yet.

"No thanks, I don't really like coffee all that much."

"Care for anything else?" He held open the door to his mini-bar, which was stocked with orange juice, some sort of health drink, water and of course coffee.

"Some orange juice would be great if you don't mind."

He grabbed two glasses and the bottle of orange juice, and brought the whole thing over to the table. I felt like we were two kids with some homework to do. He sat down and filled the two glasses, handing me one. He took a sip, nodded his head at me, and then gave me an almost fatherly smile.

"Tell me John, seriously now, what's been going on? We've never had a person do so well on a test and be so difficult to find and talk to at the same time." He asked, becoming serious with me.

"I'm a little confused with everything that's been going on around me, Mr. Pullen. Ever since my Uncle James got hurt and died, it seems like nothing has been going right; well, at least not until today when I found out that I passed the bar exam."

"Are you saying you had the impression you did not pass the bar exam?" He asked me.

"Yes. In fact, I've been studying for the past few weeks on a daily basis for the next test."

"I'd hate to see just how well you would do on the next one if you already ranked the fourth highest on the last one. Why did you think you didn't pass the bar?"

"I received a letter stating that I did not pass the bar exam, and ever since then I believed exactly that." I felt almost stupid for believing something that wasn't true for so long.

"Did you receive from us?"

"It was given to me by my last place of employment," I said, being careful to keep from mentioning names without knowing or fully understanding any relationships that there may be between the senior firm members and the Washington State Bar Examiners.

"Well John, it sounds like someone was trying to have a bit of fun with you. I don't know why or who, but it's really none of my concern nor my place. The important thing is we finally got into contact with one another and that you finally learned the truth. However, the difficult part now is to convince us that you still deserve to be a lawyer after your incident last night. We can't have just anybody become a lawyer. After all, it's the lawyer of today that will be making the powerful decisions of justice as a judge tomorrow." He told me this sounding more than ever like my grandfather, but without a forgiving tone.

"I'm sorry Mr. Pullen, but I'm really not sure what to say about anything that has happened recently. All I know is that as far as yesterday is concerned, I got the short end of the stick. I was put into jail because of debts I knew nothing of, and if I could have prevented it in any way I certainly would have. Besides, those debts are now cleared and taken care of, and so is my name. Unfortunately, the reputation that goes along with it is not in the clear, and never will be unless you let me become a lawyer and earn some respect for myself." I hoped that I sounded persuasive enough.

"To tell you the truth John, there was no real threat of you losing the chance to practice law. I talked to a few other members of the committee this morning, and we all agreed that everybody has a rocky moment in life. To let this stop your career would be a bad move on our part. I think we've all been in your shoes before, John. It's not easy, but if you put your mind to it like you did with that bar exam, I have no doubt that you'll get over any hurdle."

Pullen was trying to give me the "I've been through what you're going through, and I know you can make it" pep talk. He thought he knew what I'd been through, but I wasn't even sure if I fully understood everything that I'd had to go through -- and was still going through.

"This means I can practice law then," I asked, still trying to swallow all of the good news.

"Well, as soon as you are sworn in you can, and as a matter of fact, you'll have a chance to get sworn in next Wednesday. I think all the seats have already been taken, but I'm sure I can get somebody to squeeze in an extra seat for you. Just go down to the courthouse tomorrow sometime. I'll give them a call, and they'll have all the paper work you need to fill out so you can be sworn in."

"Thank you Mr. Pullen, you don't know how happy this makes me," I said, knowing that I still had to thank Olivia. She was the one that really deserved the credit.

"Actually its Dr. Pullen and not Mr. Pullen, but like I mentioned before, feel free to call me Richard." He was right, every lawyer earns their JD in law school, and he had every right to request being called by the appropriate title. But I'm still glad he was letting me be informal by letting me call him Richard. He held up his glass of orange juice to give a toast.

I held my glass up to his and we downed the last couple of sips in our glasses. I almost felt like I was still sleeping in the cot of the jail cell, dreaming something that I never thought possible. I guess all bad things have to come to an end sometime.

Chapter 25

I drove up Aunt Heide's driveway extra slow just to get the full feel of total satisfaction driving the Malibu with the top down. Of course, trying to draw attention to myself from Charleen peering out of the window might have had a little something to do with it as well. Charleen came running out, and greeted me with a running impact hug as I hopped out of the car.

"John I've been so worried about you. What happened? Are you okay? And how did you end up at Olivia's yesterday, or should I ask this morning?" She asked me at a million miles per hour.

I couldn't help but laugh and give her another hug. Charleen gave me a strange look with a slight smirk on her face. She didn't quite know how to react rationally to my smiling face. I squeezed her once more, shoulder to shoulder. With my arm around her, I guided her to the back porch of the house and explained the last twenty-four hours. The entire time her eyes fluttered, as mine probably did when Olivia, and then later, Dr. Pullen explained to me that I had indeed passed the bar and was going to be a sworn in lawyer. Charleen and I must have talked through the story over a dozen times before our stomachs finally took charge of our focus. We made dinner with the groceries that I had bought a few days before, and exchanged thoughts on why Dwayne Albertson and his partners had such a strong desire to keep me in a position where I was constantly under pressure by them. We decided that it was most likely a precaution taken simply in reaction to my uncle's death. They were probably worried that I might create problems with them concerning

Uncle James's death and proper ownership of the firm, which might lead to a bad name for their new firm. I wasn't sure if that was really the reason or if they were just plain cold-hearted sharks, but I did know that as far as I could tell Charleen and I were free from all of their chains, thanks to Olivia.

Before I realized it, it was already half-past eight and I hadn't even given Olivia a call. I gave her a call while loading the dishwasher, but nobody answered. I left a brief message saying that I did believe what she had told me, and that I was too tired to come over tonight but would come over first thing in the morning with the car. After I got off the phone and finished loading up the dishwasher, I gave Charleen another hug and went to bed. Even though it was only around nine O'clock and I slept in this morning, I felt like it was two in the morning and I hadn't had any coffee to keep me going.

On my way down the hallway to my bedroom I peeked into little Michelle's room. Sure enough, she's sound asleep with the teddy bear I gave her squeezed tight in her arms. Charleen is a lucky mother to have such a sweet girl, especially one whose teddy bear is almost twice her size. I closed the door with a chuckle, thinking about how many months or even years it might take until she's the same size as the teddy bear.

As soon as I made it to my bedroom I stripped down to my boxers, curled up underneath a thick layer of blankets, and before long I was out cold.

Charleen woke me up at about nine O'clock to tell me that Olivia was on the phone. For some reason I didn't feel like I just woke up, which made talking to Olivia a lot easier to deal with. I had to give a somewhat common-sensed reason when I tried to tell why I never came back over to her place yesterday and just left a message instead. I picked up the phone next to my bed on the dresser, and before I even said good morning I could hear her giving orders to somebody about something or another on the other end.

"How you doing, Olivia," I asked, trying to get her attention.

"Good morning, Sweetie. Did you sleep well?"

"Yes, thank you."

"Listen John, I'm sorry to have awoken you, but I wanted to let you know that I have to leave town on short notice and I won't be back until Wednesday evening. Don't worry about returning the car, you'll need to have something to drive around in. Just remember that car is very special to me, and to my sons too, so take good care of it okay?" She sounded somewhat hesitant about leaving me the car.

"I'll take very good care of it Olivia, I promise," I said, being extremely thankful for having a means of transportation.

"I know you will, dear, I know. However, even though I won't be in town, I need you to go over to Lisa's lab so she can fill you in on the details which you may need to know for your trial."

"Ahem, ah, excuse me, what trial is that," I asked Olivia, quickly realizing that I'd become indebted to her for getting me out of trouble and helping me realize I passed the bar exam.

"I'm sorry John, I have absolutely no time to explain. I have to fly out in an hour to go to Chicago for business, but I'll leave everything you need with Lisa. I told her you would meet her for coffee this morning in an hour-and-a-half at Susie's Seashore Café. It's easy to find, and quiet enough to understand an important conversation. Now don't let any difference in viewpoints bring the two of you to bad terms, I need you two to help each other out. Well, I've got to run John. See you soon, Sweetie. And don't worry, I'm sure you'll do just fine."

"Olivia, what are you talking about?" I was answered by a dial tone.

I put down the phone and lay in bed for a while letting all of her gibber-jabber sink in. I wasn't too certain anymore if it was truly a good thing that Olivia had helped me out. Two days ago I wasn't committed to anything except passing the bar exam; now all of a sudden I found myself going to a cafe to meet a woman that I didn't get along with in the least.

I finally was able to bring myself to hop out of bed and take my first decent shower in the past couple of days. Even though the thought of this being my first shower in a couple of days sounded bad, it wasn't like living it had been any better.

Charleen left a note on the kitchen table for me saying that she went to visit her Dad's grave sight to water any plants that may still be alive from the funeral. Made me feel a little guilty not having been to James' grave since the funeral, but I knew I'd swing by as soon as I got a chance so I tried not to think about it. I wasn't so much visiting the grave as it was feeling the memories while being at the gravesite. I missed James. I wished more than anything he and my father could be with me now. After all that I'd been through, I couldn't even tell those that probably cared the most about me becoming a lawyer.

I pulled out a telephone book and paged through it until I found the name Susie's Seashore Cafe, then I called for directions. I'd much rather pay for a two minute phone call than drive around the city completely lost for two hours wasting more money in gas than an entire phone bill. After getting directions, I grabbed a bagel out of the fridge with cream cheese and hopped in Olivia's Malibu. I left the top up; the air seemed a little too cool to let the top down, and it was more than I felt like fussing with at the moment. I thought about how I was going to act around Lisa after the way she blew up at me; I also wondered how Lisa was going to act around me. Although, I wasn't too concerned with it. After all, we didn't have to work together, all she was going to do was give whatever information Olivia had already given me. I imagined most of the information dealt with what Olivia was telling me about yesterday concerning the computer chip.

I left a little early just in case I got lost. Even though the directions seemed to be fairly clear, I wanted to make sure I wasn't going to be late (especially when it came to someone like Lisa). I didn't want to give the impression of being incompetent. I rolled into the narrow back alley of the place and parked alongside the building about twenty minutes early. Normally I'd be somewhat concerned about parking this car in a side alley, but since I was parked behind a Mercedes and in front of an older looking Porsche, I figured I was safe. Even if there was a threat of a car being stolen where I was parked, my car would be the last of the three to get stolen.

The place was crowded inside, just like all the other places I'd been to in Seattle. It had a layer of smoke so thick it almost acted as a piece of ceiling furniture or even art in the tiny cafe. I walked over to the front counter to order a hot coffee so I could wake up a little more before

Lisa arrived, when I realized that none other than Lisa herself was already there. She was standing directly in front of me and hadn't noticed me yet. I wasn't sure why, but I decided to stay unnoticed for a moment just to sort-of get the feel of her mood as she would be without me around. I heard her order an Irish Cream latte with extra honey.

"Could you make that two please?" My sudden voice coming out of nowhere startled her.

"John, I didn't even notice that you were standing behind me," she said, finding a quick response to her being startled.

"And now that you have, are you going to yell and leave the room again?"

"Listen, I'm in no mood to play games. Olivia put me in a very awkward position by having me come down here." She peered at me snobbishly.

"No chosen favor coming from my side of the court by being here either, *dear*." I put extra emphasis on the word dear with sarcasm.

"Will this be together or separate," asked the young girl behind the counter as she chewed her bubble-gum vigorously.

"I've got it." I handed a ten spot over Lisa's arm.

"Thank you," Lisa said as she took her Latte, gave me a fake smile as she tilted her head, and headed over to a table to sit down without waiting for me.

Obviously she was about as anxious to be here as I was. After I got my change I walked over to where she was sitting.

"Is it okay with you if I have a seat here," I asked, trying to be a smart-ass as I grabbed a chair and sat down before she could respond.

She pulled a fat envelope out of a soft-cover briefcase that she had beside her, and handed it to me. I opened the envelope and pulled out a pile of papers. They all looked alike to me. Each one of them was a documented record of the Schlau computer chip's development -- basically the recipe to the chip.

"Listen, I don't..." I started saying, only to be interrupted by Miss impatient.

"I know, you don't know what's going on and why you're in the middle of it. Well, I'm not really sure why you're in the middle of it either. If it was up to me I wouldn't even be here, and I certainly wouldn't be giving you, of all people, these research notes. However, I really don't think it's a risk to lose them at this point. They were already stolen from us once before, which is what brought our company into such a bind in the first place. Besides, Olivia has control of the company and she has done a fine job with it so far. I'm not going to interfere with her decision, even if it's an irrational one. Anyway, enough of that. Let me tell you what I'm supposed to tell you.

What you have there in that envelope is the backbone of our Schlau computer chip. Olivia told me she explained to you vaguely the set up of our chip, which probably means that she tried to explain it to you in the forms of 'front door, back door, offense and defense.' Bad idea. Olivia has a pretty good idea of what is involved with the design of the chip, but if you're going to get anywhere at all with this case then you need to know the design and system of this chip as well as I do. And that means knowing everything, I mean everything. Now then, as soon as you feel comfortable with all of that, you can get started on the second stack of papers. If you want to know what not to do, read this. It's an accurate record of what went on in the first trial of Schlau verses Xiborlink. As we obviously lost the first trial, I suggest you research this thoroughly and figure out exactly where they went wrong."

"Who's they?"

"They, are the three people who worked on this case long before you were even in town. Two lawyers and a paralegal."

"Where are they now," I asked, curious why they weren't working on this instead of me.

I waited for a reply, but instead I got only a hesitant expression before she continued.

"You, along with the defense, will meet with Judge Turner next Friday. It won't be an official trial; all you have to do is convince the Judge that you have enough evidence to make a case in court. Here are your directions on where it is, and at what time." She handed me yet another envelope. "I also included some papers you need to fill out and send in before you appear before the judge. I suggest you take care of them immediately since it's only a week away. And don't you dare think that you can get lazy and not do any research, because I'll be there too. I'll know whether or not you put any effort into this case, and believe me, Olivia will also find out. Thanks for the coffee, I'll see you next Friday." She picked up her soft-covered briefcase.

"That's it? You're just going to leave now," I asked, baffled by her hit and run tactic of conversation.

"I'm a scientist, and you're a lawyer. I'll stick to my job, and you can stick to yours."

She walked off with her latte in one hand and her brief case in the other. With the attitude she had, I would almost think *she* should be a lawyer.

I sat there for a few more minutes, sipping away at my coffee. Stunned with endless thoughts of what was ahead of me, I stared at the wall and began to hope that I was only dreaming, and it was almost over. I couldn't even think straight anymore. I felt like I'd just been hit by a tornado, she rattled everything off so fast. I wasn't even sure if I wanted to imagine why she didn't answer me when I asked about the three people that were working on this case before me.

Somehow, I didn't feel nearly as happy and enthusiastic as I had last night. I pushed my cup aside before finishing my Latte; I don't like that stuff anyway. I gathered all of Lisa's envelopes and headed out. Feeling the thick stacks of paper inside of the envelopes, all I could think about was how much work was ahead of me. What was Olivia thinking by giving me a job like this? I have no in-depth insight with this Schlau computer chip, nor do I have enough time to get the insight I need. I have no idea what kind of a company I'm up against, and I have absolutely no experience. Aside from all of this, I still owe eighty-four thousand, six hundred seventy-eight dollars and thirty-two cents in school loans.

I got into the Malibu but decided not to turn it on. Piling the envelopes into the passenger seat beside me, I slouched down into the seat and closed my eyes with a long sigh. I wondered for a moment how my mother was doing at the institute, and whether or not she was being cared for. The only thing I regretted about leaving Chicago is that I had to leave my mother behind. I'd make it up to her someday, someday soon I hope. I couldn't help but be concerned about Junior at the same time. What was he doing in the middle of India without any communication to us? He probably still didn't even know about his father's death. I wish James were still alive, I wish he was still in charge of that firm. Sure the firm would still be in financial hardships, but at least then it would still carry the Bowman name, Junior certainly wouldn't be on some nature hike in India, and Heide and Charleen would still have peace-of-mind. I hate those bastards, I really do.

I cracked my eyes open just a little, stuck the keys into the ignition, and turned on the radio just loud enough to hear it. I stared at the envelopes for a moment, then opened the one that had all the information from the last trial. I paged through some of the documents. They were neatly dated and titled by days and times; they even had some of the telephone conversations written down. I pieced together that the paralegal must have done all of the recording. That name was the only name that wasn't mentioned as a subject to the case, aside from minor notes. The two lawyers were Jean Benton and Chris Westhouse, and of course the names of the defense attorneys started out with none other than Dwayne Albertson, followed by the names of all of his little buddies. I couldn't help but wonder whether or not Dwayne Albertson was going to be covering this trial as well, assuming I could even convince the judge that we should have a trial. Whoever was covering the other company would be trying their very best to keep this case from ever even getting that far.

I dumped out the rest of the things in the envelope onto the passenger's seat. I looked at the items that fell out, and studied them for a minute: A computer disk labeled "case file for Schlau," an empty pocket-sized tape recorder, an empty pocket-sized camera, and some undeveloped film with a note on it stating, "research and development for Schlau." I stuffed everything back into the envelope except the film, and started up the car. My curiosity brought me to two needs: finding a computer to see what was on the disk, and finding a one-hour photo shop. I didn't have a remote idea as to where I might be able to get some film developed, so I decided to chase through a few streets until I could hunt down a photo shop. Of course I could just ask somebody if they might know where one is, but I had some time to kill. I almost enjoy driving with nowhere to go; it gives me time to slow down and think about things.

After about twenty minutes worth of driving, and thinking about what chances I had at getting this case to go to trial, I found a one-hour photo store. I parked the Malibu in a "no parking" zone in front of a fire-hydrant, and ran in to drop off the film and ran back to the Malibu before I got a ticket. The owner of the store, working with two other people on what looked like his picture developer, told me his machine was broken, but if I could wait until six O'clock to pick them up he'd give them to me for half price with free doubles. I figured a few more hours couldn't possible do any harm so I told him I'd see him at six. I walked out of the store and got ready to climb into the Malibu when I heard somebody honking a horn. I couldn't see anybody I knew, so I hopped in and pulled into traffic.

"Hey kid, what's the matter? You blind or something," I heard someone yell from the car next to me. I looked over and saw a huge grin smiling back at me from a face inside a Porsche.

"Mr. Peterson, how you doing," I shouted back at him, as we both slowed down for a red light.

"What do you say we go grab some ice-cream," he asked. He sounded like a grandfather trying to please a grandchild.

"Sure, why not. But you have to lead the way. I don't know where anything is around here." I figured I might as well do something since I had a few hours to burn before those pictures were finished. Besides, I was curious as to how things were going with Peterson and his Vegas fling.

Peterson pulled out in front of me. I followed him for about three blocks before he pointed me to a parking spot. As I pulled the Malibu into the parking spot, I could see Peterson buzz around the corner looking for a parking spot for himself. I was glad he gave me this one; it wasn't all that easy to find a parking spot that would fit a long Malibu like this one.

After locking up the car I walked around the corner and met Mr. Peterson, who was waiting in front of the door to the ice-cream shop. I didn't even have time to shake his hand before he had me in a bear hug.

"Kid, you saved me from one of the biggest headaches of my life," he said, laughing through his teeth as he inhaled a cigar. Charleen had taken the liberty of helping me out yesterday and delivered all the information, including Peterson's marriage certificate which proves everything he needs to prove, to Peterson's office yesterday. I imagine this to be the reason he's so happy.

"I take it everything went well then?" I asked as he put out his cigar and we walked into the ice-cream store.

"I'm still getting phone calls from Sharpner, just begging me to forgive her. Of course any old fool can plainly see that she is only begging to be forgiven because she's afraid of being sued."

I ordered a double-scoop cone, one scoop vanilla, the other chocolate. Even though the store had dozens of different flavors, I preferred the original above the rest. Peterson got a mix of coffee and yogurt flavors on a waffle cone. I let Peterson cover the three-dollar price, after-all, I did save his hide and *he* was the one that invited me to eat ice cream.

"And, *do* you actually plan on suing her?"

I was trying to analyze what level his morals were on, although I wasn't sure where my own morals would be if I had just gone through what he had.

"Oh no, I just get a kick out of scaring her, nothing more," said Peterson as he inhaled a good part of his ice-cream cone.

It was pretty obvious that he was excited about the whole ordeal, the way he was slurping down his ice-cream.

"So what now," I asked, curious about his future plans.

"What do you mean, what now? Now I am a free man, and I intend to live accordingly." He took another chunk out of his ice-cream cone. My cone still didn't even look like it had been touched.

"Don't you want to settle down though one of these days, and maybe fall in love," I asked, almost predicting his answer before he could give it."

"HA! I should hardly think so. I have no urge to meet another Sharpner. I may not act it John, but I'm getting too old to play those kinds of games anymore. But as for you," he said, pulling out his checkbook, "we still need to settle the score between us. It's your call, kid. What'll it be?" His pen hovered over his checkbook and he smiled, awaiting an answer from me. I thought for a moment at the tempting offer and then remembered the idiotic position that I was in. It was too dangerous taking money from him. Even though I had gotten the letter from Olivia, and I had talked to Richard Pullen about scheduling a date to be sworn in, I technically still wasn't a licensed lawyer. And if Dwyane ever found out that I had accepted money from Peterson for doing work on his case before actually having been sworn in, well, I'm quite sure it wouldn't turn out to be a very pretty scenario.

"Listen Mr. Peterson, I'm not..." I began to say, but he cut me off.

"You're not a lawyer, I know."

"You knew that?" I was completely astonished.

"Of course I knew. Your uncle's senior partners did everything they could to keep me with their firm, and even more so, keep me from talking to you. That included them telling me that you had yet to be sworn in."

"I don't understand. If you knew that I wasn't a lawyer, why did you even bother asking for my help?"

"Because I had a good feeling about you, and see, look where it brought us."

I tried to figure out exactly where it *had* brought me. *Nowhere.*

"I'm afraid that because I'm not a lawyer yet, I can't accept any money. If I were to accept anything from you, there is a good chance those senior firm members would nail me to the wall for practicing law illegally and I'm afraid I just can't risk something like that. I wish I could accept some money from you more than anybody, but thank you anyway." I watched the smile fall off of Peterson's face.

"I understand, but I sure wish I could help you out with something. Well listen, if you need anything at all you just let me know, okay?" He said it even though there really wasn't much he could do.

"Sounds good, Mr. Peterson." I shook his hand across the table while I tried to keep my ice-cream cone from dripping.

I thought for a moment about what he had just said, and realized that I'd probably never be able to ask for a favor as long as Dwayne Albertson was keeping an eye on me.

Suddenly an idea popped into my head that might just not be so bad - somewhat humbling perhaps, but at least nobody would ever be able to hold me to anything illegal.

"Mr. Peterson," I said, still holding my ice-cream cone so it wouldn't drip, "I think I just might have something that I could use your help on."

"What might that be?" A grin formed on his face; he obviously loved the idea of being able to repay me.

"Well, what are your plans for the evening?"

"I was just going to go for a jog. Other than that, nothing."

"Great. Let's go grocery shopping."

"Grocery shopping?" His tone was unbelieving.

"I know this may sound a little awkward, but Charleen and I are both very broke and we could use groceries in our fridge more than anything right now. Of course, not only would we be going grocery shopping, but we would be buying food for a cookout we'll have in celebration of your quote, unquote, ex-wife." I hoped he wouldn't find the idea too much of a hassle.

"I'd love to, John. I just can't believe you didn't say anything to me earlier."

"Well, I didn't exactly have any useful information about your marriage earlier though either." I said in response, being somewhat funny.

After we ate our ice-cream down to the cones, we decided to leave and head for some groceries. I used the payphone at the supermarket to call Charleen and let her know what was going on with dinner. She sounded pretty happy to be looking forward to a dinner for once, something other than a pizza or a frozen meal. I didn't mind the deal myself. Not that I wouldn't rather order up a fat paycheck from Mr. Peterson, but under the circumstances, I was quite content with some free food.

It took us about forty minutes to get everything we needed for the evening plus some food for the next few weeks. Needless to say, poor old Peterson had to foot one hell of a bill at the cashiers. But it wasn't as if he couldn't afford it; besides, he was getting off easy as far as I was concerned. I decided that I could just as easily pick up the pictures either tomorrow or early next week instead of at six O'clock. There certainly wasn't any reason why I would need to see them right away; I had enough in the files from Lisa to keep me busy for quite some time. In the mean time, I didn't plan on doing anything except drink a few glasses of wine with Peterson and Charleen, and enjoy a juicy grilled steak for the evening.

Peterson and Charleen's daughter seemed to hit it off right away. Peterson seemed to like the idea of acting out the grandfather scene. Charleen was sweet enough to set the dinning room table; she even put a wild bouquet in a vase on the table with a candle on either side. It almost seemed we were in a restaurant it was so perfect. Peterson and Charleen talked in the kitchen while I went outside and fired up the grill. The grill was sort-of built into the back patio with bricks and even a miniature chimney to channel the smoke. I had to do a little cleaning first, though. There were cobwebs hanging from the corners, and leaves had blown underneath. After cleaning it, I threw some charcoal into the pit and let it heat up. I loved grilling outside. I thought about my Dad and all the times we used to grill when he was still alive. That was when Mom was still with it and I didn't have to deal with a hard-ass for a stepfather. I couldn't help but deal with sad memories when grilling, but at the same time I still got the same happy feeling that I did when I was just a kid.

Charleen, her giggling daughter and Peterson joined me on the patio table. They brought a plate piled high with three fat steaks, and a hotdog for Charleen's daughter, just as the grill was getting hot enough. After throwing the steaks on (with a bit of sauce Charleen stirred up in the kitchen poured over the top to give them a bit of flavor), I went over to the table and opened up a bottle of wine which Peterson had brought outside for us. I didn't bother letting anyone smell or probe the wine, I simply filled three glasses and made a toast.

"Here's to getting rid of a wife you were never married to, and to our dinner which Mr. Peterson footed the bill for." I held up my glass to Peterson and Charleen. "I only hope it'll taste as good as the revenge on Miss Sharpner did."

Between the three of us, we polished off the first bottle of wine in less than two glasses each. Didn't seem to bother Peterson in the least, he'd bought a total of five bottles of wine plus a bottle of Southern Comfort. Before long he had two more bottles sitting on the patio table. Charleen stopped after the third glass, but Peterson and I kept at it until all three bottles were empty. The wine wasn't all that strong, so I didn't feel more than just a little buzz after we finished the third bottle.

After grilling the steaks for about fifteen minutes, along with Charleen's daughter's hot dog, we threw them onto a serving plate and brought it all inside. Charleen mixed up a salad and warmed up some French bread in the oven. Not exactly a fancy dinner, but a dinner I didn't have the chance to enjoy very often.

I didn't really want to drink all that much, but with nowhere to go and a thick steak to soak up the alcohol, I wasn't too worried. Charleen quickly learned how to have fun with two half-sober people. I didn't mind, and obviously Peterson and Charleen didn't mind. Peterson was sucking down the wine twice as fast as I was, and Charleen became an expert at refills.

"Well, those steaks were excellent. Maybe not quite as sweet as my revenge with Sharpner, but they were good. Thank you John," Peterson said with a slur.

"What are you thanking me for, you're the one that footed the bill for this dinner," I said, sounding even more slurred than Peterson.

"No, no. I don't just mean for the dinner John. I mean for getting me out of that mess with that scrawny ex of mine. And I thank you as well Charleen, John told me you had quite a bit to do with it."

Peterson put one arm around my shoulder, and the other arm around Charleen's shoulder.

"I think we're both just as happy that we didn't let you down," I said, giving him a good pat on the back as Charleen nodded her head in agreement.

Peterson gave out another happy chuckle, and then walked over to the fridge and pulled out the Southern Comfort.

"Are you two up for a shot?"

"I already stopped on my third glass of wine, but thanks for offering," answered Charleen.

"What about you John?"

"I think I'll pass on this one Mr. Peterson." I was feeling the bottles of wine we already had.

"Oh come on, John. Just have one, for me." Peterson leaned up against the fridge to keep his balance.

"Well okay. But only one," I said, thinking about what I'd be feeling like tomorrow morning. Oh-well, I had nothing to do tomorrow morning anyway, so why not. Besides, everybody knows you can't make a man drink his first shot all by himself.

"That a boy, John."

He neglected asking where he might be able to find a couple of shot glasses and simply filled our wineglasses about half full.

"Take it easy on me Mr. Peterson, I think we already gave the liquor store enough money. No need to hurry up and support them some more."

"No worries John, this will help that dinner of yours settle right in." He brought his glass up for a toast. I hesitated for a moment, and then I clinked glasses and shot it down as fast as I could. I felt it burn through my whole body. If I'd ever had symptoms of a cold before, I certainly didn't now. I didn't like drinking this much. I usually don't even get into drinking at all, but I guess Peterson had changed that for the evening.

Charleen put her daughter to bed after she finished her little ice-cream desert. I wasn't quite sure if Charleen decided to put her to bed because of Peterson and I hitting the liquor, or simply because it was eight O'clock. For no particular reason at all, I decided to pour another two shots out for Peterson and I while Charleen put her daughter to bed. I was past the point of being able to focus and reason with myself, which meant that taking a few shots at this point wasn't too hard to accept. And of course Peterson had no problems with taking another shot of Southern Comfort. In fact, he made sure I poured an even better sized offering than what I originally poured into his glass.

After Charleen came back out and joined us, we all moved into the living room. Although my balance was beginning to sway, I was able to throw a few pieces of wood into the fireplace and start a fire. It felt good to have a fire to warm us up a bit, especially since the weather decided to give us some rain outside. Every once in a while either Peterson, Charleen or I, would pour another shot of Southern Comfort into my glass.

Chapter 26

My head felt like I'd just gone ten rounds in a boxing match. Worse yet, it felt like I lost. I slowly turned my head toward the alarm clock next to me and found it was only eight O'clock Saturday morning. I tried to close my eyes again and sleep off another few hours of this headache, and then, as if predicted, the phone rang. I squeezed my eyes tight and hoped Charleen or somebody would pick it up. After about the fourth ring I gave up hope on that idea and slowly crawled out of bed. What a headache. As I pulled off the sheets I noticed I still had all of my clothes on except for my shoes and socks. I was sure, although I couldn't remember, that Charleen was to thank for putting me to bed last night. I managed to walk over to my dresser and pick up the phone on what felt like the twelfth ring.

"This is John," I answered, figuring that whoever was on the other end would either ask whom they were speaking to, or if they can speak with John. I might as well make things easy by simply saying my name off the bat.

"John," I hear, in a familiar voice, "this is James."

"Junior? Where are you, are you okay?" I was completely baffled to hear his voice.

"I'm at the Seatac airport, I just got in from India. Aside from being flat broke, I'm fine. I was sort-of wondering if you or someone else could pick me up."

"Of course, I'll be there as quick as I can."

"Look for the international terminal, I'll be waiting by the doors," said Junior, followed by a click.

I threw on some socks and shoes, and grabbed a bottle of mouthwash on my way out of the house. I checked Charleen's bedroom on the way out to see if she wanted to come with, but she was already gone. I ripped down the driveway in Olivia's Malibu and headed for the airport. I didn't make it any further than the first curve before I had to stop. I barely was able to park the car and jump out before I had to puke my guts out. I felt horrible, but getting it all out of my system was good. I waited another minute or so, until I began feeling a little better, and then hopped back into the car and headed for the airport. It's a good thing I grabbed that mouthwash, and I'm sure Junior will be thankful as well.

I was somewhat concerned about Junior. He didn't sound happy on the phone. Even though he and I had never really been the closest of friends, he'd never put down the phone with out saying good-bye. I'm sure I wouldn't be in the best of moods either if I just got back from an eighteen-hour trip.

I got to the airport in less than twenty minutes. I tried to make it as fast as possible so Junior wouldn't have to wait so long. I found the international terminal, but had no idea which airline to look under. I decided to just drive past all of them, since Junior said he'd be waiting outside the door for me. There he was, sitting on the curb eating an apple. I parallel parked in front of a car that some family was unloading, giving me enough time to greet Junior and get his stuff in the car.

"It's good to see you again. We were all getting pretty worried about you," I said, giving him a hug. "Can I grab any of your bags?"

I looked all around for some luggage, but couldn't see any aside from a backpack.

"This is it." He handed me his backpack.

We hopped into the car and headed for home. I wasn't really sure how to handle conversation with Junior. I had no idea how much he knew about his father's death, if anything. Not exactly an easy subject to bring up, and with how quiet he was he might be more down than I realized.

"What happened to all your luggage," I asked, trying to lightly break into conversation.

"Same thing that happened to my father and my job, gone." He said, leaving little room for conversation.

"Would you like to stop by his grave?" I was trying to think of something, anything, to perhaps comfort him.

"And a flower shop if you don't mind."

"I'd be happy to." I understood exactly what he was going through. I tried to imagine what he'd been through in the last few weeks, but I'm sure I wasn't even close. Our silence made the whole car feel cold, but there wasn't much that could be done about that. I knew of a flower shop that was on the way to Uncle James' grave only because I had stopped by there once before for the flowers I got for Olivia. I searched my memory as best as I could in order to find it again. Junior remained silent the whole way, which kept me silent as well. I felt like I did the morning we had the funeral, absolutely miserable. It's depressing to see a family with so much love lose a vital figure. Just like my father, I didn't think they'd ever be able to replace Uncle James, not even in memory, even though that's about as close as it gets. I was sure Charleen, Junior and Aunt Heide would pull together more and more as time went on. They may even grow to have a better understanding of and more sensitivity for one another. Whatever happened, I'd try my best to help out in any way I could for as long as I could, or until they kicked me out.

They knew Junior by name at the flower shop, and let him charge a pot of daisies to his mother's account. I didn't have that much money on me, but didn't want to go to Uncle James' grave empty handed so I bought a white rose. We both kept silent as we walked towards the grave. I could see out of the corner of my eye that Junior's eyes were teary, and the pot of flowers he was holding was shaking slightly. As we kept on walking next to each other I briefly put my hand on his shoulder and gave him a slight squeeze to let him know he wasn't alone. He didn't say a word, but he did reach over and pat me on my back as if to say, well, whatever a person says at a time like this. We came to a gentle incline. James' grave was just on the other side. Just as we topped it, we saw Charleen with her daughter hand-in-hand. We stopped where we were as soon as Junior and Charleen made eye contact. Charleen slowly tilted her head to the side with a smile, and tears began to roll down her cheeks as she dropped to her knees and covered her face with her hands. Junior immediately walked over and knelt down next to her, holding her. Charleen buried her face against Junior's chest, crying and gasping for air like a child. Junior's eyes were shut tight, his cheek pressed against the top of Charleen's head. Tears flowed endlessly from his closed eyes.

"What's wrong Mommy," Charleen's daughter asked, tugging on her shirt.

I quickly wiped tears off my own face, and walked over to pick up Charleen's daughter.

"Your mommy is just fine sweetheart. She's just a little sad because she misses your grandpa," I whispered into her ear, as I let her hold the white rose I'd bought.

"Is she going to be okay?" She looked over my shoulder at her mother.

"Your mother is going to be fine. She's a very strong girl, just like you're going to be someday."

I tried not to let any more tears run down my face in front of the girl. Her eyes remained focused on her Mom for another few seconds, then she looked at the white rose in her hand.

"Here," I said, letting her down, "why don't you take your flower and set it down on top of that stone."

I pointed to James' grave. She cracked a little smile and ran over to do what I'd said. I was trying to be careful not to say the wrong things in front of her. She may be just a little girl, but unusual moments at a young age can stick with a person for a long time. And I was sure it had to be quite dramatic for her to be watching her mother cry.

Charleen and Junior slowly got up, still holding each other, and walked over to the grave. Charleen took her daughter's hand while she clung to her mother's leg. Junior got down on one knee and set the plant down directly on the center of the still freshly dug soil. Sniffling was the only sound that could be heard aside from a soft breeze rustling through a large oak tree nearby. I walked over to Charleen and put my arm around her. I could still feel her body shivering slightly, not from the breeze, but from grief and sorrow over her father. It felt like hour after hour were going by as I watched Junior with his head leaned over the grave on his hands and knees. I could hear him whisper a prayer for his father, or maybe it was one last good-bye, but either way it was obvious where his heart was.

Charleen and I took a few steps towards Junior to comfort him as he stood. He turned to the two of us and gave both of us a hug at the same time. With Michelle in the middle of us, we stood there for about a minute arm in arm in a circle, and then began to head back to the cars. None of us really had anything to say, and if we did, it had already been said in silence in the hugs we gave each other. I saw Aunt Heide's car, the car that Charleen must have driven, parked in the parking lot. I walked them both over to the car and told them I'd meet them back at the house. I figured it was probably best for the two of them to ride together at a time like this. At the very least they could share their silence. It may not sound like a lot, but it was more than I could've asked for during the time of my own father's death.

When we got back to the house, Junior and Charleen dug out some old photos of the family, laughing and crying with each one. I left them alone in the living room while I grabbed a glass of orange juice and headed for James' old office to look at the files from Lisa. I actually wouldn't mind talking to Junior about his trip. If anybody would know something about this case that could help me out, it was definitely him. After all, he's the person Dwayne sent over to India to do some sort of check on the production line of the company. I didn't know what Junior really knew about the case, if anything, or if he'd even be able to tell me anything, as he was still working for them. This had to be one of the most awkward situations I'd ever gotten myself into. I was taking on a case which, not only did I know nothing about, but was at one time fought against in court by my uncle's own firm. All I had so far was one side of the story, and I didn't even really know or understand it.

I took three aspirin with the orange juice. Hopefully it would ease my still pounding headache and nausea. I pulled all the papers out of the envelope and began to sort them according to dates, persons, or subject matters. It felt like I was starting all over again with the Peterson case, only this time it meant a little bit more than just a few dollars. It was an entire reputation, and an entire company's future. It still made no sense to me why Olivia was so damned determined to have me working on this case. I knew for certain that it wasn't because I was an inexpensive lawyer, with all of the costs I'd made for her so far I'd probably racked up more than enough to hire a first-rate lawyer.

Chapter 27

Out of all the files and papers discussing the computer chip and the recorded case already made by the previous lawyers, I couldn't find anything that would help Schlau's case. As for learning anything more in-depth about the computer chip, forget it. I'd stick with the general definition Olivia gave me; it was a lot easier to understand then all of Lisa's notes and scribbles. Besides, understanding the actual setup of the computer chip wasn't going to help in proving its design was originally thought of and documented by Schlau and not Xiborlink. Why waste time trying to figure it out.

After about four hours of fidgeting around and getting nowhere, I decided to go to bed. I walked out to the kitchen and could still hear Charleen and Junior talking about old times. They would probably be out there most of the evening. Not that that's wrong; talking is probably the best therapy there is, especially with family. I went to the entrance of the living room, tapping my hand on the door, then gave them both a hug goodnight. They tried to invite me to stay and talk for a while, but I declined. I told them I'd take them up on it tomorrow, and headed for bed. I turned for the door, and just before I walked completely out of the living room, Junior called my name. He paused to wait for me to turn around. He just stared at me for a moment, then walked over to me and threw me a handshake.

"What's this for," I asked, joking yet truly curious.

"Thanks, John. You've done a lot for me, and I appreciate it more than you think."

"C'mon Junior, I haven't done a thing besides pick you up from the airport, and I was more than happy to do that."

"Believe me John, you've done a lot more than just that. You helped out around here, with Charleen, little Michelle, Mom, and I'm sure even more than that. It really means a lot to me John, thanks." He pulled in my arm and gave me a tight squeeze.

"You'd do the same J, I know you would." I gave him a pat on the back and then left the room. I never thought I'd see a side of Junior like this. He was a completely different person in some respects, almost in all respects. I wondered how thankful he'd be towards me once he found out what case I was working on, and for that matter, whose side I was on.

Then again, I didn't know about anything anymore. I had absolutely no idea if I was even fighting for something I felt was right. Olivia sounded convincing, and for that matter, so did Lisa. She'd gotten so perturbed with just the mention of Uncle James and his firm (ex-firm now). But on the other hand, why would Uncle James ever even consider taking a case unless he knew he was on the right side of the fence? Hopefully Junior would have some insight into the whole thing. At this point, however, I wasn't even sure if he would be able to share his thoughts on this case. If he knew anything of value and was still working for the Senior Partners, then he'd be committed to withholding any information that could help me out. Oh well, just so long as there was no conflict between the two of us, who cared. I didn't exactly see myself as a threat to Xiborlink, at least not with the information I had to go off of. And unless I got lucky with a phone call or two, like I did with Peterson's case, I highly doubted I'd even have enough to make an effort for an appeal on Friday.

For some reason I woke up two hours before my alarm usually went off. Six O'clock on a Sunday morning is an early time to wake up, but since I hadn't a sleepy bone left in my body, I got up. I took a quick shower and then headed downstairs where I met Junior. He was sitting on the back porch eating cereal and reading yesterday's newspaper. I guess he didn't care what he read at this point, just so long as it was in English and about something he could relate to, like the Seattle Seahawks. I grabbed a bowl of cereal and joined him.

"Pretty early for someone that just got done doing so much traveling," I said, clearing the first crackles of my early morning throat.

"Time change. It's the middle of the day for me over there. What's your excuse?"

"Don't have one," I said, "must be everything that's on my mind."

"I know what you mean, I think it must run in the family," Junior said, polishing off the last of his cereal. "So what is it that's on your mind?"

"Nothing. You've got enough worries of your own, you don't want mine on top of them." I knew he probably couldn't get his father's death out of his head.

"What I need is something fresh to think about, not to be left alone."

"Well, to tell you the truth, I don't know if I'm actually allowed to be discussing this with you, since you're still working for the senior partners."

"I don't think that's a problem anymore. They fired me."

"What do you mean they fired you? Even after making you go all the way to India?" I was completely baffled with their ethics.

"Looking back on the whole thing, the only reason they sent me to India was to get me out of their hair long enough to smooth things out with the firm. They knew that if I had been around I wouldn't have given in to anything, at least not the easy way. All they did was give me some bullshit union dispute to work on over there. A local lawyer in India could've done just as well while they cleaned out my office. They didn't even have the decency to let me know my own father had died until I got back."

"I'm sorry Junior, I know how much that firm, and especially your father, meant to you."

"You're right about my father, he did mean a lot to me, but not the firm. Not anymore. The only feeling I have left for that firm is spite. So don't feel like you can't discuss something because of them; they're nothing but back-stabbers."

"Well, I'm supposed to appeal the case for Schlau that they lost against Xiborlink. Do you know much about that case?" I was hoping for something that might help me out.

"To tell you the truth, I don't really know anything about that case. All I know is that Dwayne made certain he, along with his buddy Murphy, were personally in charge of that case. They didn't want anyone else to get involved. Nobody really thought anything of it at the time. We just gave in to the idea that it was because it was such a big case. But now, after all that has happened with that firm, I'm skeptical about everything that went on."

"But I thought you knew more about what was going on with that case. You went to India especially for purposes involving the production of the chip, and you were given information pertaining to the company."

"They did send me over to India because of Xiborlink, but it was only in concern over the union dispute, which was working with the production line of the company. I never got any details on the chip itself or any affairs with upper management within the States, which is where anything that has any significance in Xiborlink happens. And like I said, the only reason they sent me was to get me out of their hair long enough to reorganize."

"Do you think I should be working for Schlau, or do you think I'd be betraying your father? He must have had reasons to defend Xiborlink to begin with," I said, trying to get directly to the point of my concerns.

"My father really didn't have much to say about the case. That was a major argument between Dwayne and my father at the time, because Dwayne was supposed to go over everything with him before it was finalized. Of course, after they had a talk, this case became the first and last case that Dwayne ever handled that way." Junior was apparently disgusted by the idea of what the senior partners had done.

"So you don't think it would be wrong for me to take the opposite side on this case?"

"Wrong? Huh! Anything you can do to get back at those damn senior partners is far from wrong. And as for my Dad, he never had an actual side as far as this case was concerned. But if he were to have had a side, I'm certain he would have chosen yours, John." He'd given me the answer I was looking for.

"Even if I do end up fighting this case for Schlau, there is almost no chance for me to win using only the information I have so far." I poured some orange juice into my glass and took a hefty sip.

"Who says you need to win the case? Have you ever considered doing a merger?"

"A merger?"

"Why not. It would be the easiest, and probably the best thing for both companies. Schlau can increase their portions of any local stock they have and let it go national, while Xiborlink gains extended knowledge of any computer networking involved with this chip. I don't know anything in-depth about Schlau, but from what I've heard I'm sure Xiborlink would be more than happy to make a generous offer. If for nothing else, then to help prevent anything or anybody from endangering their reputation," said Junior with a devious look in his eyes.

"It's a good idea, but I really don't think Olivia would go for it. Nor would her family allow it." I pictured Olivia's entire family sitting down at the dining table while I tried to suggest selling out the company. Sounded like more of a suicidal nightmare to me.

"Of course they would go for it. You can write up a contract forcing Xiborlink to keep all former employee contracts with the company so that nobody loses their jobs. Then you can add on mandatory benefits, as well as a similar system of management." Junior leaned forward in his chair like he did the day he told me about Greg Finely.

I wondered if he even knew that Olivia knew all about Greg Finely and believed him to have been involved with the theft of Schlau's design? What Junior was saying, however, made a lot of sense. I wrote a paper on company mergers in law school. It was one of my favorite areas. I always dreamed of working as a corporate lawyer and being involved with just such a case. I sure liked the way the dream had turned out, problem was, it was *only* a dream.

"Wouldn't it be wiser for Schlau to stay on their own? They seem to have a secure profit margin at the business level they are currently on," I asked, still skeptical of the idea of Dwayne and Schlau joining hands.

"They certainly aren't doing bad, but they're not nearly where they would be if they were smart about getting ahead. It's obvious that the dispute over this chip doesn't have any meaning behind it as far as Xiborlink is concerned because they've already gotten what they wanted. Xiborlink has already begun production with it and will soon be making profits. On the other hand you have Schlau who hasn't made a dime off of the chip simply because they are incapable of competing. And if they think they're going to somehow win it back by appealing, well, you and I know what the chances of something like that are, especially when the company they're up against has already put a market out on it. Don't get me wrong John, I'm sure you're a fine lawyer, or so I've heard from Charleen. But even if you do somehow manage to get this appeal through and get this case back into a courtroom, there is no way any jury isn't going to be persuaded by a powerhouse like Dwayne. If Schlau really wants to stay on their own I'm sure they have the power to do so, but they would have to do it with a loss of time, effort, and potential money they could've made with the chip by doing a merger."

"If, hypothetically speaking, Schlau agrees to go through with such a thing, how exactly do I go about knocking on Xiborlink's door and asking for a merger?"

Even though I had an idea, I was still curious to hear what Junior had to say. He'd worked under Xiborlink, and he'd been around a lot longer than I had.

"You don't," he said, giving me the last answer I ever expected.

"What do you mean I don't? Is it just supposed to happen out of nothing?"

"I guarantee Xiborlink, or perhaps even Dwayne if he's still their lawyer, will approach you with the offer themselves."

"Impossible. They didn't do it during the first trial, why would they do it now," I asked, remembering what I read yesterday about the case being done by three lawyers before me.

"If Dwayne has anything to do with it, they will. I've seen him do it a hundred times before. This is exactly the type of game Dwayne likes to play. He'll get a good feel for the kind of company he's up against, financially and stressfully, and then he'll begin to suggest ideas left and right encouraging the companies to merge. For him it means a lot more money than if he were to simply go to court and try to keep a few reputations out of the dirt. Even though he realistically would have a good chance of winning this case in court anyway, he wouldn't gain nearly as much as if he were to form a merger. And that, after all, is what Dwayne is after; money and power. The only reason he probably didn't do it before is because he figured he didn't have much of a chance with Schlau. At that time they were still strong-willed and determined to win the case against Xiborlink. Now Dwayne most likely sees them as being worn down and ready to compromise, or so he hopes. And if, by some chance Dwayne doesn't approach you, well, then you can approach him. I'd wait it out a few days and see what happens."

"So do you think this is what I should do?"

"If that's what you want to do." Junior sounded like a professor trying to make a point of forcing self-reliability upon a student.

"What would you do?"

"I'm not sure. I am sure, however, that Dwayne can't be trusted. Especially after what happened while I was in India." He shook his head in puzzlement.

"Why, did something else happen there," I asked, letting my curiosity push for an answer once again.

"I'm not exactly positive about what happened. The day I got my first and only phone call from Dwayne telling me to come home, was the same day some guy I had worked with concerning some of the details of the production line wanted to meet me. He gave me a certain address and time, but when I got there nobody was in sight. I waited for about a half an hour, and then I decided nobody was going to show so I went back to my hotel. The minute I walked in, Dwayne gave me a call telling me, among other things, that it was time to come home. None of it made any sense. I didn't know that man very well at all, I can't even remember his name, but I do know he was responsible enough to always be on time. So when he told me to meet him concerning something of importance and didn't show up, well, I've got to wonder a little about what happened. I never did get a chance to find him seeing as how I had to leave that very day."

"And you're saying that Dwayne had something to do with this?"

"No. Well he might have, I really have no idea. All I'm saying is that there are a lot of strange things that happen when Dwayne is around, and usually those things aren't good when you're on the opposite side of the fence."

Silence took control of the table as we both stared down at our empty cereal bowls and pondered what we'd been talking about. Junior did have a good point. At first the idea had seemed a little absurd, but in the long run it was probably the best decision Olivia and her family could make. They would have more financial success with the manipulation of stocks once the two companies merged, and more capabilities in furthering their research. The only thing they might lose would be the amount of power and flexibility they had now. But it would be worth the sacrifice, especially considering the amount of stress that would be lifted. They might not approve of whom they'd be doing business with, but on the other hand it wasn't the firm they were going to be working with, it was Xiborlink.

Chapter 28

I decided that if I was going to get on top of this merging business I had better do it right away. I had to bring my file to the Appellate court by Friday. If this merger looked to be promising, I had to give a cancellation notice to the court at least a day prior. This meant, as much as I hated to think about it, meeting up with Lisa and going over the idea of a merger. If she liked the idea, chances were the rest of the family would too.

I didn't have to call very much before finding her. She was exactly where I expected her to be -- her main office at Schlau. Figured, even on a Sunday afternoon she didn't take one minute to stop and relax. I got directions from her and told her I was on my way. She didn't sound too happy about meeting with me to discuss the case, but I couldn't say I was thrilled to be meeting with her either.

I'd never been to the Schlau Company before, so pulling up to the entrance had me quite impressed. I could see the overwhelming design of what looked to be a seven-story building, which had to have cost a small fortune in itself. However, I had little thought on looking the place over. I simply wanted to get in and out as quickly as possible.

I asked at the front desk to have them call through to Lisa Potter's main office. After they asked for some ID and a reason for being there, they gave her a ring. She met at the bottom of the stairs, where the front desk was, and led me over to the elevators without ever bothering to shake my hand. I felt somewhat uncomfortable being there. I didn't exactly feel at ease with the idea I was about to present her with.

"So, let's hear what you have to say," Lisa said as we stepped into the elevator and she pushed the button for the fourth floor. "I have some lab partners waiting for me to do some tests, so I really don't have that much time to talk. So make it quick."

She gave me a squinting look for a half a second and then looked back up at the numbers on the elevator door.

"I'll do my best," I said, allowing my voice to sound a little agitated. "I'm going to get to the point by saying that I've gone over this case quite a few times, and I'm afraid there is nothing that can be used to win a trial. There's nothing I can do that your previous lawyers didn't do already."

"You came all the way down here to tell me we're going to lose? Schlau is the company that came up with the new chip, not Xiborlink. It's not like you have to lie, although I'm sure you lawyers are used to doing that. All you have to do is let the truth prevail."

"I'm sorry Lisa, it doesn't quite work that way. I wish I could somehow make that obvious, but Xiborlink has just as much evidence as Schlau for making an argument in court. Right now anything I could do would be absolutely pointless."

"What you're really saying is that you're too incompetent to even give this appeal a try in court. You want to pull out beforehand, am I right?"

"What I'm saying is that there may be a way around this. We can keep Schlau's research in progress, and put enough money in the bank for it to be financially secure at the same time."

The door to the elevator opened and she lead the way, with me close behind trying to finish my story.

"And what way would that be?" She was snotty, as usual.

I waited as we rounded a corner and entered her office. I closed the door behind me to let her know I really wanted her attention, then took a deep breath.

"I've done a lot of thinking, and the only way this company is going to pull out of a struggle like this is through a merger."

"A merger?"

"It's the only way this company will ever be able to move forward with its research the way you, Olivia, and the rest of your family envision it."

"You think a merger is going to do that?" Lisa asked, her voice rising. I was very happy I'd closed the door behind me when I came in.

"We can set up an agreement with Xiborlink to further develop research in joint operation. We'll keep a certain percentage of the company, to provide any profits that may come through the merger or any further growth of the company in years to come. Aside from that I'll make sure your family is set up with a retirement package that's guaranteed to be worth more than the net worth of this company."

"I suppose Xiborlink would be more than happy to let us sign on," she said, sounding sarcastic but making it hard for me to really tell.

"They would jump at the opportunity. Aside from the chance at a whole new addition to their line of computer products, they would be able to stop any potential of a muddied reputation by going to court with

Schlau. Everything, as I'm sure you know, can affect the stock of a company." I felt pretty good with the idea.

"So you feel as though you might lose if we go to court on this?"

"Yes I do. I don't like to lose, and neither do you."

"If it was up to me I would get someone else so you wouldn't have to be afraid of losing, but I can't. So instead you had better do more research and come up with a strategy to win. You're right about one thing, I don't like to lose and I don't want to lose to Xiborlink again."

"Lisa, I don't think you're getting what I'm saying. We have a next to nothing chance of winning. I have nothing that I can use to base any information off of in order to win this case. Please just think this through, Lisa. You have nothing to lose by merging with Xiborlink, but you have everything to lose by not doing it." My hands were planted on her desk; my body leaned over, hoping she was beginning to actually catch my point.

"Nothing to lose? John, you haven't read through the envelope I gave you concerning Schlau's future research plans have you?"

"No I haven't, and there is absolutely no need for it. Nothing in that envelope is going to help me win this case. I need concrete evidence to prove the chip belongs to Schlau, not a format of Schlau's future research plans. That would no more show a link to the chip than what Xiborlink could show with their future research plans." I was getting irritated.

"You don't get it at all, do you John? You know, even if you were to lose, it wouldn't bother me so much if you at least understood the importance behind this case. You aren't supposed to use Schlau's future research format to win the case, you're supposed to use it to really fully understand the importance of what the chip means. And perhaps even be motivated by it. Now, if you'll excuse me I have a lot of work to do, and I imagine you do as well. Next time don't bother stopping by unless you plan on giving an idea as to how we are going to win that chip back." She walked out the door, leaving me standing there with no chance to respond.

I let out a sigh to relieve some of the tension, then headed out of the office. Lisa had already disappeared, probably to one of her lab rooms. There wasn't much I could say to make anyone consider a merger of any sort; that was obvious. However, why they felt so strongly about it as to not even talk it through, I could only guess. Apparently, the answer was in the future plans for Schlau. I found it almost childish of Lisa to be so stubborn about it. She didn't understand where I was coming from in the least way, and because of that I had almost no leeway on this case. Lisa was living in a dreamland. No wonder the three lawyers before me lost their case. They had no solid proof other than some silly envelope filled with plans for a company that had no money to even create the dream, whatever that dream might be. I had to keep trying. Every case, as one of my law professors would always say, has a crack; it just takes some patience to find. Unfortunately, patience wouldn't be good enough with the court date less than a week away.

I dug right back into the case as soon as I got back to the house. Junior and Charleen told me they'd love to help me out when they got back from taking Michelle to the park, if it was okay with me. I told them I'd be delighted to have their help and opinions on anything they'd like to get involved with. I needed some extra hands on this case more than anything. Besides, Junior had covered over fifty cases, and had gotten to be quite the crafty lawyer by now. I had a seat in Uncle James' office and went through all of the paperwork again. Lisa's envelope with all of the research info was the only thing, aside from a brief scan, that was untouched. The papers in the envelope concerned such things as the technology of the chip moving into the field of medicine; the reason why Lisa felt this chip was so important. I understood how she felt, and I understand that she would very much like me to feel the same way about why this chip was so important to the company, but none of it was going to make a strong enough point to the jury. I could tell the jury all day long that this chip must be ours or we wouldn't have already made such secure future plans for it, but Xiborlink's leading attorney would shoot me down by copying my entire story. They could even make something up on the spot if they had to. All they would have to say is that Xiborlink had the same plans, and that we stole our future plans from Xiborlink. It would be their word against ours. I needed a little more than that to win this case. I began to read over the format the three lawyers had put together for their previous trial to see if I could find something new; something I didn't notice before or would give me an idea as to where I should be heading with the upcoming court date. Just as I got about halfway through the second page, the phone rang.

"This is John." I was not in the mood to talk.

"Hello John, this is Olivia calling. I just spoke to Lisa. She told me you're having somewhat of a hard time putting this case together. Do you think you'll be okay with it, dear?" She asked me as if I had been perfectly fine with it before.

"Olivia, why did you want me on this case so badly? I mean really, what makes you think that I, of all people, am going to be able to make something happen with it?" I was perturbed that she was making me go through something I had no intentions to.

"John, all I have is a good feeling about you."

"That's it? Come on Olivia, you can't possibly mean to say that your entire company is run off of a good feeling. You find someone you have a good feeling about and you give them a job? I have no experience, I won't be sworn in until Thursday of this week, and I have absolutely no material on this case. Olivia, please get someone who is qualified to go to court for you on Friday. It's not that I don't want to repay your favors, but I'm not the best lawyer you can get. At least with someone a little more experienced you would have a shot at winning. With me you're betting on a sure loss."

"Don't tell yourself you aren't going to win, John. I have a good feeling you're going to come through for us."

"Olivia, I'm a rookie. Doesn't that mean anything to you? What you need is a professional; an experienced professional in the field of corporate law," I said, trying to make my argument as forceful as possible without raising my voice too much.

"Listen John, just do your best and everything will turn out. I'll be back in a few days and maybe we can talk more then. Take care of yourself dear, you're a sweetheart."

She said it as if every word I'd said didn't mean a damn thing. She shouldn't be in a position like the one she's in if she couldn't tell I was in a desperate situation as far as this case went. That court was going to laugh at the case I had for them. There was nothing, absolutely nothing, that would support our appeal.

Chapter 29

The majority of Sunday evening was spent bringing Junior and Charleen up to speed with all of the details of the case. We all agreed to split the work three ways so that concentrating on more specific areas would be easier. Junior volunteered to look into any personnel that worked for Schlau to see if, at some other time, they had also worked for Xiborlink. Our good old friend Greg Finley was already part of that list. Charleen opted to research the case records to find what key points Xiborlink used to support their case at the last trial so we would know what we were up against for the upcoming trial. I took the leftovers, everything the previous lawyers had used to support Schlau in court, so I could get a feel for the level of argument we needed if we wanted to have a winning chance come Friday. Of course, Charleen and Junior were both absorbed with reading piles of papers for much longer than I could keep my attention focused. I tried to hold my eyes open past eleven, but instead I left the two of them to continue research while I hit the hay. Monday morning I got up early and went to a coffeehouse in downtown Seattle to read through more papers on the case. Sometimes it helped me think when I changed my environment. That, and the coffee. I sat in a chair up against the side of a wall facing a fireplace. The coffeehouse was long and narrow, with no windows other than the ones in the wall along the entranceway. Classical music was playing softly in the background, which helped me relax a bit. This was a good thing, considering my stress level seemed to be at a peak.

For about five hours straight I went through the case over and over again. I had almost every action that was taken by Schlau memorized. I knew virtually every right and wrong thing they did, but what did it help me if I had nothing new to go on? I tried not to think about that for the time being, and concentrated on what it was we knew so far, which wasn't much. Charleen and Junior, I was sure, were going through their sections of the case by this time of the morning as well. It was a little past eleven-thirty, and since I'd arrived here at around six-thirty, I was sure I'd worn my welcome. I threw a two-dollar tip in the tip jar as I left, so that the two girls behind the counter wouldn't be too tempted to badmouth me after I left. Generally speaking I could care less what people do or say about me, but when it comes down to it I can't help but try to keep peace amongst whomever it is that may be around. That's probably why I ended up sending Olivia those flowers, but if that had anything to do with why I was working for her right now, well, I had to wonder if it was such a good idea. As I hopped into the Malibu, I realized I still had the piece of paper from the photo shop for my pictures hanging out of the ashtray where I put it on Friday just before my little run-in with Peterson. Speaking of which, I still hadn't heard anything from Peterson. I hoped he survived the night a little better than I did. After driving around a few unfamiliar blocks, I finally came across a road I recognized from Friday. I headed in what I thought was the direction of the photo shop.

To my amazement, I found the photo shop within five minutes or so. I did an illegal parking job blocking traffic next to another car, threw on my flashers, and ran into the store. There's another lane available for traffic to get around me with, so I didn't feel too bad. I used to get mad when I first moved to Chicago and saw people do what I just did. After about a month's worth of driving around in the city and realizing that wasting more than a minute parking for a two-minute pickup was idiotic, I quickly picked up the habit myself and brought it with me to Seattle.

The same old man was in there from Friday and remembered me by name. He asked why I hadn't made it back that same night and I told him that I had a run-in with an old friend. Of course I didn't tell him my friend's name came from the comfortable south, I also didn't tell him about the headache I had the next day. I made sure I still got the deal he promised me on Friday for having to wait. Even though I didn't pick up the pictures when it was expected, it didn't matter. A deal was a deal, and I was strapped for cash. I hopped back into the Malibu before some cop could notice my illegal parking, and got back into traffic. I threw the pictures in the back seat next to Lisa's envelope, and spontaneously decided to have a talk with Richard Pullen.

I found his office building without getting lost, probably because I'd walked the entire stretch by foot from the pub the last time I went there. Stepping out of the elevator, I was greeted by the secretary by my first name. I apologized for not having an appointment, and gave a sweet smile while asking to see if I could talk to Mr. Pullen. She dialed Pullen's extension on her phone and swiveled her chair so that her back faced me so that I couldn't hear what she said. At least that's what she thought. I heard her ask if she should schedule me in for another day so I didn't disturb his lunch, and then, "yes, right away." She spun back around, gave me a smile and told me to head on into his office. I didn't even realize it until she mentioned it on the phone, but I had shown up at exactly lunchtime. Hopefully he either took an early lunch or hadn't taken it at all yet. I gave a quiet knock on the door and then walked in.

"John, what a wonderful surprise. Please, have a seat and let me get you a drink. What'll it be, orange juice, ice-water, milk?" He reminded me that I was talking to probably the only alcohol-free lawyer in Seattle. After my evening with Peterson, I'm seriously considering taking up the same habit.

"Juice would be great," I said, realizing that I was a bit thirsty.

He brought over two glasses, just like last time I was here, and a carton of orange juice. After he poured two glasses he had a seat and asked me, as if he were an old friend who was extremely concerned, what he could help me with. I was careful not to tell him any details of my case, but I filled him in on enough so that he could understand what I was up against. As soon as he got the picture, I asked him for a favor; a look at any past cases that he, or someone he knew may have dealt with that had this same type of problem. I knew I could look up history of it on my own, which I intended to do anyway, but if Pullen had any hands-on experience with a similar case then maybe I could get him to show me a few tricks. Of course I still had to be careful that he wasn't a friend of Dwayne Albertson's or any of his hot-shot buddies. That was why I was holding off on any details. If there is any connection between Pullen and Dwayne, it could work against me rather than for me to ask for a helping hand.

To my delight, Pullen's face lit up the minute I mentioned the word help. He seemed to be quite busy with a tall stack of papers when I came in, but as soon as I asked for help he picked up the phone and dialed his secretary. He told her to bring in some specific cases which he named off, then listened for a second longer and agreed to something about sending someone in. I had walked in on Pullen just before his lunch arrived. The person Pullen told his secretary to send in was none other than the pizza guy. He seemed to know Pullen on a personal basis seeing as how they spoke to each other by name. Pullen placed the pizza in front of me, still inside the box, then gave the pizza guy, Darren, a tip.

"I hope you like vegetarian pizza, because that's all I eat. I've got to stay healthy. Keeps the wife interested," he told me, as if I was interested in what he and his wife did.

Pullen placed a napkin down in front of me and pulled out a cheesy slice of pizza. He placed it down in front of me, then did the same for himself. I apologized for interrupting his lunch, but in a way I was kind-of happy to have dropped in on him when I did; I love pizza, especially when it's free. Pullen's secretary came in shortly after Darren, the pizza guy, left, and she unloaded a box full of folders. I imagined they were the folders that Pullen had requested. We didn't bother waiting until we finished our pizza to start looking over Pullen's cases. He had an entire stack in front of him and kept handing them over. Each was a specifically specialized case in their own field, but all of them were generally the same as far as the topic: patents and their rightful owners. It turned out that Pullen himself used to work for a law firm which dealt with primarily corporate law, almost as though I'd known where to look for help. I spent the majority of the afternoon there, and after discussing some of his past cases with a little more depth I began to let him know a little more about my case. I made sure to feel out the situation first by asking him questions pertaining to the two companies. Of course he had heard of Xiborlink and even Schlau, but all I really wanted to know was if he was biased towards either one in particular so that I would know whether or not to back off on telling him the whole story. He seemed fairly trustworthy. Letting him know more of the bits and pieces to the case helped us both out. He told me I had a chance if I played my cards right and stuck to concrete evidence. Unfortunately he had to agree with me about not having very many, if even more than two, concrete points to focus on. The first thing we had were the original notes and trial computer chips used to develop the prototype. The second was that we knew Schlau had ordered materials specifically for the computer chip within only a few days after proving the chip could work. This was, unfortunately, only a few days before Schlau found out that Xiborlink had copied the design of the chip. The fact that we had receipts proving that Schlau had ordered materials before Xiborlink ever did stood a chance of holding up in court. However, when it really came down to it, none of this was truly solid. If Xiborlink had their guard up, which they would, I'd need a lot more to get me anywhere.

It was good to know people like Pullan were still out there helping out poor fellows like me, and hopefully he'd continue to keep tipping me ideas as the week went on. Pullan let me keep the files until the case was over, which was good because I needed to study them a lot more before I planned a format for the Schlau case. I ended up walking out of his office at around quarter to five with a big box filled with case files, and two slices of leftover pizza. I couldn't help but feel a little excited. Even if winning the case was not yet a reality, the idea of putting up a fairly good fight was.

At home Junior and Charleen told me they'd been reading through information all day long, but still had no breakthroughs for a solid case. I told them about my day and how Richard Pullen helped steer me in a good direction. I emptied out the box of files and told them to help themselves.

As Junior had predicted, I found out Dwayne had called after I had left. He left a home phone number in case I couldn't get around to calling him during the day. I dialed his number and took the cordless out onto the porch.

"Is Dwayne available," I asked without giving my name to the woman who answered.

"May I ask who's calling?"

"Dr. Bowman," I said, trying to sound somewhat intimidating with my formal name I earned for graduating from law school with my JD. There was probably no need for it seeing as how I was probably speaking to a family member, but it helps to practice.

"This is Dwayne." I heard a familiar rusty old voice. It sounded like I might have woken him. Good.

"This is John. You called earlier?"

"John, I understand you're working the Schlau case. Is that true?" He asked as if it was impossible for a person he fired to get an important case.

"Does it matter?" I asked in response, trying to get on his bad side.

"Well son, it just so happens you're on a lucky one this time because I'm working the same case for Xiborlink. Looks to me like we can work out something to fit us both."

"And what would that be?"

"How about a merger, Xiborlink and Schlau. Come on, John. We could both win this one. It doesn't happen often you know, both sides getting a piece of the pie; especially with me. I never lose," he said, tripping on his own ego again.

"How much?"

"Why don't you come over tonight to my place and we'll talk about it."

"No thanks."

"All right. Tomorrow then, at the office."

"I already tried, Dwayne. If it was up to me I'd have already made up a contract, but my client doesn't want any part of it."

"Bring them with you to the office tomorrow. I'll talk them in to it." Dwayne kept his manipulative tongue ready to go on the sidelines.

"Sorry Dwayne, not going to happen."

"What's it gonna be then, court?"

"You guessed it."

"Like I said John, I never lose. I just hope you're ready to face up to that."

"Face up to you losing? I think I can handle it."

I could almost feel the hot air blowing from his nostrils. He told me he'd see me Friday and hung up. It was obvious he'd pull every dirty trick he could to not only win this case, but to make me look like the worst lawyer he ever came up against. Dwayne wasn't used to not having his way about things, and not getting this merger meant any frustration he couldn't contain would be directed primarily upon me.

Junior was waiting for me inside the house. As soon as I stepped inside from the porch he asked me if Dwayne offered. I told him yes, and then explained why Lisa and Olivia had said no. Junior was as astonished as I had been. There was no reasonable explanation besides the romanticized idea of what future research potential the company had.

Charleen had taken off while I was on the phone to go do some inexpensive school shopping for Michelle. With no ready-made food in the fridge, and neither one of us willing to cook anything, I remembered the two pizza slices from Richard. The two slices were not nearly enough to make our stomachs content, but it would at least hold us over for a little while.

I told Junior about the two main points that Pullan and I had come up with so far. We spent the next three or four hours brainstorming ideas of how to fit facts and notes we'd read over in the files to support the two arguing points. All we seemed to be able to come up with was a dancing skeleton. The skeleton was our format, and the dancing was the motivation. A bit ridiculous considering what we were up against. Junior and I took a short break. After about fifteen minutes we went into James' office to look over what we'd come up with so far. We both began to laugh. We'd known the format was bad, but to come back to it after working on it for so many hours only to find a few scribbles and thoughts that lead absolutely nowhere? I suppose it should've been seen as a rather serious matter, but neither one of us could help but laugh.

Junior and I both agreed to go back to the original material we had split up three ways, and try to find some supporting points for our newly made format. I was still shaking my head in laughter as I was walking out of the office to the Malibu to get Lisa's files, which I had left in the back seat from this morning. I grabbed the files along with the pictures, and headed back to the kitchen where I decided it was time for a sandwich. I pulled out some roast beef, cheese, lettuce, tomatoes, and bread, and threw it all together. I took the stack and let it heat up in the microwave for a minute or so, then sat at the kitchen table with a tall glass of plain old water. It tasted good to have something pure and clean go down rather than a bunch of carbonated chemicals. After my first bite, I reached for the pictures and pulled them out of their envelope with my free hand. I pulled the pictures out of their second, smaller envelope, while drinking some water and then my eyes glanced down towards the pictures. I choked. The water in my throat seemed to instantly freeze up. Finally I coughed and gasped for air. Quickly I filed through more pictures; they were all the same. I guessed the pictures to be of a region in Africa because of the landscape, as well as the natives. Although, I couldn't be certain. All of them were sick or dead. Those that appeared to be dead were unburied. A sheet or cloth was laid over their heads. Those appeared to be living at the time of the pictures, looked like they were desperately hanging on for dear life. Most of them were missing a leg, arm, or even both. All of them seemed to have thickly wrapped bandages somewhere on their bodies, which were pure red from bleeding that would not stop, and had come through the cloth.

I stopped to look away for a moment as I saw a small girl in one of the pictures holding the hand of a woman, a woman I have to assume must be her mother. The girl has only one eye, the other has puss and blood dried around where her eye used to be. I cringed and moved to the next picture. Lisa was in some of the pictures, along with a few others who all seemed to be trying to give whatever medical assistance they could. Lisa, as well as everyone else who was assisting, had yellow head-to-toe suits on of what looked to be a thick plastic. Strapped along side of the suits they had oxygen tanks.

Junior walked into the kitchen telling me he'd heard me coughing, and asked if I was okay. I just handed him the pictures I'd already looked through and kept looking through the rest. Towards the end of the stack I began to see pictures of a few of the people that had been helping in the yellow suits, but were now being treated themselves. One woman seemed to have blisters all over her skin. Two other men were also covered with blisters on their arms and hands. All three people are of white skin color, proving that whatever disease this specific region might have was not due to what many people might categorize as a native malnutrition problem. It looked as though the three of them had only been recently affected at the time the pictures were taken since their affections were not as severe as some of the others. Each one of them had a frightened look in their eyes, as though they knew they were faced with something that couldn't be fought.

Junior looked over at me with as much confusion in his eyes as me. I was angry that Lisa, and of course Olivia, and the rest of her family, obviously forgot to tell me a few things. It was just before ten

O'clock, but I was still quite certain Lisa was at her usual location. I called her office number, but nobody answered. Hoping desperately the only reason she wasn't answering was because she was in a different area of the building, I grabbed Junior and went for a drive to Schlau's Company building. I piled all of the pictures into my coat pocket in case Lisa tried to give me the run around when I asked her some questions. The night security guard at the front gate tried turning us away until I began to unleash a few forbidden words in his face with threats of law, which I was quite certain he had never heard before. He quickly called through to Lisa for me, who didn't sound happy to hear I was there but none the less cleared my entrance. He opened the front gate. I parked the Malibu in front of the entrance to the building. A security guard met Junior and I at the front door, and let us in. He took us up to Lisa's office on the fourth floor where Lisa was waiting.

"Afraid to talk to me alone now." She asked sarcastically, eyeing us both.

"This is James, he's helping me with your case. James this is Lisa, part owner, one could say, of Schlau." I tried not to blow up thinking of the pictures.

"I'm not interested in meeting people right now. I'm heavily into my work. I'm sure you can imagine that your timing is incredibly off to try to persuade me into another one of your bargain deals," she said, bringing my irritation level to a peak, again.

I didn't even bother to say another word to her; I just took the pictures and slammed them down on her desk. I could see Junior's eyes grow large as my temper began to flare. Lisa took a moment to observe the pictures.

"Where did you get these," she asked me in a low, and yet clearly upset voice.

"Cut the bullshit Lisa! I want the whole story on this damn company, and that includes what happened to your previous lawyers!" I pointed to the picture with the three sick people whom I assumed were the former lawyers and paralegal of Schlau.

Lisa put her face into her hands as she rested her elbows on her desk. Silence prevailed in the room as she pulled her hands from her face and looked through all of the pictures. She stopped at the picture with the small girl holding her mother's hand. I could see her holding back tears for a moment, then she composed herself and told us to follow her. She pulled a key out of her lab coat pocket as we stepped into the elevator, and put it into a keyhole located on the control panel of the elevater before pushing button number seven. Junior and I looked at each other for a moment in bewilderment. Lisa kept staring at the picture with the little girl until we reached the seventh floor. She took us down an empty hallway that smelled like medicine, to a door where she made three security checks for entrance. In order to gain clearance into the room, she had to do an eye scan, finger print scan, and a card scan. She opened the door and let Junior and I follow behind her. Neither Junior nor I made it far past the entrance. We both stopped in complete disbelief of what we were seeing.

There must have been a dozen nurses, and six or seven doctors. Most amazing of all were the patients. There had to be over three dozen patients in the room. Most of them looked healthy; there was absolutely no comparison to the pictures.

"This is our rehabilitation area for patients trying to rebuild muscle tissue that may have been cut away or surgically replaced." Lisa pointed to a row of exercise machines and very light weights.

"Rehabilitation area for patients? What *is* this place?" I was still trying to organize my thoughts so that I could make a little sense of the place.

"We like to think of it as a medical refuge for those that need it."

"A what?"

"Come on, there's more."

Patients left and right said her name, begging for attention. All of the doctors or nurses just nodded their heads as she walked by. They ignored Junior and I. Lisa took us to the other end of the room and through another hallway with yet another security door. After doing the usual three scans, we entered through the doorway and found ourselves in a small, square room with two doors aside from the one we came through.

There was an entire row of yellow colored outfits with small oxygen tanks, all lined up on the wall without a door. Lisa handed Junior and I each an outfit and pulled one down for herself. I just looked at Junior, who shook his head and looked back to Lisa for some sort of an explanation.

"If you want to go any further you need to put these suits on." She was already halfway covered with yellow material.

Junior and I gave each other one last look of desperation, and then began to put our suits on. Lisa strapped a small lightweight oxygen tank to each of us, and inserted a long tube from the tanks into a small filter device on our collars. She proceeded to place very lightweight, yellow helmets onto our heads. As a final step she double-checked all of our zippers, Velcro, and all other air escape areas.

"Don't worry about anything," she said, hooking on the rest of her helmet, "and try to keep breathing normally." She glanced at Junior. His entire faceplate was fogged up. Lisa, for the first time in a long time, gave a quick smile before walking to one of the two doors.

A computerized female voice announced a fifteen-second wait in order to check for any open leaks. Lisa explained that there was a small sensor in our suits that would alert the computer if there were any leaks. The way it worked, she explained, was by monitoring the amount of oxygen release from our suits. We should only be losing what we had already breathed in, which got pushed through a filter in front of our helmet allowing air to escape, but not to enter. If there was any other oxygen loss, the suits would send a signal to the computer which would in turn keep the door in front of us locked until we examined ourselves for any leaks.

Fortunately for us, the door opened after fifteen seconds, meaning that none of us had any leaks. Or so I hoped. As we walked through the doorway, I immediately saw more patients. There was a small area with a few couches and a TV, where the patients seemed to be gathered. Beyond the TV there was a long hallway with rooms on either side, much like a hospital. Every one of the patients in front of the TV was wearing thickly wrapped bandages on some part of their body, and all of them looked very thin. As in the other room, most of them looked to be African Americans. A few looked Hispanic, and from what I could see so far, one patient who appeared Caucasian.

"Most of the patients you see here have just recently had surgery."

"For what, what happened to them?"

"There is more to see," she said, leading us down the hallway.

Almost every room had patients. I couldn't really tell what the condition of them was, but I didn't want to be offensive by looking too much so I kept my eyes in front of me. Lisa stopped in front of a closed door of one of the last rooms in the hallway and quietly whispered, "some of the patients in these rooms will pass on, but hopefully most of them will pull through. We have one patient we've been struggling desperately to keep alive."

Lisa opened the door in front of us and held out her hand for us to walk in. I walked in with Junior behind me. There was a tall curtain surrounding a bed. I could hear a machine beeping, as well as an oxygen pump helping the patient to breathe. I stood at the end of the bed, still behind the closed curtain, and looked to Lisa who was still standing at the doorway. She nodded her head at me as if to say go ahead and pull on the curtain, so I did. My heart stopped. It was the same little girl that was holding her mother's hand in the picture. Her only eye was closed; she was sleeping. The other eye, which I could remember from the picture was no longer there, had fresh, white bandages over it going all around her head. Most of her face was covered with the bandages except for her mouth, left eye, and one side of her nose which had the tube from the oxygen pump going into it. Her neck was covered with blisters, most of them open and weeping, or even bleeding. The rest of her was covered by a sheet, except for her arm. An IV stuck into it, probably for pain. I looked to Lisa and gave her a nod to let her know I'd seen enough. Junior pulled the curtain shut and followed me out of the room. Lisa closed the door behind us. I could feel her staring at me, waiting for a response, but I didn't give one. We walked back down the hallway and into the containment room. Lisa shut the door tight, and hit a green button on the wall next to it. The female computer voice came on again, telling us to hold our arms out and spread our legs for thirty seconds; we followed the instructions. After thirty seconds went by, we were told that we could take off our suits. Junior and I both hesitated taking our suits off until we saw Lisa first strip her helmet off her head; we followed by doing the same. Thinking of the girl, I couldn't help but feel knots in my stomach. Her young age and small body, and already she had gone through so much.

"Her name is Sam. We gave her that name because she's too sick to tell us her real one. She's the only one who survived of the people you saw in those pictures. The rest either died while we were there trying to help them, or on the way back. Unfortunately, that includes Jean, Chris, and Benson, the two lawyers and paralegal you saw in the pictures." Lisa wiped a tear from her cheek. "They had grown to be much more than just a legal team, they became bonded with the spirit of hope we try to bring people. And that spirit is what they lived for... and died for."

Lisa gazed up at the ceiling for a moment, collecting herself, then pulled her ID card from the back pocket of her blue jeans and ran it through the scanner of the final door we hadn't yet entered. My curiosity at this point had been overcome by fearful images racing through my mind repeating what I had just witnessed. My stomach still felt nauseous, and my heart was still at the bedside with poor Sam.

Walking through the doorway, I found there was nothing to keep a knotted stomach over. The door we walked through from the containment area entered into another long hallway, and there were no patients.

"It took quite some time to get over the deaths of all those people, and I still have nightmares, but that's why we're doing all of this; so that we might be able to help more people like the ones you saw in those pictures."

"What exactly does Sam have? How come all of those people died? And what is it exactly that you're doing," I asked, still a bit shocked.

"Sam has a virus related to Ebola. Every characteristic of her virus runs almost parallel with that of Ebola. The only difference is that what Sam has is capable of twice the damage in half the time. Ebola feeds off of flesh and can literally deteriorate the legs, arms, or organs of a person within eight to twelve hours, depending upon how bad the condition may be. However, what Sam has is like Ebola with a catalyst making the rate at which the virus attacks speed up. We named the new form of this virus Doga-Ebola because one of the areas infected by this was Doga, Mali."

"Don't we have a cure for Ebola," I asked, in pain at the thought of such a virus.

"Well, there is no real cure, only surgery. Similar to some forms of cancer, the only way to rid the patient is by cutting, not only the infected areas themselves, but even deeper so there is little to no chance of missing any part of the virus and allowing it to spread further. This is why so many of our patients are doing rehab. We have to help them build back up any muscle tissue that we were forced to cut away. In some instances we were unable to even save the arm, leg, or body part that was infected, and we were forced to amputate. Something I detest doing. Sam is a strong fighter, but she will undergo surgery again in less than an hour. The infected areas on her neck you saw formed within only the last few hours, and if we don't do surgery again soon, she'll die."

"How many times have you done surgery on her," asked Junior.

"This will be our fifth time in just three days, but hopefully this will be the last of if."

"And if not," I asked.

"If not, then we keep trying until we can't try anymore."

Lisa continued to lead us down the hallway. I tried getting a look into some of the rooms as we walked by, but they were mostly empty. The ones that did have something in them were too dark to see into anyway. Occasionally I saw someone walk by in a white lab coat. Every one of them made sure to either say hi, or at least nod to Lisa on her way by.

"I don't really understand how you got so involved with all of this," I said, confused, "I mean, what exactly is your part in all of this and what does it have to do with Schlau?"

We stopped about halfway down the long hallway and walked into room seven-eighty-two.

"This is what it's all about," Lisa said, closing the door behind us.

There were four others in the room with us. Lisa introduced them casually, with no exchange of handshakes. All four of them were wearing white lab suits with an ID card hanging around their necks. The room really wasn't that big. We were all stuffed into a six-foot by maybe fourteen-foot room, and all of us were looking through a triple-layer glass window. The window looked through to seven small, divided areas. Each had four or five rats in them. Lab rats. On our side of the window there were computers lined up left and right, as well as all sorts of lab test equipment. There were also insulated arm extensions that reached out into each one of the divided areas on the other side, so that someone was able to work with the lab rats, yet not expose themselves to whatever chemicals they might be working with. At the end of the room there was a doorway which, from looking through the window to the other side, looked to have a containment area similar to the one Lisa had taken us through earlier, only smaller. I found myself to be completely amazed, and at the same time completely lost as to what the overall focus was of this bizarre seventh floor of Schlau.

"This is what all of *what* is about?" I asked.

"This is what our chip is all about. We're not here to make millions upon millions of dollars, but we do need enough money to keep this research alive. And *that* is the underlying importance of your case."

"What exactly is this research of yours all about?"

"Why don't you guys take a quick break," Lisa said to the four others gazing through the window, "we'll be starting on Sam again as soon as I'm done here."

She turned to us.

"Don't you get it," she asked me, almost making me feel inferior that I didn't. "This chip may find us the cure to life-threatening viruses and diseases. Ebola, cancer, sexually transmitted diseases, including maybe even AID's, and many others will all become abolished through the use of this chip."

She waited for a response. I just looked at her in awe along with Junior as I repeated in my head everything she just told me.

"Well, you certainly have my undivided attention," I said, holding my breath as I waited to see what she would say next.

She extended her hand, pointing to the chairs so we may have a seat, then pulled a chair out for herself.

"I've always pursued helping people with techniques of modern science simply because I enjoy helping those that need it. However, I've never had the opportunity to pursue something as meaningful as this. Usually I've always stuck with simple problems. More often than not, it was a matter of a sick or wounded person who simply could not afford, or did not know how to go about getting the medicine they needed in order to be nursed back to health. We didn't have to do much. We hired on a couple of part-time doctors and played off of their judgment as to what patients needed. All we had to do then was find the chemicals needed to mix up the proper medicine, and next thing we knew, we had a healthy group of fans who had no medical bills to pay."

"Let me get this straight. You're having people examined by doctors, you're mixing up generic drugs without any official license, and nobody is the least bit concerned about anything fatal happening?"

"Yes, yes we are concerned. We are very concerned, but those people need our help."

"What about the hospitals? They have medicine, they can help."

"Yes, they do have medicine, but they won't give any if you can't afford it. Besides, it isn't like we're helping people commit suicide. All we're doing is curing people of a few aches and pains, perhaps even help a single working mother deliver a child. I know it must be tough for the two of you to see past the illegalities of this whole ordeal, but it's worth a try."

At the sound of that last piercing remark both Junior and I cringed. She was right, I wasn't looking past the illegalities; yet I couldn't help it. I was a lawyer. That's what I was supposed to do.

"So where does the chip come into play?" I asked, overlooking her comment.

"It hasn't yet, but we're trying. You understand, I assume, how the original chip which you're fighting for in this case is capable of disarming security codes, right?"

"With out an in-depth understanding of the actual design, sure. I guess I have the basics."

"All we're trying to create is the same thing, only through human beings. Imagine what we could do if we were able to find out exactly where it was that our bodies weren't functioning, and why. We would be able to understand things nobody ever dreamed understanding before.

And DNA is the key. DNA is what forms us as a baby. It's basically a human body blue print that formed our every last detail, and the fact of it is, nobody really knows how it's done. The DNA structuring is so complicated, that to break down enough to match only one single strand of DNA with perhaps a murder suspect at the cop shop can take months, or even longer, if at all. Now imagine what it takes to analyze a person's *entire* DNA structure in order to find out where something may have gone wrong, and then, how to repair it. The task is virtually impossible. Science today only understands a tiny fraction of how DNA works and where our authority is in intervening with it. The endless stretch of codes involved with DNA leaves researchers clueless."

"Until now," stated Junior, starting to understand her conclusion.

"Well I don't know about now, but hopefully we're looking at sometime in the near future. Come take a look at this over here."

She rolled her chair over to a microscope attached to a computer. Junior and I scooted our chairs over to where she was. Under her microscope she had what looked to be a drop of blood spread between two small squares of thin glass. The frame of the microscope itself had a glass encasement covering the area used for examining threatening things such as the drop of blood Lisa had in there now.

"This is a drop of Sam's blood. We added enzymes, dye, and put it through electrophoresis which, to try to make it sound as simple as possible, separates the DNA strands allowing us to analyze individual strands. The stages we have to go through from here are more complex than what one might think them to be. DNA structure, or our human blue print, is much like a bank security code. DNA has thousands upon thousands of uniquely formed codes, which dictate our body's shape, form and basically, the individuals we are. However, if one of these codes was to be set up in the improper order, then our body could become vulnerable to anything from cerebral palsy at the time of birth, to becoming a victim of lung cancer at the age of forty. As I mentioned before, the idea of recognizing incorrect DNA and the purpose it serves within our body is almost untouchable by the techniques science has been using so far. Yet I believe with our Schlau chip there may be a chance of conquering such a feat. We know our chip is capable of doing such a task, it's just a matter of somehow programming the chip to recognize the unique codes of DNA. Once we have established this, we will be able to break down the DNA and find the cures to diseases that have been hindering man for centuries."

With chills running up and down my spine, I listened to the stillness of the room for a few seconds, then looked towards the rats.

"And what kind of purpose do they hold, or are they just for looks?"

"Well like I've said, we haven't had any breakthrough in analyzing DNA to the chip's fullest potential as of yet. However, we have gotten enough bits and pieces of data to give us an idea as to which direction we should be headed in. In order to test potential cures, we first expose the rats to a gas containing Doga-Ebola. This is to our advantage because the rats seem to carry the virus, but are at the same time immune to any of its fatal effects. We proceed by injecting what we think may be a potential cure through the use of our insulated laboratory arms. As of yet we've had no success, but we're going to keep trying. We're going to keep finding new ways of programming our chip until it works and can break down these codes, and we're going to keep praying for Sam to pull through for us. That's all we *can* do. We've been doing trial and error testing for over seven months now, and so far we have nothing, but that's not to say we're going to give up now."

"Why have you waited so long to show me this?" I asked.

"How was I supposed to know who to trust anymore? Had I not trusted anybody in the first place, then nobody would've had the chance to run off with our chip and you wouldn't even be here to pursue regaining it in court. Besides, what good does showing you all of this really do? Are you so extremely heartbroken, deeply touched, and perhaps so concerned for Sam that now you think you've grown to care about what we do here? I wouldn't believe you no matter how good of an actor you were. It's all money to your type."

"Listen-" Junior started, but I interrupted.

"No, she's right, Junior. All we're out for is the money. Lawyers don't have hearts do they, Junior? And even if we did, well, what the hell would it matter if money can buy everything? Well let me tell you something, Lisa. There's an old lady sitting in a nursing home that can't remember her name because she has Alzheimer's. She can't remember if she was ever married, or if she has a son, or whether or not she ever had a family she loved more dearly than anything. She also has something in her brain that causes her to have seizures and burst out in aggressive frets, and not one doctor knows why. But you are absolutely right, why should I care about an old lady like that? Why should I care about an old lady who just happens to be my mother?" My anger was no longer in check. "Let's get the hell out of here, Junior. After-all, time is money."

I stared Lisa down with raging fire. Both Junior and I walked out of the room, leaving her with an astonished look on her face as she sat sunken into her chair. Lisa may be well educated, and even extremely gifted and talented within her field of research, but to hurl one immature insult after another was downright childish. I felt my jaw forcing stress on my teeth as I clenched down on them in pure rage. I could almost feel Junior's anger building inside of him with every step we took going down the hallway. At the doorway to the containment area, we found somebody in a lab coat who carded the slot so we could get out. After finding our way to the elevator and then finally making our way outside, we hopped into the car and went home. I heard Junior make a few negative comments, and I agreed occasionally. We didn't exactly say goodnight; we just gave each other a nod and turned in.

Chapter 30

In spite of the aggravating comments by Lisa, we might very well have a chance with this case. I couldn't help but wake up around quarter to seven, and begin adding ideas to the case outline for Friday. Junior got up only a few minutes after me, and seemed to be just as enthusiastic. Of course he seemed to have a hard time looking past Lisa's comments, but we didn't let any of it get to us. Although the things Lisa said had gotten to me last night, sleep had worked most of it off. Even if it hadn't, I wouldn't let it keep me from moving on.

Sitting in the kitchen, both Junior and I agreed that if Schlau was going to have any chance at all in court on Friday, we were going to have to emphasize their medical research. If we could somehow show that Schlau's research was being done *before* Xiborlink's dates of initial design work had begun on the chip, then we'd be able to show procession. The only thing we had to sidestep was all of the illegal work that had been done by Schlau. Nobody could deny it had all been done in the very best interest of medicine and helping the sick, but if Dwayne found out Schlau had been doing anything illegal, even a few bad parking tickets, he'd turn it against us and make us pay dearly.

Junior and I talked through every last detail we'd learned yesterday, and tried to decide what material was valid for use and what was not.

After about two hours of back and forth questions and dead ends, we were left with one possibility: Mali. We had to try to concentrate on the work that was done in Mali. None of it was illegal because it had been done in a foreign country. The help Schlau had given in Mali would help us show that they had been doing research in the medical field before Xiborlink's dates of basic design work had begun. Junior and I were both gleaming with smiles when Charleen walked into the kitchen in her morning robe. We told her all that had happened, including Lisa's enlightening opinion of lawyers. Charleen got a little excited for us as well, then reminded us that we only had three days to thoroughly prepare a report for Friday. We agreed.

We heard the phone ring twice before Junior was able to reach his arm back and grab it.

"Hello," Junior said, with both Charleen and I watching curiously. "Just a second."

Junior put his hand over the phone and whispered to me that it was Lisa. I gave both Junior and Charleen a dreadful look fully indicating my thoughts of not wanting to talk with her.

"This is John," I said, expecting a long list of negative remarks, which she probably stayed up all night trying to gather.

"Hi John, this is Lisa. Listen, um, I was wondering if you could come down to my office so we could talk," she said in a very soft tone.

"What time?"

"Whenever it's good for you."

"How about right now? I need more information from you anyway," I said as professionally as possible.

"That would be fine. I'll see you in a little bit, then."

"Yup, see ya in a bit."

I hung up the phone, completely baffled. Charleen and Junior were both looking at me, wondering what that was all about. I just shook my head and told them I had to run down to Schlau for a while. They asked if I wanted some company, but I told them no. I had a feeling by the tone in Lisa's voice, that whatever she wanted to talk about would be difficult enough as it was with just one person.

After a quick shower and a bagel with cream cheese, I headed out the door and over to Schlau. Charleen and Junior decided to begin preparing a second, new outline for Friday while I was gone. Until I got more information from Lisa about the work they did in Africa, we wouldn't be able to conduct very much preparation work. I supposed that was about the only good reason she'd called so far.

The place looked different during the weekday. The parking lot was full of cars, and inside the building there were people shuffling back and forth like there was no tomorrow. I didn't have to say much more than my name at the security desk downstairs before I was escorted to the fourth floor of Lisa's office. I walked over to her door and knocked until I heard her tell me to come in. She was on the phone when I came through her office door, but that didn't keep me from coming in even further and sitting down. Sort of impolite, but I didn't care.

I stood at the door and waited until she was done.

"John, thank you so much for coming down," she said as she got up out of her chair.

She leaned against her desk. I couldn't help but be once again puzzled by her soft tone and demeanor.

"Listen," she said, "I feel absolutely rotten about the things I said last night. You have to understand I didn't mean to treat you like that." She sounded surprisingly sincere.

"Then what exactly did you mean to do?"

"I guess I've been a little too caught up in my work lately, and I've forgotten who's on my side anymore."

"I see," I said, letting her know she had better have more to say if she wanted to convince me of anything.

"And, well, I think I've forgotten that there are other people out there that have a heart besides me. Please, will you accept my apology?" She walked over to me and reached out her hand. I shook her hand and gave her a smile.

"So did you call me all the way down here so you could shake my hand, or was there something else?"

"Well, I also wanted to apologize for judging you and your uncle simply for what has happened here at Schlau. It wasn't fair of me. I don't really know you, and I never knew your uncle. It was inconsiderate of me to prejudge you the way I have, and I'm sure you had a hard enough time as it was just trying to deal with your uncle's death. So, I'm sorry. I'm sorry for everything, and I truly hope you can forgive me."

"Thank you," I said, somehow finding it very hard to hold back any softness. "I must admit I haven't exactly been all that charming myself, and I apologize for that."

"However, don't think I'm going to make life easy on you. You've still got to win this case for me. If you don't, well, I may just have to resort to my alter ego," she said, thankfully in a joking spirit.

"So how's Sam doing?" I asked, knowing that she underwent surgery shortly after Junior and I left yesterday.

"She's still in critical condition, but the surgery seems to have gone well. We still don't know if we cut all of the Doga-Ebola out of her body yet, but maybe this time we got lucky. Maybe if you can win this case we'll get very lucky and finally be able to invest a little money into this research so we can develop that chip until we get a cure."

"I certainly hope so. Listen, about the case, I think we might have a shot. After what you showed us last night, I think we might be able to scrounge up enough material to make this case a possibility."

"What do you mean? I can't afford to give out any information to the public that may put this company in jeopardy. If anybody finds out about our little hospital going on upstairs, we're through." She became quite protective.

"I realize that, and we are going to make sure that doesn't happen. Junior and I have been discussing this already this morning, and we won't use any material that may give away Schlau's current missionary work, if one can call it that. All we intend to do is use the research you did in Africa to help establish the time of existence for the Schlau chip. I give you my word, we will not go any further than that. So, what can you give me on Doga-Ebola research that was done during or for the trip to Africa?"

"Well, virtually everything we're doing on the seventh floor relates back to that trip, so if you can somehow use the info without having to involve any current medical practice that we may doing, then you're welcome to whatever you want."

"Great. Can I see the rest of the files on your research?" I hoped that she did indeed have files, and not just scribbled notes.

"Certainly. I dug them out before you came." She pulled out a box from under her desk. "Anything else?"

"How about you?"

"What about me?"

"Do you think you could take a few days off of work and fill us in on anything we might get a little confused about? I mean, we would be able to move through the material a lot faster, and you could help clear up any areas that may need some explaining. It could help us win the case."

"Can't you just give me a call whenever you don't understand something," she asked, trying to get out of it.

"Well I'm not sure I'd be able to understand everything you may describe to me over the phone, I'm a very *visual* type person." I tried to be a smart-ass and not laugh at the same time.

"What time," she asked, a slight smile peeking through.

"How about in a couple of hours? Oh, and don't forget to bring your Prozac. You're a lot easier to get along with when you're like this," I said, trying to keep the air light.

With the box of files in my hands, I made my way back down to my car and began to head home. I would've told Lisa to follow me over right away, but I wanted to get a little preview of what was in the files. Besides, I only thought it was right of me to first warn Junior and Charleen that we were going to be having a visitor.

Coming into the driveway, I found Mr. Peterson's Porsche parked in front of the garage. After I pulled up next to his smooth convertible and parked the Malibu, I heard voices coming from behind the house. I walked around the house to find Junior, Charleen, Michelle, Mr. Peterson and someone I didn't recognize. I didn't see any Southern Comfort in sight, just a couple bottles of orange juice. By the sound of the loud laughter, Peterson seemed to be sharing more of his jokes again.

"Hey John, it's about time you decided to join us. Come on up here and let me know what I can do for you this week."

I walked over to the table and greeted Peterson. He introduced his brother-in-law, Gary; he looked a little younger than Peterson, but not by much. I couldn't help but to be in a good mood whenever I saw Peterson. He never let anything bother him. Well, nothing except ex-wives.

"Well I think we've already gone over the rules of what you can and can't give me, remember?" I tried to resist the thought of asking for a fat paycheck.

"Sure do John. I just have to give you a hard time, is all. But just remember, if you ever *do* decide you need anything, anything at all, you just let me know and I'll take care of it."

"Maybe we'll go grocery shopping again sometime, only no Southern Comfort, okay?"

"To tell you the truth John, I just wanted to invite you and your family over to my cabin up north for the weekend. I'm having a sort of pre-divorce get together and it wouldn't be proper to have something like that without the true man of honor." He yanked out a cigar, but didn't light it, not yet anyway.

"I'm going to be kind-of busy this week, but if I still have enough energy by the time this weekend comes around, I'll be sure to be there."

"I'm counting on you to be there, John. Don't let me down. I've got a lot of friends that have been asking me for a good lawyer, and I want to make sure they don't look any further than you." Peterson pulled out a sheet of paper from his back pocket, and threw it down on the table. "I made up some directions on how to get there. If you get lost, just call my cell number."

He wrote down the cell number on the back of the piece of paper. It was a great thought on his part, but by the time we got done with this week I highly doubted I'd be in any sort of a mood to go party.

"Sorry to say this, but Gary and I can't stay any longer. My sister is making us some good 'ol cherry pie, and we can't be late for that," he said as they got up out of their chairs and shook hands with Charleen and Junior. Peterson gave little Michelle a pat on the head, then gave me a quick hug good-bye as if I was never going to see him again. I said good-bye and told them I hoped we'd be able to make it up to his cabin for the weekend.

After he left, I gave Junior and Charleen a run down of what happened at Lisa's office. They seemed both surprised and happy that she'd apologized the way she did, until I told them she was going to come over in about an hour or two. Even though Charleen had never met her, she cringed at the idea because of what Junior and I had said about her in the past. I explained to them what they probably already knew, about being able to do a lot better on the case with her help. Neither one of them wanted to agree, but neither one could disagree either. We gathered the half-full glasses of orange juice, and brought them into the kitchen along with the new box of files. The kitchen sounded, and was even beginning to look like a library after about fifteen minutes of digging through papers. Charleen, Junior, and I became quite absorbed. None of us openly admitted it, but we were all, especially me, stressed at the idea of having to go to court in only three days. I wasn't really sure how well prepared we were. It was hard to tell when we didn't really know how much it was going to take to convince this court to accept our appeal on Friday. By the dominating silence in the room, I was sure we weren't as well prepared as we should be.

Lisa arrived at three O'clock. She apologized to Junior, and then I introduced her to Charleen and Michelle. Lisa seemed to take a liking to the girl immediately. I can't exactly say Michelle doesn't like soaking up the attention.

We began discussing anything and everything about the chip and the research that had left us confused. We went over additional photographs, which Lisa had tanken herself on the trip, and airtight samples of blood which were tested while they were in Africa. We paged through the diaries of both lawyers and the paralegal. We discussed thoroughly the details of all the medical notes and reports made on the trip, especially those relating to the chip. And finally, we pulled apart what the last two lawyers had focused on, the employees which at one time worked for Schlau and were now working for Xiborlink.

Xiborlink was as clever as they could be. They hired over two dozen former employees of Schlau at the time they stole the chip, so that we wouldn't have any concrete proof in singling out a thief.

We struggled through each person and their former position within the Schlau Company until we could no longer stay awake. It was two in the morning by the time we finally called it a night. We had two more days before we faced Xiborlink in court, but we had a fair chance. Our strong point would be all of the work Schlau had done in the medical field involving the chip. If we could show that this work would've been impossible if Schlau hadn't designed the chip any time other than the time period in which Xiborlink claimed to have designed it, hopefully we would gain full ownership of the patent. Xiborlink had done none of what Schlau had done in the medical field, and we were going to make sure the court heard it. However, our strong point might also end up being our weak point. Xiborlink, once they figured out our emphasis, would most likely try to concentrate on the new technological advancements that they had made. Dwayne would try to manipulate anything I said and make it sound as though whatever advances Schlau had made could've easily been done at anytime. Hopefully by the time Friday came we'd be able to counter any such assertions, so that neither Dwayne nor his buddies would have a chance at shooting us down.

I also had a copy of the letter which Jean and Chris, the former lawyers of Schlau, had sent off as Schlau's brief to the Federal Court of Appeals. Originally, the case was disputed in the Federal District Court, which is the lowest level of Federal Courts. The brief stated some of the main points that we ourselves had been going over, but it didn't focus on the dates of research in Mali. It didn't really matter too much, I'd just start off talking about whatever was included in the brief and then move into my strong points. It might even be a better tactic to slowly build the court up to a strong ending climax. Maybe then Dwayne wouldn't have as much impact if I leave them with a strong impression.

I offered Lisa a guestroom so she wouldn't have to risk falling asleep on the way home, but she didn't like waking up somewhere else if she didn't have any fresh clothes or a toothbrush, and decided to go home. We agreed to meet again tomorrow, but not quite so early. Lisa had to attend to any medical needs that Sam might have, and I'd told Richard Pullen that I'd stop by his office sometime in the afternoon so he could give me more pointers.

I was glad Richard was helping me out as much as he was. If anybody knew whether or not a case had a chance and how to make it happen, it was certainly him judging from his past track records of patent law. I decided to be polite and walk Lisa to her car, it gave me the opportunity to thank her for being so helpful and recognizing the idea that not all lawyers were evil. Of course maybe a small part of me wanted to get one last look at her deep green eyes and beautiful smile before she left, but I made sure not to let her get any hint of that.

Chapter 31

I pulled off yet another early morning. I had a quick breakfast, showered, and made a thank you card out of a plain sheet of paper for Junior and Charleen thanking them for all of their help. I still made it out of the door by six thirty. Although I only got about four hours of sleep, I was feeling pretty good. I figured I'd go nestle up in a coffee shop and go over what we went over yesterday as many times as I could until I had to see Richard. If I could get to know the material so it felt like an actual part of my life, maybe I'd be able to think it through better and actually analyze what it was I was going to be telling the judge on Friday.

Even though I could've tried to stay at home and review the material there, I figured I'd be better off where nobody knew me and no phone calls could interrupt me. I left most everything we had sitting on the kitchen table at home, in case Charleen and Junior wanted to go through it like I was. All I brought with me was my notepad and tape recorder, which together contained nearly everything that we'd reviewed last night. I wasn't too particular about which coffeehouse; Seattle had more of them in one block than the rest of the country.

I ended up at "The Southern Bean". It had a South American appeal to it, with a lot of flowers in the windows. I liked it. I ordered up an Irish Cream latté with whipped cream on top. It felt great. My head was clear, and I didn't have nearly the stress I'd been feeling ever since Olivia had thrown this thing in my lap. Lisa had helped lift a lot of the stress off of my shoulders. Partially because she'd apologized, which I never would have expected, but also because she sat through our entire discussion yesterday without hesitating to get involved. It gave me the feeling that she really knew I was taking the case seriously. If I lost, then I lost. At least she would understand that I'd really tried. It almost made me want to win this case even more. First, however, I had to get this thing through the Federal Court of Appeals on Friday. If the judges weren't convinced to let the case have a second chance, then my chances and Schlau's were over.

The judges were what worried me. I'd heard many stories from old professors about the things they went through trying to appeal a case. Almost every story I could remember ended with them never even getting the case past that point. On top of that, I didn't only have to deal with a simple appeal; I had to deal with three federal judges. I didn't know who the two other judges would be, but in the letter Olivia had received from the courts I knew the name of the presiding judge, Judge Harrison. Of course I didn't know him personally, but I'd heard of him. Most of the things I'd heard, mainly coming from Junior, were that he was a fair player. That was all that mattered to me. I wouldn't have to deal with a jury, witnesses, testimonies, or any type of hard-core evidence. All I had to worry about was persuading three judges. It sounded easy thinking about it, but the reality was if the judges didn't think the case I presented to them had a good chance, and I mean really a *good* chance, of winning in front of a jury, then they wouldn't grant it. So basically I had to play this court off on Friday as though it were the real deal; all or nothing.

I went through about two lattés and decided to switch to water until two O'clock rolled around. That was when I figured it was about time to go over and get my regular dose of orange juice from Richard.

Before going to Richard's office, I stopped by a local market and picked up a Barbie doll. I couldn't really afford it, but I couldn't afford the teddy bear I'd gotten Michelle, either. Yet she'd been holding on to that bear ever since I gave it to her. Hopefully the Barbie doll would have the same effect on Sam at the hospital. I couldn't seem to get her face out of my head.

Amazingly, I didn't have to await permission at the front desk to see Richard; the secretary just smiled and waved me down the hall. The door to his office was open, so I just headed right on in. He looked the same almost every time I saw him: the bow tie, wild looking hair, the thick glasses, and the funny looking mustache, Einstein's twin. I walked in and set my notepad and tape recorder on the conference table while Einstein over there automatically got out the carton of orange juice. You'd think I was on a liquid diet.

Richard had all of his notes from last time sprawled out across the table, and he also had more case examples for us to make a few comparisons with. We first covered what I'd been going over with Lisa, Charleen and Junior. I explained to him what we felt our strong point would be, and how we were going to play off it in court on Friday. He thought it was a good idea, and that relieved me.

"Take the defense and those judges by surprise," the Einstein look-alike said. "None of them will ever expect medical data and proof of dates coming into play, and that's what counts. If nobody's prepared for it, then chances are you won't have to deal with any back talk by the defense team and you'll win. Remember, everybody in that courtroom on Friday will have reviewed the first courtroom case and the main points of argument which were explained at that time. Nobody will be expecting a complete regrouping of thoughts and arguments saying that there was to insufficient evidence. People usually don't find enough concrete evidence to support such an accusation when they try to appeal. Usually people, including me in past cases, concentrate on laying down groundwork of an unfair first trial because of either manipulation of the jury or even the judge. But I have to hand it to you, John. For a rookie lawyer, you're looking pretty good."

"Do you think I have a chance?"

"Sure do. Fact is I think you have a better chance than I had with many of my cases, and I didn't lose very often." There was that ego, again.

We spent the next few hours going over more material. Pullen related a few cases in-between the lecturing, but I listened. Most of what he had to say was exactly what I needed to know. The proper tone to have, facial expressions, to be careful to make a statement and not a full on argument; the list went on. By the time he poured the last of the orange juice into our glasses and asked the secretary to run down to the store for more, I was beginning to feel like one of his students. At quarter to seven we called it quits.

Tomorrow was my day to be sworn in as a lawyer, but Pullen said he wouldn't be able to make it to that or the dinner because he'd already made plans to celebrate he and his wife's thirty-fifth wedding anniversary. I congratulated him and told him it was no big deal if he couldn't make it. I'd only be at the dinner for about an hour, and then I was going back home to review for the appeal. Pullen wished me the best of luck, and told me he'd be watching the results on the local news.

It never occurred to me that this was something that might attract the media. But considering the size of the companies playing this case, there was good reason for the media to have an interest. It didn't bother me too much, no cameras were allowed in the courtroom itself and I didn't plan on giving a speech afterwards whether I won or lost.

I stopped by Schlau on the way home. I wasn't sure why, I could have just called instead, but I suppose part of me wanted to check on Sam. Not that I couldn't just ask Lisa how she was doing, but I guess I wanted to see for myself. Besides, I wanted to give her the Barbie doll I'd bought for her earlier today. Even though Sam was barely conscious because of all the painkillers she was taking, any little thing that might comfort her whenever she was coherent was worth while dropping off. And perhaps some part of me wanted to see Lisa.

My face was quickly recognized at the front desk. An elderly lady with glasses handed me an envelope with my name on it and told me that Lisa dropped it off yesterday for the next time I came through. I opened it up and found a "you're welcome" note attached to what looked to be an access card. I told the ladies at the front desk thanks, then headed up. Some guy in a white lab coat got into the elevator on the second floor. He looked familiar, but I couldn't place his name so I didn't bother saying anything. He looked young, about my age. He was wearing a stethoscope and a white lab coat, so I assumed he was a doctor. He had a wide frame, perfect for playing football.

"Aren't you John," he asked, finalizing my theory that I'd seen him before.

"Yeah, who are you?" I tried not to sound too rude.

"Actually I've never really met you, but I did see you the day you took Lisa's little tour on the seventh floor. My name is Jeff. I was one of the guys in the test room. Well, I was until Lisa kicked us out so she could talk to you and your friend." He glanced down at the Barbie doll I was holding in my hand.

"Yeah, sorry about that. I guess she just likes to keep things private. Well, this is my floor."

"Actually, if you're looking for Lisa, she's on the seventh floor. I usually don't do this, but since you've already seen everything there is to see, I can access you." Jeff plugged his elevator key into the panel and pushed number seven.

"Well, if Lisa won't have a problem with it."

"Problem, hardly! Your name has been coming up quite a bit lately."

"Concerning this case?"

"You could say that."

"Come again?"

"Not many guys have been able to make an impression like you have, and believe me, a lot of us have tried. By the way, I'm one of Sam's volunteer surgeons."

"Volunteer?"

"Sure, most everyone here volunteers at least a few hours a week. A few of the other surgeons and I have been putting in some extra time for Sam. She needs it."

"How is Sam," I asked, still trying to figure out where this juggling act was going.

"I'm not really sure what qualifies as good when someone has got what she has, but I think we've got ourselves a little fighter."

"So you think she'll probably live?"

"Tough call at this point," Jeff said. The elevator door opened on the seventh floor. "Here you are. Lisa will probably be in the Lab room where you saw me a few nights ago. Your ID should be scanned into the computer, so just use your card to enter through our security system. I assume you know the procedure. Well, it was nice meeting you. I've gotta run, I'm due back at my real job." He reached out and shook my hand.

"Hey, ah, what was it you were saying about Lisa again?" I asked Jeff, standing from outside of the elevator door.

"Just go with the flow of it, John. Believe me, she's worth it," he said as the elevator door closed.

I stood there for a moment in complete amazement. How could a guy I'd never even met before go off on some wild tangent (which I couldn't follow), and then just leave me hanging? I turned my back to the elevator door and walked down the hall to the three-door desensitization room. Some recovery patients were watching Jeopardy; I could see a few of their heads turn in curiosity at my unfamiliar face as I walked past them. The ID card I was given worked, and so did my fingerprint scan, but Jeff had never told me what to enter for my digital entry number. I stood back and thought for a moment, then put the last four digits of my Social Security number in - it worked. I was impressed, and almost frightened at the same time. Schlau had been able to find personal records in a very short amount of time. I hated to think what someone could do if they were trying to use fingerprints and social security numbers for something other than an entry system.

I walked through the containment area to the first door on the right, which was where Jeff said Lisa would probably be. I didn't need any type of a suit, so I just keyed my card through the slot and entered the hallway. Room seven eighty-two was locked. I twisted the doorknob back and forth in case there was someone inside, but nobody replied. I looked both ways down the long hall for a minute, then decided to head over to the side where Sam was. I got into the desensitization room and put on a suit. I managed to put it on a lot quicker this time, mainly because I knew how. I waited for fifteen seconds until the female computer voice cleared me. I could imagine growing tired of doing this as a daily routine. Even though I certainly should have felt safe being air tight in the suit, I couldn't help but feel an adrenaline rush from having thoughts of catching a life-threatening disease.

I walked down the hallway towards Sam's room. The hall was quiet. Aside from a few nurses getting their exercise by delivering dinner to some of the patients, there wasn't much going on. Nobody really seemed to pay much attention to me as I strolled down the hall. I preferred not to be noticed so that I didn't feel as though people were watching my every move.

The door to Sam's room was ajar, so I walked in. The curtain was pulled shut around Sam's bed, and there was no sign of Lisa. I unwrapped the Barbie-doll and pulled back the curtain. Poor Sam was still all wrapped up in bandages, only now she had a thick wrapping going around her neck as well. I walked over to her bedside and laid the Barbie doll down on top of her left arm, which was resting on top of her sheets. I paused for a moment, looking at her bandaged face, then turned to walk back out of the room. Suddenly, holding the curtain in one hand and getting ready to leave, I heard a quiet cough. I looked behind me to see Sam's eye open. I walked back over to her bedside.

"Hey there, kiddo. How you doing," I asked her, leaning over her bed.

I realized she couldn't talk right now, and if she could she wouldn't be speaking English, but it didn't make any difference to me. I simply wanted to make her feel comfortable by speaking peacefully. It was somewhat difficult speaking through the suit; everything echoed. I lifted Sam's arm a little and tried placing the Barbie doll in her hand, but she was so weak she couldn't even hold on to it so I just laid it back on her arm again.

"Well I certainly wish I could read your mind, Sam, so I could help you out, but I don't think we're going to get that lucky." I hoped that at least my smile would make some of her pain go away.

Sam looked at me for a moment with her brown eye, then tilted her head to the side and looked over to the nightstand. I looked over to see what she was staring at, and noticed a children's book. If I could read only one thought, this was probably it. I picked up the book and slid a chair next to her bed. I opened the book so she could see the pictures, and began to read. I still felt awkward reading a children's book from inside the suit, but I didn't think Sam really minded.

By the time I reached the last page, I noticed Sam's eyelid gradually closing. She was asleep. I pulled up her covers a little more and quietly got out of my chair. My heart jumped for a moment as I turned around and noticed someone standing by the doorway. It was Lisa. She had a huge smile on her face. Without saying anything, we closed the door behind us and began walking down the hallway.

"Since when did you start sponsoring the Barbie Corporation," Lisa asked me with a grin.

"I was looking for you, thought maybe you'd like to join us for another delightful evening in the books."

"Just so long as they're not children's books, I guess I can handle it."

Lisa followed me back to my place in her full-size Chevy pickup. I never really figured her to be the type to like trucks, but it suited her quite well. At home my faithful volunteers were at the kitchen table with a box of pizza in front of them. They didn't seem to be too stressed out, which was good. I told them about the encouragement given by Richard Pullen, and that worked to relieve even more stress.

We spent the next few hours reviewing, and also going over some of the files that Richard had given me. By eleven O'clock we called it quits. We'd had enough long days, and besides, we'd nit-picked our way through just about everything one could possibly go through for just a briefing of appeal. I wasn't worried. I felt good about the case, really good.

After the notebooks were closed, we ended up sprawling out in the living room. Junior and I got a fire going, while Charleen and Lisa made some warm milk with sugar for Michelle. She couldn't sleep, and had made sure to let everyone know it. Junior and I ended up talking about how many things had changed. For once, I opened up a bit. And for once, so did Junior. I told Junior I respected him for everything he had gone through, and how he'd been able to hold it together. And of course, I thanked him again for helping me out so much. It was like having somebody guide the trail, and for me that was one hell of a trail to follow. I really was quite happy he'd been helping me out.

Lisa walked into the living room followed by Charleen and Michelle.

"I've got to run back to the hospital for some quick work I have to do for Sam, but I'll swing by the court tomorrow for your swearing in testimony if I have time." Lisa thankfully reminded me about getting sworn in.

"Thanks again for helping us out tonight," I said as I got up so I could walk her to her car.

"Oh that's okay," said Lisa, anticipating my intentions, "Charleen said she'd walk me out."

Both girls smirked. Junior and I just gave each other questioning looks, and we both told Lisa good night.

For some reason Junior and I got into a discussion of women. I think Junior brought up the conversation on purpose so he could hammer me with a few questions about Lisa. Junior was quick to pick up on vibes, and managed to pick up on my thoughts about Lisa rather quickly. I dropped the subject just as quickly. I told Junior I thought she wasn't a bad looking woman, and I left it at that. Changing the subject, I turned the woman questions around on Junior instead. He told me of a few love battles he'd been through, but didn't have any potential opportunities at the present time.

"I've been broken one too many times to let another woman in," he told me.

After what I'd been through with Susie, I could relate quite well.

Chapter 32

There must have been a total of fifty or sixty people. Each and every one of them had gone through law school just like I had, and they all had to take the bar exam. But I'd bet none of them would want to be in my shoes right now. I'd also bet that at least half of them were working for Daddy's little law firm.

I arrived early and found a spot towards the back of the room. Charleen and Junior made their way to the very back of the courtroom area where everybody else that was here to watch was seated. Lisa must have gotten held up at work again; she wasn't here. No big deal.

"All rise please for the honorable Judge Harris," the guard said from the front of the courtroom.

That was about the last thing I really paid attention to. All I could think about was tomorrow. I'd be here, in this same courtroom, trying to convince three judges that Schlau deserved another chance with this case. Occasionally I tuned in to hear what Judge Harris had to say. He was in the middle of explaining the importance of serving justice and setting only the truth free. I tuned back out. My father came to mind. He would love to be here right now. Out of all the things in life I'd ever accomplished, this was what really mattered to him. And now, well, now I was thinking about how much I'd rather be a relaxed bartender on some far off island. I started paying attention again when the Judge had us repeat after him the unbreakable oath of becoming a lawyer. We promised to always serve justice above all else. After we were done raising our right hand

and pledging our commitments, I turned to accept hugs and congratulations from Charleen and Junior, and then we bolted for a bar.

None of us planned to drink hard, we just figured a bottle of champagne and some appetizers ought to cut it. After all, being broke was what we were trying to stay away from, and spending a lot of money on drinks wouldn't exactly be helping the issue any. We kept the budget down to some nachos, beer bread and two glasses of some very inexpensive champagne per person. Then we headed back to the house. I had two messages waiting. One of them was from some guy Jerry Cullinsworth, a friend of Richard Pullen, who reminded me of the award dinner I had tonight. I'd been trying hard to forget about it, but I didn't think there was a way to get out of it. In a way I supposed it was an honor, but that didn't mean I was going to stay there for more than an hour. Hello, thank you, and good-bye was all they were going to get from me. Junior gave me a quick compliment about receiving the fourth highest score in the state. He told me it was because I was related to him. Whatever; I just told him we'd have to wait and see if anything I'd learned would do us any good tomorrow in court. Grandma Olivia had left message number two. She'd just gotten back into town and said she'd been hearing good things about the case. She was looking forward to seeing me at court tomorrow. At least one of us was looking forward to it.

The rest of the afternoon I kicked back with the family. We didn't do much, just hung out in the back yard. Michelle loved the attention she got throwing the Frisbee around and playing catch. I had to admit, little

Michelle had quite an arm. Maybe she'd grow up to be a softball pitcher, and buy her penniless Uncle a drink when he needed it.

None of us mentioned the case even once. I think we all knew where we stood with it. Besides, as soon as my award dinner was over, we'd review all the case material one last time anyway.

I picked a wardrobe from my small selection of suits and ties, and got ready for the dinner. I was saving the suit Olivia had given me for tomorrow. I'd use anything I could if it'd help me in just the slightest way to win this case. Even if it didn't do me any good in court, it'd still score me a few points with Olivia in case my presentation didn't quite turn out.

Charleen came in to help me straighten out my tie. I'd always had problems with ties. I either made them too long, too short, or I ended up putting an entirely new look to the knot. I brushed through my hair once, squirted on some good smelling stuff and headed down to the kitchen to grab a glass of water. I asked Charleen and Junior if it would be all right if I asked for their help again this evening. I told them I would probably be home by around eight or eight-thirty at the latest. There wasn't a whole lot to go over, but I wanted them to listen to what I'd be saying in court tomorrow so that I'd feel a little more comfortable when I had to do it for real. They both told me they weren't going anywhere. I kind of expected the response, but it was better I'd asked than just assumed they'd help.

I left early to give myself a few extra minutes so if I *did* get lost trying to find this place I'd at least have some time to make up for it. The dinner was being held in the banquet room of some ritzy hotel downtown. Richard had given me directions; hopefully I could follow them.

What the odds were I didn't know, but Peterson certainly seemed to know how to beat them; out of the small handful of people I knew here in Seattle, Peterson always managed to find me in his brand new Porsche. I don't think I've gone into downtown Seattle more than once without seeing him. I rolled down my window.

"What are you doing out so late, looking for another divorcee?"

"Long day is all. I'm happy to finally go home," he said, looking tired but still holding a smile.

I couldn't believe this guy was still working at his age even though he had enough money to support my lifestyle a hundred times over.

"You didn't lose the directions to my weekend party now, did you?" He was still trying to convince me to come.

"Nope. I still have them." I made sure not to include a definite on whether or not I'd be coming.

"You going to your award dinner?"

"Yeah, how did you know about that?"

"Oh let's just say the word gets around. You're going the wrong direction though," he said as he looked at his watch, "I've got a few minutes to spare, why don't you just follow me."

"If you don't mind."

The light turned green. I let him get ahead of me, and then followed him around the block and headed in the opposite direction. I felt like I was following a taxi cab driver the way he was zipping through traffic, but I kept up. I wondered how Peterson, of all people, knew where this award dinner was being held.

Finally, after a few detours, he pointed to a free parking spot. I parallel parked the Malibu. It wasn't quite as easy as parking the BMW, but I got the job done. Peterson had his blinkers on, and waited for me until I walked over to him.

"Just walk around the corner and in the front doors."

"Thanks Mr. Peterson, I owe you one."

"I had better see you this weekend, and feel free to bring whomever you'd like," he said as he sped away.

I swear the guy stalks me sometimes. Every time I turned around, I saw him. Oh well, it might not be quite as good as seeing a beautiful dame, but at least it was better than to turn around to find Dwayne staring back at you.

JIMMY'S was the name of the hotel. I'd never heard of it, but it looked about as fancy as I'd ever seen a hotel. Then again, I hadn't seen very many fancy hotels. I saw a sign for the bar review banquet, and followed the arrow into a nearly empty room. I checked my watch, five-twenty. I was only ten minutes early. Maybe things got started later on the West Coast than they did in Chicago.

The room wasn't very big. It held four large, round tables and about thirty seats. I stood at the door of the room for a second and looked to see if I recognized anybody. There was no one.

"You must be John Bowman," I heard from behind me as I peered at the hand that was laid on my shoulder.

"Yes I am," I said, turning around to see a rather large man.

I wouldn't exactly call him muscular, nor would I call him fat. He was just one of those naturally stocky guys. He had a thick mustache and a wide nose, but it suited his large size.

"I'm Scott Henning, a friend of Richard Pullen's." He smiled, showing his three fillings.

"How did you recognize me," I asked him as I shook his hand.

"It's pretty easy to do when there are only twenty people coming and you've been working with most of them for the last ten years."

Scott led me over to a table with a few other people who all seemed to be about my age, and pointed me towards a chair. He introduced me to all of them, then walked off to talk to one of his buddies.

There were eight people sitting at the table with me, all looking at me as if I was about to give a speech. Finally the guy sitting across from me asked me how it was going. That seemed to break the ice, and suddenly everybody at the table slipped in a few words of conversation. We were all here for the same reason; all of us ranked within the top five percent of bar exam scores in the state.

It was interesting to hear other people's backgrounds, and how they managed to get where they were now. I was glad to see I wasn't the only who hadn't brought a date. Only two others had brought along their significant others. The oldest among us was thirty-six, hardly defined as old. She was an ex-cop who'd gotten fed up with seeing criminals let loose within a few days of bringing them in. That was why she'd become a lawyer. She wanted to produce a little revenge. It was hard for me to picture her being a hard-ass cop. She was very friendly and didn't seem like someone who could use brutal force, but I was sure she'd had her share of rough nights and I wasn't going to be the one to question it.

At ten to six, the so-called award evening began. Mr. Henning thanked us for coming, made a quick toast and introduced another speaker. Speaker after pointless speaker shared their words with us for about forty minutes straight, almost making enough self-righteous comments to fill out a résumé. Finally Mr. Henning appeared before us again, and asked everyone sitting at my table to join him at the podium. The five of us lined up next to him. He announced each of our names and had us take a step forward as he described each individual's background. Then he continued by stating how bright our futures would be because of our dedication. This showed through the high marks we'd obtained on our bar exams.

I got a little nervous when he had each of us stand at the podium and share what it was we were currently doing with ourselves. I was the last to go. Everyone else had listed one big law firm after another that they were working for. I decided to make it as simple as possible. I never named any law firm specifically, I just said that I was still trying to get over the fact that I'd finished law school. I told everyone that I was currently working for a private company. Nobody seemed to be unsatisfied with what I had shared, and if anybody really wanted to know whom I was working for, they could always tune in to the news tomorrow when I tried to submit a competent argument for Schlau.

The five of us had our last moment of glory as Mr. Henning awarded each one of us with a silver medallion, which he hung around our necks. I couldn't say I wasn't thankful. I'd never really gotten a meaningful award in my life, at least nothing more than a spelling-bee contest held in the fifth grade.

After the clapping, we all took our seats with our medallions and downed some champagne. I ended up staying longer than I'd figured I would. The others at my table were actually more interesting than I'd thought. Besides, it never hurt to meet a few people in a town where you didn't know anybody except your relatives and a few acquaintances.

At seven O'clock, after a delicious steak dinner, I said good-bye to Mr. Henning and the others. Before I left we all exchanged phone numbers, not so much for the sake of being social as for the sake of potential connections. I didn't really get into using people for their position. That was too much of a politician's thing I guess, but when there was help to be made available, why not use it.

At home I found J napping on the couch, and Charleen reading a story to little Michelle. I showed Charleen my Medallion. Before I could protest she had it pinned up on the refrigerator, making me feel like a little kid who'd just gotten home from a kindergarten art class. looking at the pin in disbelief of having achieved such a thing, I poured Charleen and myself two cups of herbal tea, which seemed to have been sitting on the stove simmering for a while. She informed me that Lisa would be here around eight to help out with any last minute ideas. She couldn't end it at that, and had to continue with a few romance questions. Sometimes I think I'm caught in one big dating game living here with Junior and Charleen, but I suppose they wouldn't be asking unless the sparks between Lisa and I were more than just subtle.

Instead of answering Charleen's questions, I asked her how they got along. Definitely the best question I could've asked. For about the next half-hour Charleen forgot all about what she was tying to insinuate, and told me all about those women things. Lisa and Charleen met for lunch today, and it sounded like Charleen's impression of Lisa was pretty damn good. I couldn't say I ever would have thought those two would end up being friends, but better that than enemies.

Lisa arrived shortly after eight. I got Junior off the couch and began the review. I went straight through the whole spiel. It was almost six minutes long. It was better to keep it short rather than too long. Not only would it keep the attention of the judges, but it also made me appear more competent with the material I'd be presenting. When a person had less to say, there was more focus.

Junior, Charleen, and Lisa helped me smooth over a few rough spots, carrying us all the way to ten O'clock. I felt very confident. If we weren't prepared enough to convince the judges by now, then we most likely never would be.

I didn't want to stay up too late, so I was glad to be finished and ready to go. We were to be in court by nine O'clock sharp tomorrow. Only I would be allowed to be seated in front of the judges at the table in court tomorrow, and of course, the same went for Dwayne. On one hand that would be good because it wouldn't give Dwayne the chance to intimidate me with a table of suits sitting across from me, but on the other hand I wouldn't have Junior nearby to help me out if I had any questions. However, I wouldn't be completely out in the cold. Junior, Charleen, and Lisa would all be seated directly behind the council's table in the first row of the public seating. Everybody, including Olivia, Dwayne's suits, perhaps Richard and probably a dozen or so media people would be seated there as well. Either way, if I ever got totally lost about anything I could just turn around for an encouraging nod. Whether or not I would be getting anything useful was another issue, but it was a comforting thought. Besides, it wasn't like anything would get too complicated. All I had to do was present my six-minute argument as to why Schlau deserved a second trial. Dwayne would present his argument after I did. Whoever sounded more convincing would have the ruling in their favor. However, nobody would be getting an answer tomorrow. It would be at least a week, maybe more before the judges got back to us with an answer. Usually, even if it wasn't bluntly stated the day of the appeal, one could almost feel which argument the judges favored.

Lisa grabbed her coat hanging on the kitchen chair. I quickly tried to be a gentleman and helped her into it.

"So, would you prefer Charleen to escort you out again, or do lawyers have special privileges this evening," I asked, getting both Charleen and Lisa to smile.

I saw Charleen and Lisa give each other a wink out of the corner of my eye, then Lisa hooked her arm around mine making her choice quite obvious. Junior gave me an elbow to my hip from his chair as we left.

I began walking her towards her car, but she leaned me towards the pond beside the house.

"I've eyed this view a few times already, but never really had the chance to enjoy it," she said softly as we walked out onto the dock and had a seat at the end. She let go of my arm, but our knees touched as she sat beside me.

"So, do you still have any grudges against me, or am I in the clear?" I asked.

She glanced at me briefly with her bright green eyes, and cracked a smile.

"I'll admit, I was in the wrong trying to associate you with the mishap of Schlau, but can you blame me for having had those feelings? It would be impossible for anyone in my shoes to be open minded under those circumstances, even you."

"What exactly was it that finally brought you around to your senses in trusting me?"

"Who says I trust you," Lisa said as she leaned over and stared me in the eyes.

I suddenly felt shaky, and weak. I could feel her warm breath hit me in the cool evening air. She crossed her arms and pulled herself tight to show she was cold. She wanted to be held, and I had no complaints about doing just that.

I swiveled one leg very smoothly so that I was directly behind her, and gently wrapped my arms around her waist. She let her back rest against my chest and brought her head to my shoulder so her face was next to mine. Our cheeks were almost touching. Her clean, soft smell filled me with thoughts. I could almost feel her holding my face with her touch. She softly rubbed her cheek against mine, and I did the same. Completely innocent yet completely indulged. I could feel my heart almost gasping.

Suddenly, a patio light. Someone opened a door.

"John, telephone. Its important," I heard Charleen whisper.
"Sorry," she added just as she turned off the patio light and shut the door.

I apologized to Lisa, getting caught again by her gaze. After a few seconds, we both broke into a smile and said goodnight to one another.   As I got back into the house I could see Lisa getting in her truck just as I picked up the phone.

"This is John," I said, thinking of what I'd just missed out on.

"Can't you sound a little happier to hear from an old friend?"

"Hey Blacky," I said, trying to sound enthused. It wasn't too difficult to recognize a man who's raspy voice couldn't possibly be imitated by another. "So tell me, everything work out for you?"

"Well, I certainly wouldn't have minded making some money off the situation, but considering all that I was being convicted of I'd have to say I made out pretty damn clean. And of course this is all thanks to you, my good friend."

"That's great, Blacky. I'm happy it turned out for you," I said, checking my watch to see that it was going on eleven O'clock. Sleep; nothing else was on my mind, but Blacky had decided tonight would be a good time to catch up on things. "So, what's the program," I asked, trying to get to the point of his phone call.

"I heard you've got a little case going on over there in Washington with some big shot computer company."

"How does something like that get around to a guy who lives in Chicago? Outside of perhaps a handful of people, nobody from around here has even gotten word of it."

"You know me, Johnny. I've always got one ear to the door," he said, as though I should expect him to always be one up on me. "I figured you could use a little help. I've got a few cards on those computer guys, probably pretty good cards."

"Like what?" I was skeptical but curious.

"To tell you the truth John, I'd rather talk to you in person about this stuff."

"Just tell it to me over the phone. I'm sure it isn't anything I haven't heard before. Besides, I've gone through everything there is to go through on this case, so I'm sure it won't have any effect."

"I've gotta make a flight into town tomorrow. I'll give you a call sometime later in the evening and we'll get a couple of beers, on me of course."

"I'll talk to you tomorrow, then." There really wasn't much he could possibly have to tell me, and my meeting with him tomorrow seems almost pointless. I'd already have stated my reason for appeal in court by the time he got in town. But I might as well have a beer with him. Once Blacky put his mind to something, he became dead set on it until got what he wanted.

Chapter 33

Today was the day that everything depended upon. If today weren't a go, then nothing would be. The only thing that would matter was what those three judges thought when we were through. Without a winning argument today, there would be no trial. No trial, no exclusive rights on the chip. No exclusive rights on the chip, no future medical research for Schlau. But I wasn't worried. My cause for appeal was just. All my arguing points were factually supported. I had rehearsed my speech more times than I'd watched my favorite Jerry Lewis movie. I had no reason to panic. If anybody should be panicking, it was Dwayne. I couldn't wait to see him squirm when I pulled a fast one on him. He had no idea what was coming, and watching him stutter for an excuse in front of those three judges ought to be a pleasure. I poured myself a glass of water to keep my hands from becoming too jittery. I took an occasional short, quick sip to keep my mind from going ballistic while waiting for this shindig to get started.

Junior, Charleen and Lisa were directly behind me as we'd planned. I hadn't paid much attention to who else was in the courtroom. However, I couldn't help but notice a few reporters fiddling around with their tape recorders and notepads. I hadn't said anything to anybody since I'd had a seat. I was trying to find my character role for the judges.

The three judges' names were Grunwald, Smith and Johnson. Johnson was the final decision-maker of the three, but that didn't mean making a good impression for the other two wasn't important. With all of the preparations made, I hoped my impressions would be competent at the very least.

It felt strange to be here as a true lawyer who had indeed passed the bar. My old man would have loved to be here right now. In a way, I was glad he wasn't. I'd be intimidated by the idea of screwing up in front of him.

I heard shuffling. It was Dwayne; he was piling his table full of notes and papers. All of his buddies, including Richard Murphy, were seated directly behind him as I'd predicted. None of them even bothered to look at me, which was fine. On a regular day I'd criticize their Armani suits, but I was in the same category wearing the suit Olivia had given me. It made me feel good though, like somebody who knew what they were talking about. It sounds superficial, but appearance truly plays a role in one's self-confidence. I just try to be careful not to rely on it. After all, I only had one nice suit. What would happen for the rest of the week when I was wearing my regular old sweats? For the time being, I'd enjoy the threads.

The bailiff announced the usual. "All rise." Dwayne and I give each other a quick glance as we stood to our feet as though one of us was about to receive the death sentence. If only he had even the slightest idea of what I was about to drop in his lap.

I suddenly felt as though my eyes were playing tricks. The three judges walked in. The third judge was Johnson; Gary Johnson. The same guy Peterson had introduced as his brother-in-law. I turned around to view the public seating area. Sure enough, Peterson was seated in the back next to the entrance. I could see him back there with an extra large

smile; he winked. I just gave him a subtle nod in return to let him know
I'd caught on to his "favor".

I took another quick glance at Dwayne; his nose was so high in
the air it reeked of over-confidence. I could feel my fists clench as we
were told we may be seated. Judge Johnson took a minute to state the
reason we were gathered here today, then stated our names along with
the side of the appellant, me, and the defendant, Mr. Albertson. Johnson
then explained that it was decided by he and the other two judges that no
cameras of any sort were permitted in the court room, only tape recorders
and hand-written notes. It didn't really bother me what the media had
back there, just so long as they were behind me. Out of sight, out of
mind. Johnson then asked if either Dwayne or I had anything to settle
before we began.

"Mr. Bowman, anything you wish to say?"

"Not at this time, your honor." My first words to go on record in
court.

"Mr. Albertson?"

"Yes your honor, if I could have the court's attention for a
moment. I have no recollection of Mr. Bowman's name being stated on
my copy of Schlau's briefing statement. I would like to ask that we
postpone today's meeting for appeal until Schlau is able to proceed with
either the appellant who was stated in the briefing, or until they are able
to file a new one."

Dwayne was being just as sleazy as I thought he might be.
Anything he could do to prolong, interrupt, or even discontinue today's
appeal, he'd do it. My stomach dropped, but as soon as I saw Johnson's

scowling face I felt somewhat relieved. I could tell already that Johnson didn't like Dwayne. Anybody that had spent even a little time in the business of Law understood what Dwayne's type was all about. Sharks like Dwayne loved to nit pick at anything they could, just to see if they could slip the issue. Even if it generally didn't work, they'd still try to use it to wear down or intimidate the opposing legal team. As far as I was concerned, Dwayne was more then welcome to try his strategy. The more he made Johnson grit his teeth, the more favored I'd be when I had something crucial to say.

"Schlau's former lawyers are deceased, and Mr. Bowman is the replacement," said Johnson, sounding rather impatient. The judges probably had a Friday afternoon golf game to attend, and one guess said Peterson would probably join them.

"I'm also lead to believe Mr. Bowman is not a licensed lawyer, and I request the court ask him for his official bar card," Albertson sated without hesitation.

"We received his official bar records last week; fourth highest score in the state. Now, if you have nothing further Mr. Albertson, and I strongly urge you not to have anything further, then we will proceed with this hearing.

"Yes your honor."

I took one more quick sip of water, then stood to my feet and circled around to the front of my table. As I walked around I gave Dwayne a half smirk to let him know he had just made a complete fool of himself. He looked away.

I took a long deep breath. "My statement for grounds of appeal rest upon insufficient evidence throughout the first trial. I would like to support my appeal for a retrial by identifying important evidence which was overlooked in the first trial."

"Excuse me Mr. Bowman, we are not here to perform a trial. There is to be no new evidence submitted at this appeal, only sufficient cause for belief that the first trial was somehow manipulated or wrongly swayed for one reason or another."

"Your Honor, I can indeed show that the original trial was manipulated if you'll give me a chance to present my material."

"Very well. Careful of false accusations."

Johnson wasn't telling me this to be cruel, but to keep me from getting myself into a vulnerable position. One of the easiest ways for a lawyer to fall into a lawsuit was in falsely accusing a person or company, which could blacken their reputation. If this happened, they could sue and claim to have experienced a loss of public respect or even a loss of money if it involved a business issue.

I turned around and grabbed a folder off my table. The moment I'd been waiting for had arrived. I opened the folder and pulled out my heavyweight. I gave three copies of my file to the judges, and one to Dwayne.

"This is a copy of a list of persons who formerly worked for Schlau and then proceeded to work for Xiborlink. At the time of the first trial, Schlau attained a court order to research employees' background records who, prior to working for Xiborlink, worked for Schlau. The reference list you have has twenty-three names, the only twenty-three names Schlau received at the time of the first trial." I pulled out another four sheets from my folder and handed them out. "Jerry Frohlauski, number twenty-four. At least, that's what he should've been on that list. A general background check at City Hall on Mr. Frohlauski showed us that he has been connected with information scandals and embezzlements in the past. We have checked into his income taxes for the past year. A portion of what Mr. Frohlauski filed was from income by Schlau. However, another large portion was filed under income made by Xiborlink, which proves he has worked for Xiborlink. Mr. Frohlauski resigned from Schlau at approximately the same time a large portion of Schlau's computer chip data was declared missing. Therefore, we believe that this crucial information on Jerry Frolauski was purposely with held by the defense in the first trial. Withholding evidence is a form of manipulation in court, and in effect I request a retrial with the submission of employee records and whatever else might be connected with those records that were with held by the defense."

Complete silence. Everyone was in awe, including me. I remained standing about halfway between the bench and my table for a few seconds.

"That's all your honor," I said, and I took my seat.

I couldn't really tell what Dwayne's reaction was because he had his head buried in his many notes, shuffling through them in what I hoped was panic. I did get a look at a few of the media people. All of them seemed to be scurrying to make notes. As I sat down I observed the judges for a moment, and could see them giving each other bewildered looks while occasionally referring back to a few of the papers I had given them. The courtroom was almost appalled at the idea of such a large corporation taking advantage of a privately owned company. I had everyone on the edge of their seats. I absolutely loved it.

"Mr. Albertson, your statement," Johnson said. He seemed almost as curious to hear the response as I was.

I had to admit, I didn't think my statement was going to go over as well as it did. Dwayne appeared to surprisingly calm and collected as he gathered his papers and stood before the defense table. While he might convey himself on the outside as being calm, on the inside I was sure he'd just now begun to realize the definition of the word squirm.

"In all fairness, I believe the corporation I'm representing deserves more respect and honorability than the appellant's accusations are displaying. I can assure this court that Xiborlink holds nothing but the utmost qualities of integrity with their conduct of business. What Mr. Bowman had to say was absolutely correct, but unfortunately he left out some rather important details."

Dwayne handed out some papers to the judges and I.

"This is a copy of Jerry Frohlauski's work history with Xiborlink. As you can see, he has been working for Xiborlink since the late 80's. Xiborlink was aware of his past records, but felt his skills as an employee could be used to their benefit so long as they limited the amount of authorization he had in the company. Although Xiborlink went to such an extent, there were still problems. Just over a year ago, Jerry Frohlauski claimed a serious back injury, putting him out of work. Xiborlink paid for his unemployment time, as well as all hospital bills and an extra amount for compensation. During his supposed recovery stage, he began work for Schlau without our knowledge. It is then with understanding that one can see why Mr. Frohlauski claimed two different sources of income on his last income statements. Keeping in mind that Mr. Frohlauski worked with Xiborlink's department of research and development, we, not Schlau, should be the ones to have suspicion of stolen research developments. It is obvious in our eyes that there was indeed some form of advancement made by Schlau due to the knowledge of our former employee Jerry Frohlauski. Now, preceding Xiborlink's recent understanding of Frohlauski's relationship with Schlau, we fired him. We also began to file a lawsuit against him for developing research for another company while still being an employee of Xiborlink. Mr. Frohlauski has left the country, most likely as a fairly wealthy man. Furthermore, Xiborlink holds no connection to Schlau of any fashion. Even though we have probable cause to claim a lawsuit settlement, Xiborlink wishes not to file one. Xiborlink simply would like to continue conducting business as usual, leaving this issue in the past." Dwayne glanced towards me. "That's all I have, your honors."

I couldn't believe that son-uv-abitch. He knew! He knew about everything I was going to say before I ever said it. He had to have, or else how could he have prepared these documents and defended my argument so well? Who could have told him? I turned my head and began scanning through the people in the courtroom. I looked back at Dwayne who had just taken his seat. His eyes couldn't come close to covering up the tremendous ego flaming inside of him. I stared right through him as he held a sleazy grin on his face. I noticed his eyes shift behind me for a split second just before he turned forward again. I looked behind me, past Lisa, Junior and Charleen. It was Pullen. Richard Pullen told him everything. It was written all over his face; he wouldn't even look at me. That wrinkled piece of dried fruit! Nothing but a two-timing Bastard is all he was.

Judge Johnson told us we could expect a decision in a letter by mail about two to five weeks from now, and then dismissed us. Usually it took longer, but this case would determine a large sum of financial worth, and therefore became prioritized. It didn't matter anyway, everyone in the courtroom already knew who had dominated today's appeal.

As I leaned my head into my hands on the table after we were dismissed, I could feel hands on my shoulders and back. I was sure it was Charleen and Junior, and if Lisa wasn't upset with me, then maybe hers too. I finally decided to stand to my feet and gather my things. I realized I was right about the hands as I stood up; even Lisa, and unexpectedly, Olivia as well. None of us really said anything, but we all understood. I looked over to see Dwayne standing about five feet away, getting ready to leave. I just stared.

"Tough luck, huh buddy? I guess it runs in the family," Albertson said.

I lunged at him. I knew I shouldn't, and I also knew a lot of my reputation was resting on it, but I hated him. He put his arm out to try and block me as I came towards him, but it didn't slow me down. In a matter of seconds I had his arm twisted, forcing him to his knees. I got ready to drill a fist into his jaw with my free hand, but somebody grabbed me. It was Junior. I didn't really comprehend what anybody was saying to me or to anybody else. I could see Dwayne yelling, but I purposely blocked it out and remained focused on my hatred of him while Junior held my arms. The bailiff didn't waste any time getting across the room, and before I knew it, I had cuffs on.

I was being arrested for being disruptive in a courtroom. It didn't matter that the court was already dismissed. It's supposed to be respected at all times, and I'd overstepped my boundaries. I didn't bust out into a rage after the bailiff got to me. I just kept my teeth gritted and walk out one of the side doors of the courtroom with the bailiff tightly gripping my arm.

My second time in jail in two months. Johnson had me sanctioned for being disruptive in a court of law. I couldn't say I blamed him, if I were a judge I'd have probably done the same thing. After all, he had to maintain a level of respect, especially with his colleagues all around him.

Before I'd left the courtroom I had heard Junior say something about how he'd try to get me out. It didn't really matter anymore. I had absolutely nowhere to go.

I was in a temporary holding cell with two other people; needless to say, I was the only one wearing a suit. One of them tried striking up a conversation, but I wasn't feeling very social. I sat on the floor against the wall on the other side. For some reason the guy took a liking to me, and sat next to me, offering a cigarette. The guards took cigarettes and all other such processions away when you came in here, but apparently he'd been through this sort of thing before and had learned the tricks of the trade. I shook my head no.

He was an older guy; a black man with white hair and a tattoo on his left forearm. He didn't look like he had a job, and I could smell old cigarette smoke on his clothes. The smell of liquor seemed to linger about him. He lit up his cigarette and started humming the tune to "skies of blue" by Louie Armstrong -- same song my father used to sing all the time while he'd work in the garden. I didn't tell this man that, but it did make me think about things.

"Life sure can be hard," he said, stopping his humming and looking to me for a response.

I had nothing to say.

"I used to be like you," he continued, trying to spark my intereet in conversation. "Sure I was. I was always searching for the right direction and meaning of life. It took me a long time to figure out what it was. You know, I had to make my first million dollars to find out what money really meant to me: nothing. When it all started I let greed run me, and after time, greed was the only love in life I ever knew."

"Listen old man, I'm not like you okay? Money has never driven me, and it never will."

His insinuations perturbed me. He just laughed for a moment.

"My friend, there are lots of things that can drive a person for the wrong reason. I never said you were driven by money, I'm just saying money is what seems to get the best of 'em," the old man said as though it were some kind of a plague.

"So enlighten me, what's the true meaning of life?"

"I can't tell you. It's in your heart, my friend, deep within your heart. It's what sets you free and lets you finally live with true dignity."

He was very sincere. I paused for a moment and thought about what he'd just said.

"And you, what did it take for you?" I asked.

"Maybe you. I don't need much. Setting someone else free gives me my freedom. Sure, you think I'm a crazy old fool, but you'll realize I'm not so crazy when you become an old fool like me." He quickly hid his cigarette to the side and tried to blow all the smoke away as the guard walked up to the door and unlocked it.

"James Bowman," the guard said, looking over at me. Junior must have already talked to the judge and made bail for me.

I made my way to the door of the jail cell, but turned around just before I exited and took a long look at the old man. He nodded his head and laughed.

"In your heart, my friend, that's where you'll find it."

I nodded my head, then I left. Seemed like everybody was waiting for me when I made it to the front desk. Junior, who had Johnson set bail for me so they could get me out, Charleen and Michelle, Lisa, Olivia, and even Aunt Heide whom I hadn't seen since Uncle James passed away. They were all there to pick me up. Aunt Heide had just come in on an early flight today. I was glad she was back. They all gave me a quick hug aside from Junior and Lisa, who just gave me a strong pat on the shoulder. It felt good to have everybody here for me. It took away some of the stress of today's appeal.

In the parking lot I got ready to give back the keys to Olivia's Malibu, but she told me to hold on to it for a few more days and bring it over when I came for dinner. Olivia tried to say this with enthusiasm to make me feel better, but I knew how she'd had her hopes up about this case. I gave her one more hug just before we both left to go home. As I let go of Olivia, I whispered to her how sorry I was. She placed her hand on my cheek, and told me she already knew and I shouldn't worry myself over it. I still felt miserable, but it was comforting to hear.

I told Lisa I'd give her a call tomorrow and bring back her files, and she nodded. I gave her a half smile to let her know how sorry I was. She returned the smile and looked away. I could tell her heart had been broken. She, like her grandmother, tried to hide her feelings. I could easily see straight through her, and it was with understanding. This had meant a lot to her, damn near everything as far as her career was concerned. Even more, relative to how much she cared for those in need. I felt terrible. I had an ache in my gut that I could feel all the way to the top of my throat. I never should've trusted Pullen; I never should've been the one to take this case. Now Schlau had no chance for continuing their research, not even for the sake of Sam. If I could, I'd fund the research myself, but I couldn't even fund my own debt. All I could do was try to somehow make it up to Olivia and Lisa in the passing of time. I wasn't sure exactly how, but whenever I got the chance, big or small, I'd make the most of it.

Chapter 34

I thought I was hallucinating when I noticed Blacky looking down at me. The man was right there in my living room, leaning over the end of my couch and blowing puffs of cigar smoke directly into my face. All I remembered was dozing off to take a little nap, and suddenly I had to wake up and deal with this guy. The nerve.

"Blacky?"

"I tried calling earlier, but nobody answered. So I figured I'd just swing by."

"Just swing by," I asked him, completely baffled that he was there. "How'd you know where I lived? And how'd you get in here?"

"I knew where you lived months ago, remember? I sent over those files for you to look over." He refreshed my memory of his devious ways. "As far as coming in, well, your door was unlocked so I guess I just helped myself."

"What time is it?" I looked for a watch.

"About eleven O'clock."

"In the morning or evening," I asked, feeling completely turned upside down.

"Evening. Friday evening that is," Blacky said as I tried to block out thoughts of the court appeal earlier that day.

"Listen John, I know this is probably a bad time for you, but I have to go back to Chicago tonight and I figured you might want to hear what I have to say about this computer bit. So what do you say we go grab a shot of good whiskey and lay some ideas for your case out on the table?"

"It's too late," I said, rolling over on the couch trying desperately to forget about the whole thing and go back to sleep.

"What's over, the trial?"

"There was no trial, just an appeal, and it's finished." I was still disgusted with how it ended.

"Well it ain't over yet, John. I need you to help me prove it."

He yanked on my arm to get me off the couch. I turned over and crawled to a stand. Blacky poured two shots of something or other, kept one for himself, and tried handing the other one to me.

"No thanks. I've got a headache as it is. Besides, I just woke up."

"I'll get you one later, then. You'll need it." He took the second shot himself and got me to follow him outside to his fat, white Mercedes Benz.

I didn't bother telling anybody at the house where I was going. They were probably all asleep anyway. As soon as we'd come back from getting me out of jail we had all changed into some comfortable clothes and hit the beds. I think we were all exhausted from the stress.

I was still half asleep and very disoriented, but I already knew that there was no way for me to avoid talking to Blacky when he had something to say, so I might as well enjoy the ride and give him a listen. He had one of his sidekicks driving the car. It looked like the same guy that had brought me Blacky's files. Inside the car Blacky had classical music playing. He also had a mini-bar in arm's reach. I was sure whatever was inside was the strongest liquor the market had to offer.

Nothing was said for about the first four or five miles of driving, and then Blacky finally set in. I'd had my head resting back on the headrest, but I looked up at Blacky as he talked.

"There are a lot of crooked people in this world, John, and I'm one of them. You've got good crooks and you've got bad crooks, and then you've got evil. Now I may have pulled some pretty rotten stuff in my time. Certainly rotten enough to surpass being a good crook, and very much so a bad crook, but I'm not exactly evil." He told me this as he took the last hit of his cigar. "I know all about Xiborlink, I know all about your friend Mr. Albertson, and I even know all about the digital security code systems," Blacky said, gaining my attention but by no means impressing me.

For all I knew, he might have gotten some of this stuff off the news. After all, I certainly hadn't been listening to the TV or any other form of Media. That'd been the last thing I needed, something to bring me down even more than I was.

"So what about it?"

Blacky gazed out the window and didn't answer. I could tell he was becoming quite serious with this conversation. As brutal as Blacky might appear to be on the outside, he was a sincere and emotional type guy on the inside. He just had a strange way of showing it sometimes. That's why he had to do things like look out the window; it let him open his heart. I wasn't sure how I always seemed to be the one he opened himself up to. I never knew what to say or do. Some things were just the way they were, and no questions should be asked.

"A few years ago I got pretty sick. Sick to the point where I couldn't do anything but sleep most of the day because I felt so weak. It eventually got to the point where I couldn't even make it to the bathroom, and I had to endure going in the bed like an old man in a nursing home. I had no pride left. I thought I was going to die, and I should have. I had a private doctor come in, and he diagnosed me with terminal cancer. It was in my kidneys and a few surrounding organs. Deadly."

"What happened," I asked, devastated by what he was saying.

"A friend of mine, at least he was until he died, brought me somewhere I would never have thought in a million years could have existed, at least not in our country. I suppose I'm thankful, but how can a man have gratitude for something he doesn't deserve to receive?"

Blacky held the cross from his necklace in his hand. I'd never seen him this way; his eyes were on the edge of tearing.

"It was an underground hospital; an advanced hospital. They had a cure for me, for my cancer. A rare herb out of the South American jungle contained a certain type of vitamin substantial for the human body to fight off the type of cancer I had. It took me a long time to recover, but I was alive and well.

"That's when the problems set in. Nobody was supposed to know about this place, at least not somebody like me. It's top secret. Basically a test lab for Military Intelligence, but at the same time an advanced health facility for top people in the military, CIA, FBI, and the list goes on. It kept the important and privileged ones alive. My good friend had his own connection through politics, but his connection wasn't meant to be used for me or my health. I was a nobody to them, worth nothing relative to their needs and demands. In fact, I was seen as a threat. No outsider was to know about this facility. Needless to say, my friend died in his sleep. That's what the police record said. Quite a coincidence how this was right around the same time my good friend got done bringing me back to health. If they were smart, they would've killed me right along with my buddy, but they let me live and go about my regular routine. They wanted to see if I was going to maintain a stable health condition concerning any symptoms of cancer. I was their personal lab rat. Before I left they gave me some bullshit about how the medicine they practice is on the verge of being handed over to the public, and they're in the process of testing the magnitude of its effects. They only told me this so that I'd keep my mouth shut long enough for them to finish analyzing me, and then finish me, period. However, I knew this, and I knew it was only a matter of time before it happened.

"While they were occupied making periodical medical tests on me, I was clever enough to figure out a way to keep myself alive. It didn't take me long to figure out the main man keeping this whole operation together was Sam Harrison, a coincidental friend of Jerry Frohlauski, that *loyal* friend of Schlau's. It took some time and persuasion, but eventually I was able to convince making an exchange with Sam. His protection to ensure my life, for my goods and services. Don't ask me to go into details concerning the goods and services. Let's just say they weren't exactly legal. Either way, I'm still alive, at least so far. But to tell you the truth John, I'd almost rather be dead. It's been getting to me. Knowing there are people all over the face of this Earth who are dying and are in desperate need of medicine, and these bastards won't give out their secrets... it sickens me, absolutely sickens me."

"I don't understand. Why wouldn't they want to help the sick if they can? Isn't that what their research is for?"

"Well sure, that's what it's supposed to be for, but do you actually think they'd want to give up millions upon millions of dollars in medical insurance just to be ethical? These guys knew what they were doing from the very start, pure manipulation. Imagine all the money that is profited from people who are infected in one way or another by disease or some kind of sickness. The more chemotherapy that is needed, the more doctor's appointments that are made and the more needles and pills that are provided, the more money they dish in. And believe me, every one of the people that is involved with this underground operation has a very good handle on the investments within the medical markets. Now, picture having a cure to diseases that people have been plagued with for decades, if not centuries; huge losses would be taken. Perhaps this underground government facility doesn't have the cure to all the sicknesses in the world, but they certainly know who does or is on the brink of providing them." Blacky looked directly at me.

"You mean Schlau?"

He nodded.

"How'd you know," I asked incredulously.

"They know about every type of research and medical development facility there is, no matter how well hidden it may be. That includes the seventh floor of Schlau. Why do you think your partner Lisa has been having such a difficult time determining the cure for Doga

Ebola, and everything else she attempts to experiment with? Why do you think Jerry Frohlauski worked at Schlau? Xiborlink was never your real opponent, the government was. They just used Xiborlink as a scapegoat to keep Schlau from ever getting enough money together to develop an efficient research program. Believe me, these guys know exactly what they're doing. They spend months of planning so that it's always someone else who takes the fall for government purposes. Do you think Xiborlink ever really knew the real purpose behind this whole ordeal? Maybe Xiborlink's lawyers are in on the conspiracy, but Xiborlink's corporate group itself knows nothing of it. Of course, this doesn't mean Xiborlink wasn't guilty of stealing the chip from Schlau, but the government was partially to blame for having Jerry Frohlauski do a number on Schlau by handing their technology over to Xiborlink. The government knew all along that Schlau needed the money from the production of that chip in order to continue research, and that's exactly why they created the conflict between the two companies. It's all about keeping a tight grip on medical research to these guys, and they're damn good at doing it."

"How the hell did anybody find out about Lisa's research? And just what are you trying to say, that the only reason her research hasn't been successful is because it's been tampered with?"

"John, we're talking about the CIA, FBI, Military specialists, and probably some groups we've never even heard of. If they really wanted to, they could plant a bug in the White House and nobody would ever find out about it. These guys will do everything they can to make sure profits from medical cost keep coming in. If that means taking down an outside research program, or perhaps tampering with Schlau's experiments so nothing will come of them, then that is exactly what they'll do."

Blacky poured two shots of Jack Daniel's. This time I took one and downed it.

"So what happens now?"

"Now," Blacky repeated thoughtfully, "now it's time for the truth. We've got to go public. I'm sick of these bastards, and it makes me even more sick to think I might have become one of them by trying to hide their scandal like the rest."

"Go public? With what, a testimony coming from a man of your background? That's pure suicide."

Blacky pulled out an envelope with a small hard case inside of it.

"My friend didn't only die because he decided to help me out, he died because he stole some pretty valuable stuff. I'm not sure if he intended to use it to bribe someone, or if he had something a little more righteous planned out, but he never got a chance to do either of them."

He pulled out a small computer CD inside a clear case, about two inches in diameter, and held it in front of us.

"This is what he died for: a black list. I imagine that before my friend's killer ever got to him, he made a copy of the original and then had this delivered to my driver, Smiles. He's the only person besides me that you can trust."

Smiles was a bald black man, about six foot four and wider than the car itself.

"Nobody ever found out that my friend had made a copy of the original, so nobody ever bothered coming after me. This little baby holds everything. Every procedure that was followed, command that was given, date that it happened on and person that was involved. Everything is backed with official government security codes and computerized signatures, so you shouldn't have any problems proving this is legitimate."

Blacky handed me the CD inside its case after he slipped it back inside the envelope. My hands were shaking slightly as I took it from him. I thought for a moment, then decided to stuff it down my jeans in my underwear. A somewhat crazy action to take, but considering the importance, I felt no shame in it. I could feel sweat beginning to form on my forehead; I wiped it off on my T-shirt.

"Now, it gets tricky. I've had this disc for some time now, and many of the recent names involved with the underground facility may not be on it, but there is a way to access it. I have to warn you that to do so is risky. The main file that this CD came from is located on a database at the Pentagon. If you go on-line using this disc as your entrance key for all the security checks and codes, you will be able to request an updated download from the Pentagon database. This disc will enable you to pass through all the security blocks except one; you'll have to know the name of my friend, along with his mother's maiden name." He wrote the password on a napkin from the mini-bar and handed it to me.

"Well that seems easy enough," I said, wondering what else there was.

"Only a handful of people have these discs, so security tends to take care of itself. But there is one more catch that goes with the name." He grabbed a stainless steel box from under the mini-bar. "You'll need this," he said as he handed it to me.

The stainless steel box felt cold as I held it in my hands. I opened it. All I could see was the corner of a plastic zip-lock bag barried underneath some crushed ice. I pulled it out and almost dropped it as I realized what I was holding. Yet, I wasn't entirely shocked. It was a cut off hand, red from bloodstain.

"The hand will need to be laser scanned as you enter the ID. I imagine you'll be able to get access to the equipment needed. Once you get the updated version of the file, you'll have everything you need to put the axe to every last one of those sons-uv-bitches. However, like I said, this is where it gets a little tricky. Once you begin to download from the Pentagon file, you'll be traced. It will take them about five minutes to trace you back to your location, and another five minutes get there. That gives you a total of ten minutes to do what you have to do and get the hell out of there. The rest is up to you. I wish I could stick around and help you out John, but by the time this hits the fan I'll be lucky if I make it out of the country with a pulse. Just make sure to watch your back."

I suddenly felt nauseous. I didn't know what to think or feel. I just sat there with an empty shot glass in my hand and a priceless disc in my shorts. Twenty-four hours from now, Blacky would be sipping Margaritas with a beautiful woman on some deserted island beach, while I'd be chopped up in a million pieces in a plastic bag, never to be found again. I didn't know if I should do it.

We pulled up to Aunt Heide's driveway. Smiles pulled the car up to the front door. Seemed like Blacky and I were ending the conversation the same way we'd started it, in silence. Finally I looked over to him and reached out my hand.

"Take care, Blacky," I said sincerely.

"Bring 'em down kid, bring 'em down as hard as they can fall."

Chapter 35

Back inside the house, I sat down for a moment at the kitchen counter and sorted my thoughts. Everybody in the house was still asleep, and unless I woke them they'd probably stay that way. Besides, the fewer people involved the better. When this was all over, if I was still alive, then I'd tell them all about it. But there was no point in escalating the stakes by getting them involved in this nightmare ordeal.

I stared down at the table for a while thinking of what to do next, and then it hit me. Peterson. His directions to the weekend party were still hanging on the fridge under a magnet where Charleen had put them. Gary Johnson would be there, *Judge Johnson*; perfect. I had to get this disc printed. I'd already thought about this as Blacky and I were driving along. Schlau's computer system was going to buy me the extra time I needed. If I could get Lisa to help me set up a Schlau chip and code scrambler when I got on-line with this disc, I should be able to buy a little extra time. Hopefully, just enough extra time for me to get what I needed and then get out to Peterson's so I could let Johnson know what was going on.

I called Lisa. I didn't bother calling her at the lab, I doubted she'd want to be there after what happened earlier today. I reached her at Olivia's house. She sounded like she'd just woken up. I didn't give her any details, I just asked her to meet me down at the lab right away. She was full of questions, but I told her to just go, and then I hung up. I snagged the directions off of the fridge, and I split.

I rode the Malibu pretty hard on the way over. My hands were still shaking, but I didn't care. All I could think about was putting those greedy bastards to the dirt. Maybe I was turning into a righteous nark, but I didn't care. Blacky was right, even if his conscience was a bit late; these guys had to go down. Lisa still wasn't there when I pulled up to the front doors. The security guard let me in, and I used the card Lisa gave me to get through the door scans on the way up to her office, where I'd asked the security guard to have Lisa meet me. I pulled out her phone book and quickly thumbed through it until I found a major news channel. I ended up calling three different channels in case one of them thought I was trying to pull some kind of a bluff. I told all three of them the same thing: meet me at about ten-thirty at the address Peterson had given me, and wait for me if I'm not there. Of course they all wanted to know what it was concerning; I just told them Judge Johnson would be there to help explain things. With his name in the picture, I was sure they'd be there twenty minutes early. I wanted to make positively sure this thing didn't get covered up again, and what better way to make sure of that than the media.

"Are you okay?" Lisa asked as she came through her office door.

I didn't even know how to respond. After tonight, Schlau would have every opportunity to pursue their research. At the same time, I was scared shitless it wouldn't work out and we'd all end up on somebody's hit list.

I didn't waste any time, I got right to the point in telling Lisa what we needed to do. To find a laser scanner to ID the hand was somewhat difficult, but we rigged the computer to a fingerprint scanner Schlau used for their security check. As we began to set up what we needed with the computer, I told her the gist of what Blacky told me. Lisa's eyes said it all, shock, thrill and disgust all at the same time. I understood exactly how she felt.

Finally we were ready. The computer was already loaded with a Schlau security system chip that would slow any trace program, and Lisa had routed a scrambler into the computer that I'd be working on. The scrambler was routed from her notebook computer stationed next to mine. From the exact second I went on-line to the Pentagon, she'd be working on scrambling any type of trace that might be too fast for the Schlau security system to block. Hopefully, this would also give us some spare time to work with. With the two systems working together, we'd be able to avoid an immediate trace, giving us just enough time to do what we needed to do.

I took one last deep breath before inserting the disc, and then proceeded. I opened up the current existing file. My eyes began to widen; I could hardly believe what I was seeing. Blacky was right. A pot full of Senators, even a couple of governors, an extended list of commanding Military leaders, and of course a mixed group of FBI and CIA were all in the report. Each was identified with their individual position and background, relative to the underground facility. The facility Blacky had been brought to wasn't the only one mentioned, there were more. Some located in the States; some located in foreign countries.

Now came the tricky part, to update the file. I began my request to the Pentagon to download the updated version of the file. Everything was happening just as Blacky had described. I gave the password, gave the Maiden name, and then it asked for a fingerprint scan. I wasn't quite sure if this was going to even work. The hand wasn't even at room temperature, and I could only pray this wouldn't effect the laser scan. I took the hand out of the zip-lock bag, placed it on the scanner, and then placed my hand directly on top of the cut off hand and pressed down to help receive a good reading. After the scan was done I removed the hand and placed it back into the zip-lock bag, and then into the container. The hand left a wine colored hand print on the scanner from the blood covering the hand, but I didn't care. I didn't care about anything except getting into this file. We just waited in silence until the computer gave us a reply. It worked. We got in. It wouldn't take more than about two minutes or so to download all the information. Meanwhile, I began to print so that we'd have a hard copy of everything just in case something was to happen to the disc. I could hear Lisa typing desperately, trying to keep the trace scrambled. I impatiently watched the percentage bar across the middle of the screen, which stated I had about eighty percent saved so far. That means we had about another thirty seconds or so to go. I'd gotten about twenty pages printed out so far from the original file. If Lisa could continue to scramble the trace until we were off line, I'd try printing out the updated information as well.

I took the pages I had so far and stuffed them into a folder. I looked back to the screen - we were downloaded. I quickly got off line. I was sure that somehow the trace had been made, or would be within the next few minutes. We had to hurry, even if Lisa did keep them scrambled while I was on-line. I waited for the last few pages of the updated version to print. I glanced at a few of the pages. I was appalled. Greg

Finely, who was the man that initially caused all the grief within my uncle's firm, Dwayne, Richard Murphy, Blacky (who I planned to delete from the file's records), Richard Pullen, Jerry Frohlauski and countless others were all involved with the underground government conspiracy against research development towards medical advancements. My rage was extreme at this point, but I acted calmly and continued waiting for the last couple of pages to print out. Every last detail about the plot against Schlau was included in the report. Dwayne's name was one of the main names to appear in procedures.

We were done. Lisa grabbed the last couple of pages from the printer and stuffed them in with the rest of the documents in the folder. I had the disc in its case sitting in my front pocket. I also had the directions to Harrison's house. Lisa and I began heading at a fast pace toward the elevators. She stopped me.

Lisa pointed to the security monitor sitting behind the front desk on her floor. It was Dwayne and Pullen. They must have somehow gotten word on us downloading the disc. They were coming through the main entrance of the building. I wasn't sure what happened to the security guard, but I could see on the monitor that Dwayne and Pullen both had a small handgun. Lisa quickly grabbed my arm, and we headed for an exit sign at the other end of the hall. It was a fire escape. I threw my shoulder against it as we came up to it so we wouldn't slow down. We both halted immediately as we stepped out onto the fire escape. Murphy was coming up from below. He saw us, but didn't have a clear shot. Lisa and I dodged back inside. We began to jam the doorway shut with a tall filing cabinet, but suddenly we were dodging a bullet. I turned to see Dwayne standing at the end of the hallway in front of the elevators, getting ready to pull off another shot. I quickly shoved Lisa behind the wall where it took a right turn. I pushed myself the opposite way as I pushed Lisa, so that I'd end up directly behind the wall on the other side of the hall where the hallway turned left instead of right, but it was too late. Dwayne pulled off another shot. I felt a sudden sharp sting in my arm, just below my shoulder. I looked down to see blood spilling down my arm, but I was still all right. I knew if I didn't pull it together, I'd end up dead and not just wounded. I looked up to see Lisa on the other side of the hall; she was fine. We had a few seconds to react; I could hear Dwayne making his way down the hall. I motioned for Lisa to meet me upstairs on the seventh floor. On Lisa's side of the hall there were stairs that would take her to the seventh floor. On my side of the building, there was a freight elevator. If we could both make it up there, we'd be able to get out of reach, and hopefully we'd have some time to think of a way out. Nobody but Lisa and I had security cards to scan through the doors on that level.

We didn't waste any time. Lisa headed her way; I headed mine. I went around the corner and raced down the hallway, holding my wounded arm until I reached the freight elevator. I pushed on the elevator button like crazy. I could feel my adrenaline pumping. I didn't feel any pain from my am. I kept looking down the hall, waiting for Dwayne's face to appear until finally, the elevator door slid open. I pulled up the old gate, got in and quickly pushed for the seventh floor. It wouldn't go. Damn it. I forgot I had no security key for the elevator to get me to the seventh floor. I pushed for the sixth floor.

I left the gate open as I got out of the elevator on the sixth floor so that nobody else would be able to use it. I headed across to the other side of the building so I could take the stairs Lisa had to take to the seventh floor. I stepped around each hallway corner with extreme caution, leaving my bloody mark, and then scurried to the next corner. Finally I made it all the way to the stairway. I held my head against the door and listened first before opening it. I heard the loud sound of a door closing. It must be the door Lisa had just scanned through to get to the seventh floor. I listened for a moment longer for any other footsteps coming up the stairs... nothing. I opened the door just a crack so I could peek through. It was empty. I bolted up to the seventh floor, grabbing my card and scanning through the entrance. Smooth. I entered again with caution. We were on the experimental area of the seventh floor, where Lisa had her rat laboratory. Carefully, I began to walk down the hallway, being cautious around the corners. Suddenly I heard Dwayne's voice. He wasn't talking to me though; it sounded distant. I looked all around me in fear, but no one was in sight. I listened to see where the sounds were coming from, then made my way closer and peeked around the corner.

"Damn it, you little Bitch! Where the hell is he?"

Lisa didn't respond. Dwayne had his arm around her neck with the barrel of his handgun pointing directly at her forehead. He must have snagged her as she came up the stairs; I was too late. He was obviously waiting for me to come up to the seventh floor in the freight elevator, as he was facing it. I could tell Lisa was struggling and scared. She tried giving him a few elbows, but nothing worked. Dwayne simply grew more furious. He was damn close to just letting his finger slip on his trigger. I had to do something, fast.

I saw a loudspeaker in the corner, and remembered that this floor had an intercom system. I quietly ran the other direction to Lisa's lab and got on the intercom.

"Come to room 782 if you want the disc," I said, although I really had no plan.

I thought for a moment and came up with an idea. I shuffled to get the disc from my front shirt pocket into the computer. I brought up all the information on the computer screen so Dwayne would know I wasn't jerking him around, then quickly transferred it to E-mail. I scurried to get an E-mail address for the biggest Seattle Media station in town. After that, all I did was keep my finger on the return key and wait for Dwayne to come through the door.

Dwayne entered slowly, with Lisa still at gunpoint wrapped behind his arm. Her eyes were teary, but she was holding herself together quite well. I tried to remain cool and collected, unlike Dwayne who had sweat running down his forehead. At first nothing was said, then he noticed the screen. I was baffled at his reaction.

"You think we never thought you might try to do something like this?" He gave a gritty little laugh. "We tapped all your computer lines so that, if it was necessary, we'd be able to intercept any information that was being communicated going either in or out of this building."

"You're lying," I said with squinted eyes. "If you were simply able to intercept whatever you wanted, you would've been able to intercept this disc before I ever downloaded anything onto it."

"We would've done just that, but all of our signals on that line were being scrambled. No big deal, just means we'll have to do things a bit differently."

He took the gun off of Lisa's head and pointed it at me. I didn't trust a word Dwayne said, so I hit the return key anyway. For once Dwayne wasn't lying. The computer screen read, "Error, incapable of processing E-mail delivery."

Dwayne's gun was still pointed at me. He cocked it back.

"It's really a shame that all you Bowmans are so much alike; always trying to prove your moral character instead of understanding what true capitalism is all about." Dwayne straightened his arm to shoot.

Even in her hindered position Lisa threw her leg up, hitting his extended arm. The gun fired. The bullet passed to the right of me, barreling a hole straight through the computer monitor. I didn't hesitate for a second. I leapt from my chair and punched Dwayne directly in his throat as hard as I possibly could with my one working arm. He let go of Lisa to hold his neck, but still tried to get off another shot with the gun in his right hand. I grabbed his forearm and smashed it up against the corner of a wall, tossing the gun from his hand. Then I elbowed him to the nose. He dropped, unconscious.

Murphy and Pullen were still in the building, and who knew who else had joined them by now. I quickly grabbed the disc out of the computer and slipped it back into its case and into my front pocket. Neither Lisa nor I had said a single word. We were both still in shock. I couldn't help but take a seat. I was feeling weak from the loss of blood. Lisa quickly tore a strip of cloth from her shirt and wrapped it tightly around my arm to slow the bleeding. It felt a little too tight from the amount of pain, but better this way than too loose. We were both breathing hard. Lisa leaned on the counter next to me.

"We need to find a way out of this building without getting caught by those bafoons, and before the police get here," I said, hoping she knew of another way out.

If the police managed to get a hold of us, it would only be a matter of hours before the government would get word and take control of the issue, or should I say, our asses.

"The only ways out are the same ways we took in," Lisa said.

I closed my eyes for a moment and tried to brainstorm for an idea. Meanwhile, Lisa took a clothes hanger and tightly wrapped Dwayne's hands together behind his back. One of the lab rats accidentally banged up against the window from the other side; I opened my eyes from the noise and watched the rat as he ran around a little more. Then it hit me. I focused in on what looked like a small tranquilizer gun sitting in the hand of the robotic arm within the lab. They used it to target the lab rats with their injection shots.

"Do you have any more of those," I asked Lisa, pointing at the gun.

"Yes, of course."

She opened a cabinet door. I grabbed two of them, and gave one to Lisa. Lisa just looked at me with bewildered eyes as I looked around the room. I found just what I was looking for, a tray of tranquilizer darts already containing an injection.

"How do you load these?"

"John, those darts contain a very dangerous virus."

"I don't care. How do you load them?"

She grabbed the darts and loaded each gun carefully.

"These guns don't have any range, John. Maybe fifteen feet at the most. We won't be able to protect ourselves," Lisa said, becoming frantic.

I edged my head out into the hallway and spotted a wheelchair, which I quickly grabbed and brought back to the lab room. Lisa watched me intently.

"Help me put him into the chair," I said, grabbing Dwayne as best I could with one arm.

Lisa began to catch on, and helped me throw Dwayne into the wheelchair. He was slowly waking up. I grabbed a small towel I saw hanging from the cabinet door, and stuffed as much of it as I could into his mouth to keep him quiet. I took the tranquilizer gun and pressed it against his neck, just as he began to move around and get squirmy.

"How'd you like to die watching your flesh being eaten off your bones," I asked him.

That seemed to calm him down rather quickly. We didn't really say much as we headed to the main elevators. As we stepped into the elevator and turned around, we both took one last deep breath before pushing for the ground floor.

"Just stay calm, no matter what. They won't do anything to us as long as we've got Dwayne at our mercy. If you see anybody getting trigger happy, fire your tranquilizer at them, but that's only if you really have to." I tried to stay calm and collected myself.

Ground floor. Lisa had her tranquilizer pointing straight ahead, her arms completely extended as the doors opened. My gun was still pressed up against Dwayne's neck. Murphy and Pullen were standing straight ahead, about fifteen feet away with their guns pointed directly at us. Amazingly, nobody panicked; we all just looked at each other and analyzed the predicament. Pullen seemed to be the most relaxed, Murphy's hand was shaking pretty bad.

"Now, let's take it real slow and easy here so nobody ends up getting bloody."

Lisa and I stepped slowly out of the elevator before the door shut itself. I could see Pullen checking out the gun I was pressing against Dwayne's neck. He was probably just now figuring out what was in the dart. Hopefully he realized that tranquilizer fluid wasn't red.

"Now then, I'm going to count to three, and when I say three, I want both of you to slowly put down your guns and kick them to Lisa. Then you're going to put your hands on your heads, and lay face down on the floor. And if I see anybody twitch, even a little, I'll plug your hero here with the worst case of health problems you've ever seen."

I wasn't too worried about Murphy; he was too damn scared not to do what I said. Pullen looked like he was thinking things through, but hopefully by the time I got to the number three he'd have passed on being courageous.

"One. Two." I paused a little longer after two. "Three."

I could breath again; they both put down their guns and kicked them over to Lisa. Lisa picked them both up and handed one to me. We waited until they both lay down on the floor, then we slowly began to head for the front doors. I slipped the handgun into my back pocket, keeping the tranquilizer gun pressed against Dwayne's neck. We rolled him right along with us to the door, just in case we needed him. Lisa kept an eye on Pullen and Murphy to make sure they stayed where they were. Once we were outside and realized nobody else was around to create any sort of a threat, Lisa and I left Dwayne at the front doors and ran for the Malibu. I pulled out the papers from beneath my shirt as I got in, and handed them to Lisa. Within seconds I started up the car and we were out of the parking lot. I could see Pullen and Murphy frantically getting Dwayne out of the wheelchair in my rearview mirror as we left. It seemed somewhat comical, actually. I tossed both the tranquilizer gun and the handgun into the back seat, and Lisa did the same. She read the directions to Peterson's place as I drove with my one good arm.

As luck would have it, my briefcase was in the back seat, which still had the notebook computer we had used for court. I handed Lisa the disc. While trying to maintain a steady balance as I swung around curves like a madman, she turned on the computer and popped in the disc. She searched for all of Blacky's files and deleted them. He was in the clear, and rightfully so. Then, before shutting down the computer, Lisa downloaded the disc onto the hard drive, just in case. Amazingly, the computer had enough memory to store all the info.

Sure enough, the yard of Peterson's weekend home had been turned into a media campground. There must have been about six media vans parked in his driveway. It was amazing how rumors could spread. Even if nobody knew exactly what it was all about, they would still try to be part of it.

We pulled into the driveway and parked about two-thirds of the way up; we couldn't make it any further because of the media vans. Within seconds there seemed to be a media mob outside the car, something I never dreamed I'd have to experience. I looked over to Lisa; her eyes were straight ahead, no movement. She was nervous. So was I. I saw her hand lying flat against the side of her leg, I reached my hand over to squeeze it. That seemed to calm her, and it certainly calmed me.

"You ready?" I asked her as I stared out the window at cameras being flashed in our faces.

"Yeah," she whispered.

The reporters mobbed all around us as we got out of the car and made our way to the front door. I could see Peterson's face in one of the windows; hopefully he and Gary would get the front door for us. The reporters were loud. I couldn't make out one clear word, just mixed shouting. Lisa was holding on to my good arm, the same arm carrying the papers and disc. The front door opened, Judge Johnson standing at the doorway. He analyzed the moment. He saw my bloody arm, and he also recognized Lisa from court. The entire group of reporters turned silent and seemed to almost make space for Harrison and I, but they were still shooting off as many photos as possible. I let the silence carry for a while longer, and then I spoke.

"Sorry about all this, but I know I can trust you to do the right thing." I handed him the disc and papers, catching his eye for a moment. He just stood there for a moment holding the papers and disc, still in silence.

Lisa and I turned and headed back towards the car. We could've stuck around and helped explain things, but why? Everything the Judge needed to know was right there in front of him. Besides, I think Lisa and I had certainly done our share of risking life and limb. On top of that, I hated being bothered by the media. Even if I *was* the one who had called the media, that didn't mean I had to stick around and talk to them. I figured Johnson could handle things from here.

As soon as Lisa and I started heading back for the car, the silence erupted. Cameras, questions, and blindness from all the flash photos being taken surrounded Lisa and I back to the car. The majority of the group, however, stayed back with Johnson to take snapshots of him. I looked back up to the doorway just before getting into the Malibu and paused; Gary Johnson nodded his head slightly. I wasn't exactly sure if he knew what he was about to get into, but at least I knew he'd council this issue to the very end. I nodded back, got in the passenger side of the Malibu, and let Lisa drive me to the nearest emergency room. The night finally gave us peace.

Chapter 36

Within hours the conspiracy had broken through to national and international media. It marked history with one of the biggest scandals ever to be uncovered. Even after three weeks, investigators were still locking away some of the best political and military scam artists on a daily basis. I was released from the hospital after recuperating from surgery. They had removed the bullet from my shoulder. I guess I got pretty damn lucky. The bullet missed a main nerve by just a few millimeters. Any deeper and I would've had a paralyzed arm forever. I didn't really know how to handle the incident, I'm not sure anybody would.

I'd been dodging the media ever since leaving the hospital. I didn't mind saying a few words to them here and there, but in general I was just camera shy. None-the-less, my face, along with Lisa's and Judge Johnson's, had landed on the cover of every popular magazine in the country. I wasn't really sure how to act when people pointed at me, I usually just tried to ignore it. It was like reality hadn't had a chance to catch up with me yet. One night I'd been running for my life, and then the next morning I woke up in a hospital staring at a TV where I was being portrayed by the media as a national hero. Couldn't say I exactly disliked the new image. Of course, my life wasn't all that had changed.

Sam was once again on her way to being just another little girl, and putting on some healthy weight. After putting an end to the medical conspiracy intervening with Lisa's research, Lisa was able to uncover several answers in her DNA research. One of those answers gave Sam her life back. Sam wouldn't be the last to be cured either. Lisa had developed one of the most incredible medical breakthroughs in history by finding a way to break down DNA and reform it. In time it would hopefully lead to cures in many other fields as well: cancer, STDs, tumors, nerve dysfunction's and maybe even problems that develop before birth.

For now, I was just glad to see Sam getting stronger. Even though we couldn't really talk because of the language barrier, I went in to rehab with her about four or five times a week. She was trying to build up her strength, while I tried to bring my arm back to normal. Originally I thought I was going to be the one to have an easier time, but Sam astonished me along with most of the staff at the hospital. I grew close to her, and hoped to keep in touch with her even if she decided to go back and live with some of her surviving relatives in Africa. I eventually bought Sam a box of LEGO's, since she had been so happy about the little doll I had given her; she was fascinated for hours at a time building things. It was good for her, keeping her mind off of missing her family.

Lisa helped Sam with her rehab as well, but it was usually one-on-one, and I hardly ever saw Lisa myself. I hadn't had a chance to kiss or even hold her. I missed her. I wasn't really sure where things with her were going to go from here. She had some sort-of a new project she was working on, and told me things would slow down once she got everything under control with it. I wasn't sure I believed it would change things and slow things down, but I certainly wasn't going to give up hope.

Olivia granted me the favor of having my mother transferred from her nursing home in Chicago to put under the care of Schlau's medical research team here in Seattle. Slowly, they were going to try to reverse her Alzheimer's if it was at all possible. If they helped Sam recover, I was sure they'd be able to at least improve the condition of my Mom. Even if it wasn't possible, I was just happy to have her close to me and away from that damn stepfather of mine. Besides, nobody ever went to visit her back in Chicago; at least here she'd have Aunt Heide and the rest of the Bowman family.

Dwayne and his fellow partners, including Pullen, a few scummy executives from Xiborlink and anybody else that was in on destroying Schlau's medical research, are all facing life long terms in prison. Rightfully so; for every medical opportunity those asses let go undiscovered, there were people who died because nobody had a known cure. That was as evil as murder.

On the brighter side of things, now that Dwayne was out of the picture, the firm took new ownership. The old firm went back to Aunt Heide and the family under a previously signed contract Uncle Bowman had written and signed himself. It entitled the Bowman family all business rights to the firm if there were to be any illegal actions taken under the new ownership. Almost as though good 'ol Bowman knew what was going to happen. Junior wanted me to join him in the firm and start it out with some fresh views. I can't say I didn't consider the idea, but it wasn't where I wanted to be. I'd come to realize some things in the past few months. For one thing, I felt the good behind "law" and what it could do for a good cause. A *lot* of good causes. Certainly that would always remain clear to me after what I had gone through. I think I finally related to my father and why he kept pushing me into law. He understood the good it can do for society when one uses it in the proper ways. But there was more. I didn't care about making tons of money, I never really had. I'd had a lot of offers from different law firms and corporations, but none of them appealed to me, except one. A new organization was just getting off the ground here in Seattle. They were trying to establish medical availability to those who were incapable of receiving it on their own. There had been organizations like these in the past, but this one was different. Most nonprofit organizations that tried to benefit the community medically usually had incompetent doctors and limited technology. This particular organization had the best of both, and it wanted to make certain that every health program in the country would follow by example. Of course an eventual goal was to reach out to other areas of the world as well, but the States would be the first in line. As soon as I discovered this organization, my thoughts became consumed by the idea of working for them. I wouldn't be getting paid very much, but at least I'd know I'd actually be helping somebody. No longer would only the rich or insured be able to seek medical attention. Now those with little more than just their name to show for themselves would be able to seek help.

The woman I was supposed to be having an interview with was going to meet me at the same café where I had met Lisa the week before we went to court. The actual meeting wasn't until two, but I liked being early for things like this.

I walked in, ordered myself a hot chocolate with Bailey's and a bit of ice cream on top, and carried my cup with my good arm to a seat in the corner. My other arm was still in a sling. I wasn't sure whom it was I would be meeting with. I was pretty sure I had the job according to the letter they'd sent me, and I think the person interviewing me was going to be my partner. I wasn't really sure about any of that though, the letter was too vague to tell anything for sure. The secretary didn't give me a name or a description, she just told me to be here at two and that whoever it was I'd be meeting with would approach *me*.

I spooned out some ice cream, and sipped my hot chocolate for a while. Then, to my surprise, I saw Lisa walk in. It was very unlike her to be taking a break in the middle of the day for some coffee. She ordered herself a drink and sat down. She didn't see me sitting in the corner. I watched her for a couple of minutes as she sipped her drink and looked through the window, and then I decided to drop in and pay her my regards.

"Is this seat by any chance taken?"

"I believe it is, by a very handsome man who happens to have become a national hero within the past few weeks." She got to her feet to give me a hug. "I've missed seeing you."

"Well, I'm not the one with the new project who can't spare any time," I said, flirting.

She smiled. I felt a little awkward after not having seen her for so long, but she didn't seem to view me any differently than before. That was a good thing.

"So I hear you've been spending a little time in our rehab center with Sam," Lisa said.

"Yeah, she's a pretty sweet little girl."

"And how's your Mom doing?"

"I think she'll be doing a lot better now that she's with a medical team I actually have some confidence in. Thanks for letting me move her to your facility, Lisa. It means a lot to me."

"Hey, after what you did for us, anything. So do you always come here in the middle of the afternoon?"

"I was about to ask you the same thing."

"Me? I'm always here. Helps me think when I can just get away from it all," she said as though it was a normal routine.

"What are you doing here?" She asked me.

"I'm meeting with somebody for an interview. A new organization is just getting under way. Hopefully they'll take me."

"Oh, really? What have you heard about this new organization?"

"Not much. All I know is that they're looking to focus their purpose on developing available medicine to those who otherwise wouldn't be able to have it."

"And do you believe in that?"

"If it can help people like Sam, or my mother, than I believe in it with all my heart."

"So this is really what you want to do, help the sick?"

"Yes it is. Why, something wrong with that?"

"No, not at all. I just never saw you as the type."

"Well, I guess some things change."

"I guess so. And what about a partner, will you have one of those too?"

"Probably. I mean, I'm not really sure, but I would imagine so."

"Do you think you might ever get intimately involved with whomever it is you're working with?"

"Lisa, why are you asking me all these questions?"

She paused, looked down at the table and grabbed my hand. She looked back up at me, slowly bringing her face to mine, and kissed me on the lips, slowly, and softly.

"Just making sure we won't run into any problems when we're working together, partner."

The End.

Part of Life

During the period of time it took to write this novel, I went through a total of three old, broken down computers, thirty-two discs, four note pads

of paper, a bunch of pens and

pencils, nine separate

addresses, ten or eleven

girlfriends (It's eleven

girlfriends if one can count a

two week relationship as

having a girlfriend, and only

ten if not...and I believe one of

those women may have truly

been a bit psycho), two vehicles,

two umbrellas, my car being

broken into where the bag with

the discs to this novel were

stolen, a police report for the

stolen bag and items, a phone

call from the police saying they

may have my bag, a police

report proving the bag with the

discs to this novel found in a

lake by some old woman was

indeed mine, one six-pack of

cold beer celebrating the fact

that, although the discs were

absolutely soaked when I

received them, they still worked

after being dried out, many

bottomless cans of *Mountain Dew*, three messy roommates, nine clean roommates, one *very* messy roommate, and two really cute roommates, three speeding tickets, one snowboard, three surfboards (a sport which inspired me to write, well, that was always my excuse), a really mean cat (but at least the cat attacked the neighbors dog which always pooped in my yard, that was a good day), selling my saxophone to make rent one month, and amongst other things, many countless packages of cookies and cakes baked by dear old Mom, and

sent by dear old Dad, from the

<u>best</u> land in the World....da

land of da <u>Green Bay</u>

<u>Packers</u>!!!